Saved

Forged by Magic, Book 3

M.P. Starkweather

PHOENIX ECLIPSE PUBLISHING

First paperback and e-book edition 2020

(Originally published as The Pit of Pierus)

Second paperback and e-book edition 2021

Substantive editing by Joe Fryman

Copy editing by Hayley Blair

Cover images by Depositphotos

Phoenix Eclipse Publishing

romance that transforms

I want to dedicate this book to my two biggest fans, my husband Josh and my son Thom, who will probably never read any of my books. Thanks for pushing me to chase my dream. I love you both to the moon and back.

Acknowledgments

I would like to thank:

My author besties, who encourage me to keep writing, even when it's hard;

My amazing PA, Gwen, who is my twinsie;

My Alpha Team who tries hard to keep me on track;

My Editing Team who does their best to make sure my books make sense and have as few typos as possible;

My Cover Artist, Ravin DeMarco, who's responsible for the gorgeous images on the front of this book

and My ARC Team, who catch some of the things the rest of us miss.

Contents

one

Mack

KYRO WOKE ME FROM the deadest sleep I'd ever had. It was so dark, almost like being buried alive. "Where are we?" I asked him in a whisper. Places like this were never safe.

"I'm not sure. I think the girls are across the hall. I hear something. Someone is coming. Maybe we'll find out where we are." He kept his voice at a whisper.

I tilted my head to the side. Yeah, that was a scuffling noise coming down the hallway, like someone who doesn't quite pick their feet up as they walk, along with the click of someone who made sure their footsteps were pronounced.

I was more worried about the girls than us, I felt Ky, and I could handle ourselves. Of course, the footfalls stopped just between the two doors. I was too short to see anything, but I knew Ky and Quinn could see it all. I was sure we were still prisoners of The Order, but when that guy started threatening the girls, I lost my temper. The guard must have knocked me out, and from the sound of it, Kyro too. I looked around the cell for Jack, but he wasn't with us.

There was a clanking noise as the key was inserted in the lock, jiggled, then turned to open our door. Standing there were two guards with torches to light the path. They looked unremarkable, just two average guys in jeans and t-shirts. They were of average height and weight, with medium brown hair. It was difficult for me to glean anything from this encounter.

They didn't look like they were carrying weapons, but there was no way to be sure without starting a fight and seeing what happened. It would probably be better to do what they asked and see how this plays out. There would be plenty of time to fight if it came to that. Besides, we'd never find out what happened to the girls if we got ourselves killed here today. I was itching to fight our way out of here, but I kept it controlled for Quinn.

"Come with us." One of the guards spoke as the other pointed. We nodded and followed them down the hall. They guided us around one corner, then another, and yet another, until it felt as though we were walking in circles. I had no idea how to get back to the girls, which was probably the point. We were led through a door, then one of the guards pointed at two chairs on one side of a table. Ky and I took that to mean we needed to sit, so we did. The guards turned and left, locking the door behind them. At least it wasn't dark here. But that was the only difference between this room and the last, save the table and chairs, that is.

"Do you have any ideas about this?" I didn't figure Ky knew any more than I did, but it never hurts to ask. You never know when a demigod will get a message from home.

"Nothing yet, Mack. I'm worried about the girls. I'm glad we hid the important stuff before we got taken. I don't think we're gonna be able to talk our way out of this." I nodded.

It was hard being away from Quinn, not knowing if she was all right. Falling for her has been an adjustment, but I felt more and more that it was one I didn't mind. I enjoyed being with her, and I was pretty sure she felt the same.

Being locked in this room was almost as bad as that dungeon room had been. Here, we had no way to know if we were being spied on, so we couldn't discuss anything important. It seemed like the dungeon room allowed more privacy, but they could have had that bugged too. There was no way for us to tell.

TWO

Zoey

Waiting had always been hard for me to handle. I got anxious about not knowing what was coming next. I remembered when my parents had left me on Calliope. I was fifteen, so it wasn't like they had abandoned a baby, but it was still hard. They had come home from time to time, like my graduation, but they always left too soon. I think, in some ways, that made it more difficult. I might have been better adjusted if they had just abandoned me.

Our neighbors had watched over me, and my parents had a messaging system set up so I could reach them if there were an emergency. I knew their work was secret and vital, but that was all I was permitted to know.

Race was the one who got me through the anxiety attacks that came daily back then. It was hard to believe that he was gone. He was all I had for a long time after they had left. And I had loved him, even if I didn't want to marry him.

We heard the guards come and take the guys. I was terrified of what that meant for us. A while later, two guards came for us as well. The door opened, and one of the guards said, "Come on."

The other pointed down the pitch-black hallway, motioning for us to get moving. Fortunately, they each had a torch, so our path was illuminated, but the hall in front and behind us was black with no light at all.

They snaked us through a series of turns that seemed to be designed to make us disoriented. It worked. We couldn't have made our way back to those cells if we had wanted to. Of course, we didn't. When we arrived at a door, one of the guards unlocked it, then pointed at the table and chairs in the middle of the room.

Q and I both lit up when we saw Mack and Kyro sitting there. We burst into the room, running toward them. "Sit," the guard commanded. I stopped in my tracks. They were pretty intimidating, so we complied, with Q taking the seat across from Mack and myself sitting across from Kyro.

"Are you OK?" I asked them both as I stretched my hand across the table, and Ky gave me a small smile as he took it.

"Aye, we're all right. What about you lassies?" Mack mirrored my movement toward Q as he spoke. My heart swelled when she took his hand.

"We're OK. Just a bit rattled." The guards stared us down, so we kept the answers short. Once they were sure we would cooperate, the guards left, locking the door behind them.

I looked from Kyro to Mack and back again. "Where's Jack?" I probably should have led with that, but I was so concerned about Mack and Kyro that it took a while to register that Jack wasn't there.

Neither of them spoke because at that moment, Jack opened the door and escorted 'Race' into the room. I had already guessed it was some sort of spell that made this guy look like my ex-boyfriend, but it was still highly upsetting to witness. I couldn't figure out exactly how he had done it.

I stood up as he walked into the room. "Jack! Are you OK?" I couldn't stop myself from asking.

He nodded. "I'm fine, Zoey, and you are too. Sit back down. We're safe here. No more running. The Chairman will protect us all." He gestured to 'Race,' and then I realized what had happened.

The Chairman. Not Race. So that's what had happened. The Chairman had killed Race and taken his form. I wasn't sure how that was possible, but that had to be what happened. It made me sick.

I couldn't figure out why Jack was working for him, though. It was so out of character. Race was his best friend. There had to be something making Jack work for this asshole. I didn't care how many times Jack tried to convince us that the Chairman would take care of us; I would always try to escape.

Before any of us could respond, the Chairman took a step forward. "You'll all be guests of mine for the foreseeable future. You'd better be on your best behavior, or there will be consequences."

"You'd better let us go, or you'll be the one suffering the consequences." Q summoned a fireball and threw it at The Chairman. Jack stepped in front of it, blocked the attack, and then walked over to Q and decked her. She was knocked out instantly. Mack caught her before she could hit the floor. Jack didn't even acknowledge the fact that he'd just been hit with a sphere of fire. His shirt was smoking and singed, but he acted as though the flames never hit him.

Of course, Mack didn't like that Jack had knocked Q out, so after laying her down on the floor carefully, he jumped over the table and attacked Jack. Mack screamed out a war cry as a man possessed. He got a couple of good hits in before Jack reacted. This time, Jack's fist met Mack's face, and the dwarf had no chance. He was knocked out as well, and neither myself nor Kyro made a move to catch him. I winced as he hit the floor with a thud.

"Have them taken to the Pit. They want to fight, we'll let them fight." The Chairman said to Jack, who nodded and then hurried off to get the guards.

The Chairman turned to Kyro and me. "Would either of you like to join them?"

We stared at him in response. Neither of us spoke or moved. I didn't know what the Pit was, but it sounded bad.

"Good. I'm glad to see you're both more levelheaded than your friends. I think you'll make a lovely addition to my harem." He gestured to me.

I shook my head as Kyro started to stand. "I will never join your harem or anything else of yours."

"Even if it saves your boyfriend's life? I'll give you some time in solitude to think about it. I can be quite persuasive." Then he turned to Kyro. "As for you, I think you'd do well in the mining camp. You can harvest gems and precious metals for me."

Jack came back with four guards who picked up Q and Mack and carried them away. Two more guards entered the room once the first four were gone. Those two took Kyro to the mines. That left me alone with Jack and The Chairman. They escorted me to my new room and locked me in.

The next morning, Jack brought my breakfast. He was alone, which told me that The Chairman had control of him somehow. There was no way he would trust a guy who, until yesterday, was out to get him. There had to be a spell, or microchip, or something. I needed more information before I could find a way out of this.

"Jack? Can I ask you something?" I tried to sound innocent.

He turned and looked at me as he placed my breakfast tray on the table. "Of course, Zoey. I'm here to help you with your transition. You can ask me anything." His behavior was so creepy. It was like he was a totally different person than the guy I grew up with.

"Well, that statement does bring forth more questions, so thanks for that. First, what is the Pit? And why were Q and Mack taken there?"

He nodded as if he had expected this to be what I asked. "The Pit of Pierus is where uncooperative people are taken. They are given a chance to get the fight out of their system. Some will decide after a few days that they'd rather cooperate with The Chairman and will move to the mines instead. Others will stay in the Pit indefinitely because they're too volatile. There are a few who don't make it very long, but don't worry about that. The bodies are burned so they can't be reanimated."

My jaw dropped. "Bodies...burned? Reanimated? You mean people DIE in the Pit? But Mack and Q are our friends, we can't just let them die!"

Jack's expression was blank. "Then they will have to cooperate. They shouldn't have attacked The Chairman. They have to learn respect."

"But Jack, they're our friends. We have to save them. There has to be a way to get them out of here." By this time, Jack had stopped paying attention to me and was headed for the door. I didn't stop him.

Over the next few days, I learned more about our captor and his organization. The Chairman had been lying when he said he had a harem. As far as anyone knew, he didn't take lovers or wives. I did hear some rumors about the type of things he liked to do while being pleasured. That made me want to work even harder to get out of here.

He hadn't been lying when he said he planned to keep me, though. He sent a doctor to check over me and make sure I was healthy. I begged the doctor to get me out of here. The best he could do was tell the Chairman I was ill and would have to recover before intimacy was an option. A part of me hated pretending to have a sexually transmitted illness, but if it kept that bastard from raping me, it was worth the lie.

THree

9

I KNEW THIS WASN'T the hardest thing I'd ever been through, but it still sucked hardcore. Parts of it reminded me of the training I went through before I could join the Resistance. Which reminds me, I'm seriously pissed at all of them! I can't believe none of them had managed to find us yet. It had to be because the boss has it out for me. They would have come after any other agent in half this amount of time.

In their defense, I had made it pretty clear I didn't need their help, and I wanted them to stay out of my way on this mission. So, I guess if anyone was to blame for our current predicament, it would be me. And that really sucked, because I couldn't even call them to admit I had been wrong. Ugh.

Mack and I had been thrown in iron cages. These bastards had locked cuffs on my wrists that blocked me from using my powers. It was like they knew we'd try to escape. I couldn't blame them for thinking that, because if it hadn't been for the cuffs that I'd woken with after being knocked out, I would have fried them all.

Every day was exactly the same. The first guards would wake us at dawn. The only reason I knew it was dawn was that there was one small window on the other side of the Pit from where our cages were, and I could see it from my cage.

After kicking the bars to wake us, the guards would throw breakfast at us. Most days it was a granola bar and a bottle of water. But the Pit champion from the day before was given bacon and eggs with toast and coffee. That was enough motivation for most of us in these cages to fight. Of course, the other motivation was fear of death. There was nothing keeping our competitors from killing us.

We had watched it happen several times. The winner got carried away and landed a deadly blow. That never changed the outcome of the fights. The guards just cleaned up and moved on. The survivors were taken back to the cages until the next fight they were scheduled to take part in.

We were only given two meals a day, and most days we were lucky if both meals were granola and water. Sometimes it was just bread. And since there was no privacy in the cells, if we needed to go to the bathroom our choices were to hold it until the two times a day we were escorted to the actual bathroom or use a bucket. I could see how living like this could break a person.

Just when I thought it couldn't get any worse, the Chairman started coming to watch the fights. If we didn't put on a good enough show for him, he would have fighters executed. It got even worse when he started making Zoey come down to watch our fights. He didn't make her watch anyone else, just Mack and myself. I knew it was a ploy to convince her she could save us, and I hoped it didn't work. I would gladly fight every day for the rest of my life to spare her from becoming his concubine.

I had also seen a dark-haired woman sneaking around by the Pit. She obviously thought she was being stealthy, but if anyone had really been paying attention, they would have noticed her. I wondered who she was and what she wanted. It didn't matter, because I didn't trust anyone around here anyway.

I spent my days either training in my cell or fighting in the Pit. Nights were spent trying to sleep, then giving up and talking to Mack. He seemed to be having the same problem. It was hard to get comfortable enough to rest when you had no idea if someone would come to kill you in your sleep. We didn't get to see much of the compound outside the cages and the Pit.

I wondered if either Kyro or Zoey was able to scope the place out and plot an escape route. I was guessing they were in pretty much the same position as Mack and me, just without the physically fighting for their lives part.

It was hard to stave off the depression that reared its ugly head. Spending so much time in the dark had never been good for me. I knew our captors didn't care about my mental health. After all, they didn't even bother to treat physical injuries unless they prevented someone from fighting.

The first few days we were here, it seemed like someone was always trying to escape. It was bad for them but good for us. We learned really quickly what wouldn't work. All that was left was to figure out what would. Mack and I had been working on it for days and still hadn't finalized a plan. It was hard to strategize when we weren't allowed out of our cages at the same time.

Every time the guards came and took him to fight in the Pit, I was sick with worry until they led him back. He was always bruised and bloodied, but he was alive. That was the important part. We had to stay alive. I had to concentrate on that thought when the guards took me to the Pit for my fights.

In the beginning, the fights were fairly easy, as if they were trying to gauge our skill. Mack and I discussed each fight afterward, trying to plot strategy and prepare for the next battle. Each fight became progressively more challenging. I wasn't sure if they had one massive guy that we would end up pitted against, or if they would start doing multi-person fights.

There was a part of me that loved the fighting. It was exhilarating and filled me with adrenaline. It was what I had trained for. Another part of me just wanted to be free of this place. I wanted to escape it all and run away with Mack. For once, I was making plans for the future. I had a pretty good idea that Mack felt the same way, but neither of us said it out loud.

Four

Zoey

IT DIDN'T TAKE LONG to figure out exactly what the Chairman meant when he said he would keep me. He seemed to have access to Race's memories, at least in part, and tried to use them to steer me toward a relationship with him. It would have been like old times. Except this guy isn't Race, and I had no interest in a relationship with him.

I saw Jack every day, but he wasn't himself. I couldn't figure out why, but he acted like the Chairman was Race. The Chairman tried to force me to love him. He tried ordering it, and when that didn't work, he tried beating me. That was the one thing Jack wouldn't tolerate. And I knew it would get him killed if he kept going up against our captor. Jack was the reason I conceded. I couldn't stand the thought of him getting hurt or killed because he stood up for me.

I resisted at first, but the punishments kept getting more severe until I gave up and started going along with it. The first punishment was simply being locked in my room without food or water for a day.

The next was the same plus lashes with a whip. There was a point when they tried magic on me, and I decided that was my out. I could pretend this imposter was my ex-boyfriend, but I refused to act like I was interested in dating him. When I stopped fighting, I started treating him like I had Race. Friendly but distant was the best I could offer. Their mage either didn't notice that his spell had no effect on me, or he didn't care enough to tell his boss. I suspected from his attitude toward the Chairman that it was the latter.

Once I gave in and pretended that the mage's spell had worked, the Chairman started giving me gifts and would get upset if I didn't wear them. I indulged him to keep my friends safe. He was the most enthusiastic about a silver filigree bracelet. He insisted that I wear it and never take it off. He even began popping in my room randomly to see if I was wearing it. He was definitely a strange man.

After a few weeks, I heard reports that Q and Mack were doing well in the fights that were held in the Pit. I also heard that Kyro had been killed in a cave-in, but I suspected that was just a story the Chairman made up to force me to get over my feelings for Kyro. It didn't work. I wouldn't believe that he was gone even if someone had shown me a body.

It seemed like we'd been trapped here forever. After a while, the days all ran together. It became harder to remember exactly how we got here. I could feel my memories fade but couldn't do anything to stop it. I tried to hold onto names and faces, but it didn't work. I tried to figure out exactly what had changed before I lost all of my memories, but I couldn't get the pieces to fit together.

I woke with a sense of dread tugging at my consciousness. Something was wrong. I couldn't remember anything before the past two weeks. I had that nagging feeling I was forgetting something important. I just couldn't put my finger on what it could be. I took a chance and asked Jack about it when he came to pick me up.

I remembered I was going somewhere with Jack and Race but still felt like I was forgetting something. As soon as he knocked on the door, I started questioning him.

"Jack, I feel like I'm forgetting something important. Any idea what it might be?"

He looked puzzled. "No idea. Maybe Race will know. We need to get moving so we're not late."

"Give me a minute." I stepped back into the bathroom and looked around. Maybe this would help me remember. I caught my reflection in the mirror. It was me, but something was different.

I couldn't explain it, but there was a strange glow around my reflection. For a second, I thought the reflection flickered, almost as if another face had replaced mine. I blinked and then looked again, but it was just me. The glow had faded. I knew Jack was getting impatient, so I grabbed a hair tie and walked back to the other room.

"OK, let's go. Maybe Race will know what it is I'm forgetting. Or maybe it's just not that important." I couldn't shrug off the feeling that something about this whole situation was wrong.

We walked down the corridor, chatting as usual. It was obvious Jack didn't have the same nagging feeling I did. I guessed I would have to stop obsessing over it and hope it came to me. I could ask Race, but something inside me was screaming not to tell him about that feeling or about what had happened with the mirror. I tried to put it all out of my mind for a bit so I could focus on hanging out with the guys.

We arrived at the Pit before Race got there. Jack and I took our seats in the VIP section and waited. It seemed odd to me that Race had suddenly become so interested in fighting. He had insisted on coming here every day this week so far. It wasn't bad to watch unless one of the fighters got out of control. These athletes were very skilled though. Sometimes they made it look as though it was a fight to the death. And everyone stayed in character. The special effects were fantastic.

There were two fighters I enjoyed watching the most. Both had red hair, but one was a dwarven man and the other was a woman who looked to be of elven descent. They never fought at the same time, which seemed odd to me, because their fighting styles were eerily similar. At times, it was almost as if I knew what their next move would be before they did it. I had noticed Race staring at me when I watched these two but hadn't worked up the courage to ask him why. It seemed like he was gauging my reaction to what they went through.

As we sat there waiting, I hoped my favorites would be fighting today. The bouts seemed to go by faster when those two were involved, and there weren't any overly dramatic theatrics. It was just fighting, then they left the ring. Some of the others would make a show of winning with some dance or fancy fighting moves as they went around the ring after the bout. It was a bit much if you asked me.

FIVE

Jack

AFTER THE FIRST NIGHT, I forgot why I'd been so angry with Race. Something bugged me about the way he was acting, but not enough to say anything. He sent me to escort Zoey around the complex every day. He explained that our jobs here were sensitive, and the area was dangerous. Apparently, we were supposed to be investigating the fighting pit.

So, I kept my mouth shut and my eyes open. I didn't quite trust him. I couldn't do anything without proof he was doing something illegal though. I decided protecting Zoey would be my top priority before Race even said anything.

I didn't say anything to Zoey, but Race seemed different. It was almost as if he was a totally different person. I felt like I barely knew him. Zoey seemed the same as always, so there had to be something about Race that was different. I had to figure out what had changed.

We spent almost every day at the Pit, watching the fights and trying to solidify our cover. Or at least that was what Race told me. He told Zoey he was just really interested in this fighting reenactment club, and he enjoyed watching the actors play these characters. It didn't make sense that he wouldn't just tell Zoey we were undercover. I had already told her about me working for her mom and the Patrol. Race insisted she be kept in the dark about our mission for her safety.

It seemed to me if he was concerned for her safety, he wouldn't be parading her around here like she was a prize he won. For whatever reason, Mama Bear had chosen him to lead this mission, and she was apparently fine with her daughter potentially being used as bait.

Even though the whole thing seemed fishy to me, I couldn't prove anything, and being undercover prevented contacting Mama Bear myself. All I could do was follow orders and protect Zoey. That wouldn't stop me from doing some digging on my off time, but Race didn't need to know about that.

After the most recent bout of fights, Race decided we all needed to check out the mining camp in the compound. Of course, he walked in the front and had me follow behind with Zoey. It made sense with our cover story that she was his girlfriend and I was their bodyguard. This place was crazy. If I didn't know better, I would think these people were being held prisoner. Race assured me that it was just part of the entertainment experience of the camp, but something just didn't feel right about it. I kept my eyes and ears open as we walked.

He stopped at the mouth of a cave and turned to us. "I'd like to check this one out. You can come along or go back to your room." He had directed his statement to Zoey.

I knew she hated being locked up in her room all the time. "We'll tag along if that's OK with you." I didn't give her a chance to refuse. She gave me a smile in response. It seemed strange to me that she was being really quiet. It wasn't like her. Maybe she was catching on to all the odd things happening around us. I'd have to talk to her about it later.

"Very well. Let's go." Race marched off into the cave as if he owned the place. At this point, I was beginning to wonder if he really did. Zoey and I followed quickly behind him.

He inspected some jewels and gold that had been harvested, then had some words with one of the mine overseers. I couldn't make out what he was saying because they had stepped away from us. I didn't pay much attention anyway. Zoey seemed to be happy to be out of her room for longer than usual.

"Are you OK?" I asked cautiously.

Her distracted expression faded to confusion. "I'm fine. This all just seems strange. Maybe we can talk about it later? Let's give Race a moment to talk with his friend." Zoey started to walk in the opposite direction from where Race was talking. I followed her to make sure nothing happened. She turned left and started down a tunnel, running a hand over the wall as she walked.

"Isn't it creepy down here? The cave is beautiful, but the atmosphere is like a story I read about people being forced into slavery and mining for the land baron." Zoey and her books. It was so rare not to see her with a book in her hand. I guess with us traveling, there was no way she could risk bringing any with her.

I chuckled, "I didn't read that one, but of course you'd have a book to compare life to right now."

She smiled sheepishly before turning away again. It was nice that we were able to spend this time together, no matter the reason for it. I loved being around her. I followed as she explored further.

We came upon a man sitting down who appeared to be chained to a spot on the floor. He had just enough chain attached to his ankle to reach the wall. He stood up quickly as if he had been startled by our approach. His face lit up when he saw us. Just as he started to speak, Race stomped up behind us.

"Jack, you were supposed to keep her at the front of the cave. This part is dangerous. I just found out that these people in chains are criminals. We need to go."

I shot him a puzzled look, then walked over to Zoey. She seemed to be entranced by the chained man, who looked oddly familiar. With his olive skin and dark brown curls, I was pretty sure I would have remembered meeting him. There were so many things about this whole mission that just didn't make sense.

"Come on, Zoey, we have to go now." I gently grabbed her arm and turned her back toward the entrance of the cave. She looked over her shoulder at the man again and, with a sad expression, turned and walked with me.

"I just don't understand why I can't talk to anyone here. It's almost like I'm a prisoner. I know I sound like a spoiled child, but I hate it here." Zoey's disdain was obvious.

I shook my head again, trying to think of how to explain it to her without giving her any confidential information. "I'm sorry you feel that way. You know Race and I are working for your mom. And for some reason, she decided you'd be better off here with us. That's really all I can tell you." Trying to smooth things over for Race just felt wrong when I knew I was the one who was really in love with her.

It made me wish we'd never made that promise all those years ago to not pursue things. I hated watching her with Race. It was worse knowing she wasn't really interested in him. I was terrified he would convince her to marry him, and she would be stuck. I couldn't stand watching her wilt again under his thumb, especially when I knew he was sleeping with other women. He always slept with other women. Race was the least faithful man I'd ever known.

SIX

Shannon

When I'd heard of the Chairman's success, I had to see for myself. I knew I'd betrayed my son by giving up his location, but it wasn't the first time I'd done something he and his father would look down on me for. Those two had always thought they were better than me. I'd show them. I'd show them all. I was pretty impressed with the fact I'd bargained to keep the little shit out of the Pit, and I was planning to let him know that one was all me.

I'd given myself to the Chairman for years in exchange for the promise that he'd spare my son. They were so close to finding a way to transfer powers without killing the donor, and I wanted Kyro's powers, but I wanted him to see me with them. It wouldn't be any fun to steal his powers if I couldn't rub it in his face while I used them as he was just a lousy powerless human.

All I had to do was play along with whatever sick fantasy the Chairman had, and I got what I wanted. It wasn't so bad, especially since his new look was way more attractive than the last one. Not that Dmitri hadn't been a handsome man, I just prefer younger ones.

Watching the Chairman kill him and take over his identity had been thrilling, though I'd never admit it to anyone but myself. I figured Dmitri had it coming for betraying the Boss in the first place. It was no secret he'd run off with a prisoner years ago and that the Boss had spent so much time hunting him down. The amusing part was that he got caught trying to get back into the Order. I guess he hadn't learned anything by finding a way out.

The ability to change bodies at will was a perk of being a doppelganger. Magical beings had it so much better than the rest of us. Not that I'd know much about magic, since I wasn't born with any. What little I'd managed to steal hadn't lasted long enough to even cast a decent spell. As soon as Jeremy figured out the transfer, I'd know true power. And Kyro would know what it was like to be human, struggling while everyone around him used magic to their advantage. He would suffer the way I'd suffered since I gave birth to him. Then we'd finally be even.

I waited a few days before taking the chance of going to see him. I'd heard he had something going with one of the girls he'd been brought in with. I figured I'd check them all out first. Everyone was talking about the red-haired half-elf who got taken to the Pit, and I figured that was as good a place to start as any. She sounded like the type he'd go for.

I took a few hours to myself after the Chairman was finished with me. I snuck down to the Pits to watch the fights. It wasn't anything I hadn't done before, but I was being careful not to be noticed. I wanted to check out my son's potential girlfriend without anyone realizing what I was doing. The Chairman was the only one who knew Kyro was my son, and I wanted to keep it that way.

I sat in the third row of the bleachers that were set up around the Pit. I planned to watch the fights for a while before I went to track her down. The first fight was over way too quickly, but the pairing was uneven. They did that from time to time, to give the bigger guys a break and to weed out the weak. If the smaller guy could win, he deserved to live.

The second match was a large man, well over six feet tall and probably close to three hundred pounds of pure muscle. That's what you needed to survive the Pit. It was obvious he'd been here for a while. He looked seasoned and a bit disinterested in the whole process. That could be dangerous. People died when they became complacent. You had to keep your guard up at all times in this world, or you'd get yourself killed.

His opponent didn't look thrilled to be shoved into the ring, and I didn't blame him. I was fairly sure the poor little guy didn't have a chance. He was about two feet shorter than the big guy and might have weighed one-fifty, but that was being generous. He had red hair braided into two plaits on each side, and his beard had braids through it as well. I hadn't seen him before, so he must have come in with Kyro. This should be over quickly, then I'd go look for the girl.

The big guy stomped forward after the gong that signaled the start of the fight. The little guy just stood there. He was either brave or stupid. Maybe he had a death wish. It was hard to tell. At the moment the big guy reached him though, he crouched low and dodged the first swing.

This fight was designed to be unfair because neither of them was allowed weapons. Of course, that meant it probably wasn't meant to be a fight to the death. I couldn't imagine how it wouldn't be though, as much of a difference in size as there was. As soon as the thought crossed my mind, the big guy fell to the ground hard.

The little guy had managed to not only knock him down but to knock him out as well. The fight was over, and the little guy had won. These fights were the only thing that resulted in rules being enforced in the Pit. The little guy wouldn't be touched for a week because he had bested an opponent twice his size. After that week was up, though, he would probably have to fight every day just to prove himself.

I followed the guards as they escorted the little guy back to his cage. I figured it was the easiest way to find the girl. Turns out, their cages were right next to each other. From the look on her face when he was thrown into the cage, she wasn't Kyro's girl. It appeared they were trying to hide their relationship to protect each other in the fights, but it was obvious from the way she looked at him. She belonged to this guy. I didn't really care who she slept with, but it was a little disappointing she wasn't the one. I would have had fun with her. Oh, well, I knew there was another girl who had come in with them, I just had to find her. I wandered off toward my room to start looking.

It took me a couple of days to find her, and, to be honest, I didn't understand the attraction. She was blue. I don't mean sad. I mean, like, her skin was literally blue. How could he find that attractive? Maybe she did something special for him. Maybe she was wild in bed. Whatever. It really didn't matter. I wondered if she'd still like him once his powers were stripped. I wondered if she had powers of her own. I would have to look into that. I needed to ask Jeremy if he could make the power stripping spell to take both of their powers and give them to me permanently.

I watched her for a few minutes. I had planned to talk to her, maybe play a little cat and mouse, but I wasn't fond of aliens and decided she wasn't worth my time. Not that I'm racist or anything, I just preferred my own people over those who were different. I mean, my son is a demi-god, so I can't be racist, right?

I decided I'd rather go see my boy. I was still keeping his parentage hidden, so I treated it like the Chairman had sent me to the mines to question him for something. No one would dare to challenge me.

I walked up to the idiot guard who was supervising Kyro as he mined for gems and metals. "I need to talk to this one."

He nodded. "Hey, you. Come here."

Kyro did as he was told. I was impressed he didn't react when he saw me. The coldness in his eyes told me everything I needed to know.

"Go with her," the guard said as he unlocked the ankle chains and shoved Kyro at me.

I turned and started walking away, not even looking to see if he was following me. I knew he was. He wanted answers and knew that would be the only way to get them. I could feel the hate in his gaze on the back of my neck, but his opinion never really mattered to me.

I took him into a conference room over by the Pit. Describing it as a conference room may be an overstatement since this room was typically used to beat confessions out of people. I offered him a chair, but he crossed his arms and leaned against the wall.

"I'm sure you have questions," I started.

He glared and nodded. "What do you want?"

"To talk to my only son, of course. What else would I possibly want?" I poured the words out as though they were coated with honey.

He rolled his eyes and his words were coated with acid. "Like that ever mattered to you. What do you want, *Shannon*?"

"Ouch, son. You'll make me feel like you're upset with me for something. After everything I've done to protect you, I can't believe you'd talk to me like this." I sniffed a little, as though I was going to cry.

"Dry it up, Shannon. We both know you don't actually care about me, other than your crazy idea to take my powers. Is that what this is about? Did you finally figure out how to do it?" His words were as cold as his eyes, and it did sting a little bit to hear my own flesh and blood talk to me this way, but I'd never admit it to him.

"No, but I'm close. You should be thanking me. You could have ended up in the Pit, literally fighting for your life every day like your friends are. Even worse, you could have been killed. I kept that from happening to you." I wanted him to know I was taking care of him, I just wasn't prepared to tell him exactly why.

"Gee, *Mom*, thanks so much. I'm sure you're doing this out of the kindness of your heart, and not because you're trying to find a way to steal my powers and kill me." Sarcasm dripped from his words, and for a moment, it was like a knife twisting in my heart.

I had made so many mistakes with him. Probably the biggest one was trying to take his powers. I should have just taken them from someone else, but I knew he would try to stop me. And to be honest, he was the strongest magic user I'd ever met. I wanted his powers, even if it killed him.

The sad thing was that he knew it. That made him dangerous. I would have to push Jeremy a little harder to get the power transfer spell done.

seven

KYRO

SHANNON TOOK ME BACK to the mines as soon as she realized I wasn't going to be friendly or helpful. She made veiled threats against my friends, which pissed me off. I knew she couldn't touch Zoey because the Chairman was interested in her, but there was nothing I could do to protect the others. I almost gave in when she threatened them, but I know I'd never get away from her if I bowed to her demands.

I still didn't know what her demands were, but it didn't matter, I would never agree to help her with anything. She hadn't done anything for me since I was small, so why would I think she wanted to protect me now? She was a power-hungry liar, and I refused to even listen to her latest scheme.

It scared me to think she had faked her own death just to hide the fact she was still after my powers. There was nothing I could do to stop her, given my current situation. I spent my days mining for gems and metals, and my nights dreaming of Zoey and cursing these damned cuffs that kept me from astral projecting to her.

I tried to figure out a way to remove the cuffs but hadn't been able to sneak any tools or make any in my room. If I could manage to get the cuffs off, I knew I could find a way to get all of us out of here. Unfortunately for me, I was heavily guarded when I was around the tools. Probably for just that reason. It didn't help that the tools were locked up at night too, so it would do no good to sneak out and try to steal them. It was amusing that the tools were locked up better than the prisoners were.

Shannon had done one thing for me though. She showed me how to get to the Pit. I needed to check on Mack and Q. I was desperate to check on Zoey, but I knew that would be nearly impossible, especially with Jack guarding her. I'd heard guards in the mines talk about her and how he's always with her. I guess I should take comfort in that, but it just makes me angry.

I couldn't figure out why Jack would suddenly switch sides on us. He seemed so adamant that the Chairman had killed his friend, and now he was working for the murdering asshole. There had to be more to it than I could see.

I had figured out how to get out of my room the first night but hadn't acted on it, because I wasn't sure how often the guards patrolled. The hinges weren't the strongest I'd encountered, and with a little bit of effort, I was able to remove the door from them just enough to slip out. After a few days of watching while pretending to be asleep, I had the schedule down. As long as no one tried to escape, I'd be fine.

I eased the door open a crack to see out. As expected, there was no one around. I crept out and followed the path Shannon had inadvertently shown me to the Pit. It wasn't hard to find the cages after that. I kept to the shadows to avoid being seen. A few minutes later, I found myself standing outside Mack's cage. Q's cage was right next to his. I figured that was a manipulation tactic of the Chairman.

"Psst, Mack. Wake up," I whispered.

"Hmm?" He responded.

"Mack, it's me. I need to talk to you. Wake up." I whispered again, a little louder, but very cautious about waking anyone else.

"Kyro?" The question came in hushed tones from Q's cage.

"Yeah. I can't stay long, but I had to check on you two. Are you guys OK? Have you seen Zoey?" I couldn't stop myself from asking about her, even though I was sure I already knew the answer.

"We're as OK as we can be right now. Unfortunately, yeah, we've seen her. Sometimes he makes her come watch us fight. I think he's trying to use us to get to her. I hope it's not working, but we both know her and how soft she is. He may have done something to her; she doesn't seem to have the same look in her eyes that she did when we got caught."

I hoped Zoey could hold out a little longer. I needed to come up with a plan.

"I have to go before I get caught. I'll come back in a few days. I can't risk being gone every night. Someone will notice." I hated leaving them in cages like this, but I had no choice. I couldn't break them out until I had a way to get all of us together and out of here.

She nodded. "Be careful. I'll tell Mack what he missed in the morning before they take us to fight."

I crept back to my room, which was more like a cell, and silently closed the door, locking it carefully. Just as I laid down on my cot, I heard the guard doing his rounds. I had just made it. My heart pounded in my chest. It took a while to calm down after being so close to getting caught. I could only imagine what fresh hell I would have been subjected to if the guard had caught me outside the cell.

It didn't take long to find out, though, because one of the guys whose cell was a few down from mine had apparently figured out how to jimmy the lock too. I heard the sirens announce a break, then the guards as they stomped through checking every cell. I pretended they had woken me from sleep when they slammed the door open and searched my room.

They all cheered when they caught the guy. I heard one guard say he was really close to one of the exits. I made a decision to talk to that guy tomorrow. I needed to know where the exits were.

Unfortunately, when I looked for him the next day, I couldn't find him. I played dumb about the escape attempt and asked a guard where he was.

"Hey, where's the other guy? You know, the scrawny one whose cell is a few down from mine. I haven't seen him today," I asked as though I was just curious.

"He tried to escape last night. That's what all the commotion was about. Don't worry, he's being strung up in the Pit as we speak. Now get back to work." The guard was gruff and motioned at me with his gun, so I turned and went back to the wall I had been mining.

So much for trying to get help with our escape. And now I knew what they did with people who tried to get out. I just had to find a way to make sure that didn't happen to us.

EIGHT

Jack

No matter how hard I tried, I couldn't break the control spell the Chairman had put on me. His goons had sedated me and put this amulet around my neck while I was knocked out. I couldn't make a move to take it off, and I couldn't say anything about it. During the day, I get caught up in the spell and believed the things he made me say about everything being better here. At night, alone in my room, I knew the truth. I wasn't sure if that was part of the spell, or if I was more able to resist when I was alone.

I hated having to escort Zoey to her 'dates' with him. I was impressed she had managed to convince the doctor to lie for her and fake test results to keep the Chairman out of her bed. Every time I looked at him, wearing my best friend's face, I wanted to beat the shit out of him. That stupid amulet kept me in line. I despised the feeling of not being in control of myself. It took me right back to Chris and Katie's boat when they had implanted mind-control chips into me and Zoey. Her friends had rescued us from that, so I was trusting them to save us from this as well.

I hoped that Zoey knew this wasn't me, that there was a reason I was acting this way. Every time I tried to talk to her about it, my words got changed around and came out meaningless. After a few attempts, I gave up trying.

From my time spent as the Chairman's lackey, I learned he was a doppelganger who could take on the appearance of anyone he had killed. That gave me definitive proof that he was the one responsible for Race's death, not that I'd been able to share that info with the Patrol to clear Zoey's name.

Even though I was under his control, he kept me away from everyone but Zoey. I was allowed to interact with his servants, him, and Zoey. That was it. No one else was allowed to speak to me, and I wasn't able to speak to anyone else. I wished I had Zoey's ability to astral project.

Of course, there was no way to know if I'd even be successful using magic while I was wearing this thing around my neck. It didn't matter anyway because I didn't have magic, so I was forced to do the Chairman's bidding. I was glad he hadn't made me do anything except escort Zoey from her room to wherever he wanted her to go. I guess he figured I'd protect her better than anyone else, although I'm sure Kyro would argue about that with me if he had the chance.

More often than not, the Chairman wanted to see Zoey alone. In those situations, I guess I served as a chaperone, though I couldn't have stopped him if he'd attacked her. I noticed he didn't put magic-blocking cuffs on her, which seemed odd to me. Maybe he didn't realize she had powers. I really didn't know the extent of what she had, just that she had them.

On our trips to the Pit for Zoey to watch the fights with the Chairman, I noticed that several of the captives were wearing the same cuffs as I'd seen on Kyro and Q. I deduced that those were the magic users and the cuffs were how the Order kept them from fighting back.

NINE

Mack

MY HEART DROPPED WHEN the Chairman had arrived at our cages and announced that Quinn and I had been taken to the Pit. I should have known that was where we were when we'd woken up in cages. I'd heard of the Pit of Pierus over the years and none of it was good. At least he'd decided to spare Zoey and Kyro from it. Given that the Order had somehow managed to take control of Jack's mind and turn him into a mindless goon, I figured getting out of here was going to be way more difficult than originally anticipated.

Quinn and I were escorted down to the cells near the Pit. Of course, we weren't allowed to stay together, but at least our cells were close enough that we could still talk and even touch hands if the guards weren't around. We learned in the first few days that the guards only checked on us twice a day unless there was an escape attempt. That would cause a lockdown and guards would be everywhere until they were sure we were secure.

I spent my days in the cell praying to Hestia that we would find peace after this trial was completed. I never received a sign, but my faith did not waver. My family had prayed to the Goddess of Hearth and Home for as long as I could remember, and she had always protected us. I continued praying even when they started taking us to fight in the Pit.

I spent my evenings quietly trying to reassure Quinn that someday we would escape this hell and be free again.

"Are you all right, love?" I whispered to her, as the guards swarmed and searched for the guy who had tried to escape. We had seen where he ran and knew there was little chance, he'd make it out of here alone.

She gave a slight nod without looking at me. "I'd be better if we weren't in cages waiting to find out how we're going to die. Given the situation, I'm glad to be with you."

I knew she'd been crying, though she'd never admit it. She kept her face turned away from me a lot since we'd been put in these cages. I knew that because I spent my days staring at her unless one of us was taken to fight.

Her words were bittersweet and laced with sadness. I feared she would give up on ever tasting freedom again if something didn't happen soon. We waited out the guards, keeping to ourselves so we didn't draw attention to our relationship. I knew that was something that could be used against us down here.

She had been dragged out of her cell early. It had been more than an hour ago. I was worried that the worst had happened. We'd been forced to fight for our lives in the Pit on a nearly daily basis since we were locked up here. The fights usually lasted between ten and twenty minutes, depending on the skill of the opponent.

I always hated the look in her eyes when she returned. Even though they had found a way to keep her from being able to use her fire magic, she was always triumphant. I knew she had spent years training for this type of thing. That didn't mean I had to like what it was doing to her.

The guards came to get me, and she still hadn't returned. After the first few days, they had stopped putting shackles on us to take us to the Pit, so the guard just opened the door to my cage and gestured for me to come out. "Please, what's happened to the lass from the cage next to mine?" I decided it couldn't hurt to ask.

The response I got was dark and ominous. "You'll find out in a minute." He shoved me to get me moving, then every few seconds he would shove me again to keep me moving.

I struggled with what he might mean by that. I found myself face to face with the ugly truth of my situation moments later. I stood next to Quinn in the center of the Pit. Her fists were bloody, and her face was streaked with dirt and tears. Her clothes were tattered, but her flame-red hair was still tied back in the same braid that had held it this morning, though tendrils of it curled and stuck to her neck with sweat. My heart went crazy being this close to her with no bars between us. I knew I still couldn't touch her, or even proclaim my feelings for her. I had to keep her safe no matter what.

My eyes were drawn to the spectator box ahead of us, where the Chairman usually sat to watch the fights. He was standing there, wearing the face of a dead man, with an evil smirk skewing his features. By this time, I had almost certainly figured out what he had in mind, and I knew how this would end. There would be no way to deny my love for Quinn after what was about to occur. I prayed she would survive and be able to forgive herself.

The Chairman met my eyes and nodded in recognition. "You will fight...to the death. If you refuse, you will both be killed. You will begin when the gong sounds." With that, he took his seat.

Q looked down at me, tears spilling from her autumn eyes. "I can't. I won't."

"You must, love. I need you to live, and make him pay for what he's done to our family."

She shook her head violently. "Mack, I...I'm not strong enough. I can't live without you."

I couldn't tell her that I wasn't sure if I was strong enough to go through with it. I had to do it. For her.

Ten

q

MACK INSISTED THAT I would be the one to kill him, so I would be able to live. I couldn't do it. I wouldn't do it. Even if it meant I would die instead. I was prepared to give my life for him. At that moment, if it hadn't been for the cuffs that prevented me from using my fire magic, I knew I would have fried them all. I hated being able to feel my magic building inside me but not having a way to release it.

The Chairman sounded a gong, and weapons were thrown down for Mack and me to use. Neither of us made a move to pick up the swords at our feet.

"You will fight to the death, or both of you will die." I knew from what Zoey told us that this guy was somehow wearing her ex-boyfriend's face. The face was beautiful, but it didn't disguise the ugliness inside this beast. He seemed to be enjoying the fear and pain he was causing. He spoke again. "Let's see how this plays out, shall we?"

He turned to the guards stationed around the Pit. "If they don't pick up the swords and start fighting, shoot them. Not to kill, just to maim." The guards all nodded, and I heard guns cocking all around us.

Mack picked up both swords, turned to me and held one out. "We have to, love. There's no way out of it. Please, just take the sword."

I nodded reluctantly and took the sword he held out to me. I was determined not to use it, no matter how many times these assholes shot me.

"OK, love, now let's spar. Just like practicing on the boat. It's alright, nobody's going to get hurt." Mack said as he gently swung the sword at me, allowing plenty of time for me to react and block his swing. We parried back and forth for a while until Mack noticed the Chairman getting frustrated.

"It has to happen now, love. It's time." His eyes never wavered from mine as he spoke. I knew what he wanted me to do, but I couldn't bring myself to actually do it. I held the sword off to the side, pointing away from him.

"Mack...I can't." I couldn't find the right words. I couldn't be expected to kill the man I love. That was cruel, and I refused to cooperate with that idea. The Chairman must have noticed my attitude about his plan because he sent some of his henchmen into the Pit to kill us both if we didn't comply. Although I couldn't figure out why they didn't just shoot us. I was guessing it was all part of that sick bastard's plan.

I was ready to fight by Mack's side. I took a defensive stance, crouched and ready to spring at the six men as they headed our way. Before I had the chance, I heard Mack beside me. I turned my head towards the oncoming guards and I almost missed his whisper.

"Forgive me, love. I'm doing this for you." And before the words could even register in my mind, Mack was chest-deep on my sword. I didn't have time to react before his body went slack. He was gone. By my own hand. This couldn't be real. I blinked a few times to clear the tears that were streaming down my face.

At that moment, something inside me broke. I felt numb as I watched myself go through the motions. I heard a feral scream, then realized it was coming from me. I released the sword and watched Mack fall backward. I knew he had done it to save me, but I still felt responsible. I would never be able to forgive myself. I had killed the one man who truly loved me and made me feel worthy of that love.

With another scream, I threw my hands in the air, curled my fingers into fists, and brought them back to my sides. I felt the power inside myself bubble to the boiling point, until I felt as though I was on fire from the inside out. I glanced at my left wrist and watched in amusement as the power blocking cuff melted off my wrist and fell to the ground. I turned my head just in time to watch the one from my right wrist do the same. I now had full access to my powers, and no reason to reign them in.

I felt the flames take over before I even saw them. When I looked down again, there were trails of flames covering my skin like veins. It didn't burn me, but it helped to release some of the pent-up magic that had been suppressed since we got here. A wicked smirk crossed my lips as I zeroed in on my prey.

I turned toward the six men who had stopped in their tracks as this scene played out. I held my left hand out, turned my palm up towards the ceiling, and created a fireball the size of a basketball. I launched the flaming sphere at these men, who I blamed for the death of my love. I watched three of them burst into flames, as the other three kept coming at me. I sent three more fireballs at the remaining men, taking each of them out of the picture and watching their flesh melt from their bones. I had never had an issue with killing for a purpose before, but this was different.

I killed these men for revenge. For myself. For Mack. And I enjoyed it. I didn't just kill them, I burned them alive. I set them on fire and watched their flesh melt from their bones. It scared me how much I reveled in their deaths. But that didn't matter to me at the moment. There was more to do before I was finished. I might consider the moral ramifications later, but for now, I was a woman on a mission.

I turned my attention to the Chairman. Or at least where the Chairman had been before Mack died. The chair was empty, and the room appeared to have been locked down. That wouldn't stop me. I would have my revenge, and my friends and I would be free once more. Not that freedom meant anything to me at that moment, but I knew I owed it to Mack to grant his last request. Once our friends were freed, I was going to burn this compound to the ground. With any luck, I'd take the Chairman down with it. If I find out he escaped, I'll hunt him down like the animal he is. He will die at my hand, no matter the cost.

ELeven

KYRO

I HEARD THE COMMOTION from the mines. People were running from the pits as though something was chasing them. I tried to get a good look, but the guard who was watching my section shouted for us to keep working. I heard him call someone on the radio but couldn't understand the response.

It was hard to keep track of the days down here, so I wasn't sure just how long it had been since I'd seen Zoey. All I knew was that I had seen Mack and Q after the Chairman had taken Zoey away. Or rather after he had Jack take Zoey away. I didn't understand that either. Jack had seemed like a pretty tough guy, but he was manipulated so easily.

I spent most of my days down there thinking about everything and trying to figure it out. I had no idea why Mack and Q had been selected for the Pit, but I had been sent to the mines. I hadn't come up with a good reason for it, other than maybe he thought we were less of a threat if we were split up. I couldn't get past the feeling that there had to be more to his reasoning, but I hadn't figured it out yet. Unless Shannon had been telling the truth, and she was the one who kept me from going to the Pit—that made the most sense, but she'd never done anything to help me before, so it seemed unlikely. Whether she was lying or not, I knew I couldn't trust her.

I tried really hard to stay off the radar by doing what I was told and not talking to anyone. I was starting to worry about Zoey. And with that big commotion going on, it seemed like the perfect time to at least consider trying to escape.

I knew I wouldn't get very far as long as that guard was here. Especially with him holding that gun. The screams were getting closer, and I could smell ash, as though something nearby was on fire.

I saw the fireball come into the cavern before I recognized the source. It hit the guard square in the back as he was currently focused on me and the other prisoners who were forced to mine for metals and precious gems. When he realized he had been set on fire, his screams echoed down the caverns. He started to melt before he even had a chance to stop, drop, and roll.

As the fire went out, I realized that the other guards had disappeared. I was still chained in place, but there was no longer the threat of being shot if I stopped working. I dropped my pickaxe and turned to the opening of the cave. There was a familiar shadow in the entrance.

Q stood there, watching the guard die. She hadn't even seemed to notice me. I knew they had put cuffs on her to keep her powers blocked, and I had no idea how she had managed to remove them.

"Q! Come help me get this chain off my leg. Then we can go find the others and get out of here." I yelled at her, and while her expression didn't change, she did turn her head and look in my direction.

She walked towards me, conjuring a small fireball in her right hand as she moved. Her eyes met mine, and I could feel her pain. I had no idea what had happened, but just then, for the first time, I was terrified of her. I knew she held more power than any of us realized, but even I hadn't expected this. For a moment, her eyes blazed red.

I knew there was no way I could fight her, as I still wore the power blocking cuffs on my wrists. All I could do was try to talk her out of it.

"Q? Are you OK? You remember me, right? It's Kyro. Just take a minute and breathe."

Her expression still didn't change, and she didn't drop the fireball. When she spoke, her voice was flat and emotionless, although her eyes gave her away. "Don't worry Kyro, I'm not planning to hurt you. I'm freeing you. I'm going to kill all of them, though." As she spoke, she released the fireball at a target behind me.

Once the ball of flame hit, I realized another guard had been coming up behind me. She had just saved my life. I stood there in shock as she carefully melted the chain from my ankle.

"This may hurt, but I can get those cuffs off of you if you want." Q's voice was still flat and emotionless as she held out a glowing hand.

"It's fine, just get them off," I said.

I placed my wrist in her hand and watched the cuff melt away, then gave her my other wrist for the second cuff. She was right, it did hurt. It was worth a little pain to have these things off and be able to use my powers again. Besides, Mack would be able to heal the burns.

"Let's go. We need to get Mack, Zoey, and Jack and get out of here," I said when she was finished with the cuffs.

I noticed that she stiffened when I said their names. That couldn't be good. She turned away from me and started to walk.

"Q? Please tell me what happened. Is it Zoey? Did something happen before you came to free me?" I chased after her as I spoke.

She refused to look at me and wouldn't even slow down. "As far as I know, she's fine. We'll go get her and Jack, then we'll head back to the boat."

I didn't understand how she could plan to leave Mack behind. "What about Mack? We can't just leave him behind. We have to get him too."

She stopped abruptly but didn't turn to face me, instead turning her face towards the ground. "Mack's dead, Kyro. I killed him. We don't have time to discuss it, we need to get the others and go."

She started walking again. I was floored by her admission. How could she have killed Mack? Why would she do that? I had so many questions but knew they would have to wait. I ran to catch up with her.

We headed to the servant's quarters next to free Jack. I wasn't sure how we would be able to do that when he seemed to be under the Chairman's control. Q and I split up to search the rooms for him. I found him and yelled to Q. She yelled back for me to get him and Zoey and then meet up with her.

"Jack, we need to leave." I figured it couldn't hurt to try and reason with him.

He looked at me, confused. "Why would we do that? We're happy here."

"What do you mean? Have you lost your mind?" He sounded like a crazy person.

"Race told me. You run the mines, Zoey and Race got back together, Mack is working in the foundry, and Q is teaching classes on fighting. Everyone is happy." He seemed to genuinely believe what he was saying.

"None of that is true, Jack. Wait—did he give you anything? A gift that he insists you need to keep with you or on you all the time?" Maybe it was an enchanted item. Without Mack, a spell could be our undoing here.

Jack looked confused, then showed me the chain around his neck. "Race gave me this. He said it was a protection pendant. I'm not supposed to take it off. It keeps me safe from being controlled by magic."

I knew it was a huge risk since Jack was a lot bigger than me, but I needed him on my side. I stepped closer, reached my hand out, and tore the chain from his neck. Then I threw my hands up in front of my face to block the punch I was sure would be coming at me.

Jack blinked a few times, shook his head a bit, and took a step towards me. I flinched. He wrapped his arms around me and picked me up in a huge bear hug. "Thank you. I'd been trying to figure out how to get that damn thing off my neck since that bastard put it there. He's a sneaky one. I couldn't even control my own words. It was torture."

"Thank the gods." I looked around and noticed Q hadn't come to us yet. We still had time to get Zoey. "OK, before Q gets here...don't ask about Mack. I'll explain it once we're all back on the boat. And don't mention that she's acting differently. We need to find Zoey and get out of here."

TWELVE

Jack

I NODDED. IT DIDN'T matter to me how she was acting, if Q was helping us get out of here, I'd just go along with it. As for Mack, I wanted that story but had enough respect for Kyro to do as he asked. And I agreed with him, we needed to find Zoey.

"I know where he's keeping her. I just hope he didn't give her one of those pendants. There's no telling the kind of things he'd have her doing if he did." I shuddered at the thought. Being mind controlled was no fun, especially when it was an evil bastard who was wearing your dead best friend's face.

"It looks like Q is hunting the Chairman, so it's just gonna be you and me going after Zoey. Do you think we can get her?" Kyro was obviously in love with Zoey and didn't hide it well.

"Come on, follow me. We'll get her. Then we'll find Q and drag her out of here if we have to." I turned and started walking in the direction of the private chambers. Kyro fell into step behind me.

We climbed the three flights of stairs that led up to the Chairman's private rooms. I knew this was where he had been keeping Zoey. I slowed my steps and motioned to Kyro to stay quiet. Even with the commotion that Q had caused, I didn't want to just bust in like we owned the place.

We crept up to the third door on the left. I tried the knob, and it was locked. I mouthed that the door was locked to Kyro. He reached into his pocket and pulled out a thin piece of metal. He looked at me and raised an eyebrow as if to ask if I knew how to pick a lock. I nodded and took the tool from him.

I motioned for him to watch my back while I worked on the lock. It took a few minutes to get the tumblers to cooperate, but I managed to unlock the door. So far all the action had been confined to the Pit, the mines, and the guards' quarters. It sounded like Q was killing them all.

I carefully turned the knob and inched the door open. Zoey was laying on the bed. It was hard to tell if she was breathing, she was lying so still. Once we were sure it wasn't a trap, Kyro pushed past me and ran to her. I stepped into the room and pushed the door closed quietly.

"She's chained to the bed. And she's knocked out." Kyro sounded concerned. To be honest, I was too. I hated to think of the horrors she may have dealt with while we were captive here.

I nodded to him and walked over to pick the lock on the chains. They were easier to unlock than the door had been. Once the chains were removed, Zoey started to stir.

"What's going on here? Am I dreaming? What day is it?" Zoey mumbled in frustration.

I suspected that the chains had been to keep her unconscious, but magic wasn't my thing. "Did he hurt you? We're getting out of here." I was so far beyond pissed about being mind-controlled a second time that I could have killed the entire Order myself in that moment.

She shook her head. I wasn't sure if that was her trying to tell me that the Chairman hadn't hurt her or if she was not going to go with us willingly. Luckily, Kyro stepped between us and took over. He pulled a silver filigree bracelet from her wrist, and her eyes seemed to clear a bit.

"Zoey, it's OK. I'm here. We're going home now, sweetheart. I need you to help me. We're going to have to run, and I need to know that you can do that for me. Can you?" He spoke to her softly and gently, as if speaking to a spooked animal or a small child.

This time she nodded. It was obvious she was still coming out of whatever had been keeping her unconscious, whether it was a drug or a spell. Kyro helped her to her feet, and we headed back to where all the chaos was happening. We had to find Q and get out of here.

I spotted her across the room, surrounded by guards. I started to run towards her to help get her out, then I saw why she hadn't tried to run. She was making a fireball far larger than a basketball. I grabbed Kyro and Zoey and pulled them backward, turning my back to Q and covering them with my body.

Kyro realized what was happening and covered Zoey's ears with his hands, so I covered his ears with my hands. It left me slightly vulnerable, but I trusted him to get us all out of this. I heard the deafening boom as the guards' guns all blew up. I felt the shrapnel hit my back and I flinched.

I was scared to turn around, for fear that Q had blown herself up. I knew if I didn't, it would be Zoey who discovered her, and I wasn't ready to see that. I turned to Kyro. "You get Zoey, I'll get Q. We have to get out of here. I know the path out. Follow me. Stay close." I knew I was speaking louder than I meant to, given that I couldn't hear anything.

I ran over to Q, who had been blasted with shrapnel as well. The difference between the two of us was that I acknowledged the pain, whereas she was just staring out into space. "Q! We have to go! Now! Come on!" I yelled.

She didn't answer, didn't even turn her head to look at me. She stared off into the distance, with a vacant look and no emotion. I picked her up, threw her over my shoulder, and took off running towards the path I knew led out of here. I thought if we could get to the boat, we'd be all right. I knew the Chairman hadn't done anything to it, as he'd had me check on it a few times. I think he was planning to offer it to Zoey as a wedding gift. Yuck. I didn't want to think about what he had planned to blackmail her with. I can't believe that almost happened. That guy may have had more in common with Race than I thought.

We ran down the path, ducking into crevices when guards came along and managed to get to the boat. I put Q down on the deck, Kyro had Zoey sit with her, and we ran off to get the boat launched. I didn't think we'd make it out without the boat getting sunk, but I was wrong. A handful of guards noticed us leaving and shot a few rounds, but the girls were protected by crates. Kyro and I were pretty good at avoiding the bullets; fortunately for us, these guys were horrible shots.

Once the boat was out on the water, Kyro leaned over the edge of the boat and somehow pushed the boat to go faster. Zoey held onto his waistband to keep him from falling off. I looked over at Zoey, and she nodded. Then she let go of Kyro and stood up, her eyes went white and she raised her hands. It looked as though the water had come up and engulfed the boat. I must have looked horrified because Kyro yelled over at me.

"She's cloaking the boat so we can get away from here. To the Order, it'll look like we sank. To anyone around us, it'll look like smooth water, just like we don't exist. It's OK, Jack, I promise. We practiced it a lot before she disappeared."

I blinked a few times. "How do you know that's what she's doing?"

Kyro laughed. "We have a connection. Sometimes we can communicate through it. I can't really explain it other than that. We've both tried to fight it, but there's no use."

I decided that was as good an answer as anything else I'd heard lately. Once we were far enough away from the chaos to feel somewhat safe, I took Q down to her room. I tried to get her to switch rooms with me and take her old one back so she didn't have to deal with Mack's memory being everywhere, but she refused. I still had no idea what had happened to him.

"If you want to talk, I'm here," I told her as I pulled the blanket over her. She just looked at me blankly.

I wasn't sure what to do, and the whole thing was extremely awkward. "OK, I'm going to go now. If you need anything, please let us know."

She nodded while staring across the room. Her expression didn't change. It was really creepy.

THIRTEEN

Gill

When the chaos started, I knew this would be the only chance Trav and I had to escape. It was now or never. I looked over at him, and he nodded. I grabbed his hand, and together we blew the door off our cell with air magic.

At this point, the guards had all headed toward the Pit, where there was something bad happening. It sounded like someone was trying to escape. Which wasn't something you could usually do if you got taken to the Pit.

We managed to make it unnoticed to the docks, where I noticed Kyro's boat. We ran straight for it and boarded before the commotion made it to us. I dragged Trav downstairs to make sure the boat was stocked enough to get us out of here. We still hadn't spoken; I think we were terrified we'd be caught if we made any noise.

Just as we were heading back up to the deck, the boat started to move. Not just move, it started to fly. I knew there was only one way that could happen. Kyro had managed to escape and was on the boat. His power was the only thing that could make the boat move that fast.

This could either be really good for us or really bad. It just depended on who was with him and how pissed they were that I had betrayed them. I was pretty sure Trav would be safe, though, so that was comforting. I turned around and headed back down to the storage area off the galley. I figured there was less chance of being found right away if we hid in there. I pulled Trav along with me.

We hid for days, although Trav would have exposed us a dozen times if I hadn't stopped him. He didn't understand exactly what had happened. I snuck around and got us food and water while trying to figure out who was on the boat with Kyro.

I had caught glimpses of a green guy I didn't know and Zoey, but other than that Mateo had been the only other person I'd seen. I wondered where Mack and Q were. I knew if I ran into her it would be bad since I'd left her for dead. The only reason I knew she was alive was that I had overheard a conversation about her.

It had been almost a week since we stowed away on the boat when I got caught. I was swiping food from the galley and hadn't heard the footsteps behind me. I turned around and ran right into the big green guy.

"Who are you? What are you doing here?" He was pretty intimidating. I knew it wouldn't do any good to try and fight or run once his large hand clamped down on my arm.

"Please, you have to let me go. I'll get off the boat when it comes to port again. I promise. Please just don't tell anyone you saw me." I figured it was pointless to beg, but it wasn't just my life on the line. I had to protect Trav.

"Not a chance, pal. We're gonna see if Kyro wants to throw you overboard or lock you up. Either way, I'm not letting go." This guy was scary. I almost peed myself when he growled at me. His grip tightened to the point of pain, and I gave up trying to break free.

"OK, OK, I'll go see Kyro. You don't have to drag me." I tried to reason with him as he dragged me up the stairs to the deck. When I glanced over my shoulder, I saw Trav hiding. I shook my head at him to make him go hide again. I tripped on the steps, and the big guy just picked me up, throwing me over his shoulder and never breaking stride.

It was obvious my warning to Trav didn't work when he followed us up on deck. The big guy was so focused on me that he didn't even notice. At least I had that going for me. I watched Trav follow us, and I kept trying to get him to stop without getting caught.

"Kyro! We have a stowaway. Do you want me to throw him overboard?" The big guy yelled at Kyro as soon as we came out the door onto the deck.

"Jack? What are you talking about? What stowaway?" Kyro responded as he headed towards us. I wondered how he'd react to seeing me again.

I didn't have long to wonder. The moment Kyro saw me, he started walking faster and didn't stop until his fist was buried in my face.

"What the fuck are you doing here? Didn't you cause enough problems the last time? Did the Chairman send you after us again?" He kept punching until I felt blood running down my face, and we both heard something behind us. A throat cleared, then someone spoke quietly.

"Excuse me. Would you please stop punching my husband? I'd like to talk to you." Trav stepped up next to the big guy, who had just been watching Kyro beat the shit out of me until this point.

"Who are you?" The big guy asked.

"Trav, no! Get out of here!" I yelled at him to get him to go hide. I tried to run over to him, but Kyro stopped me. Of course, Trav didn't listen. And Kyro punched me again.

The next thing I know, Kyro and I are being pulled apart by an invisible force, and the big guy is being held in place. All three of us turned our heads and looked at Trav.

"I know, I have some things to explain. And I will, but I need the three of you to chill out so we can talk. Got it?" Trav said as he held us in place with powers I didn't even know he had. "I'm sorry we stowed away, I wanted to come forward as soon as the boat left the Order's hideout, but Gill insisted that we hide. Please let's just talk about this like civilized people."

At that moment, Zoey walked up. "What's going on?" She was obviously as confused about the situation as I was.

Trav had taken over and answered her question in a chipper tone. "Hi. I'm Trav, Gill's husband. We stowed away on your boat to escape the Chairman. I'd like the chance to talk it over before these guys kill my husband. Would you be willing to help with that?"

Zoey looked him up and down. She nodded. "I think that's a reasonable request. You're gonna have to let them go first. Don't worry, they'll behave. Won't you?" She gave the three of us a look, and we all nodded. There was no way I was going to go up against her. Not after hearing why the Chairman wanted her. I think Trav was banking on that because he knew what she was too.

Trav released us, then Zoey gestured to some chairs over by the workout area.

"Let's sit and have a conversation, shall we?" She was calm and collected, even though you could see the power coursing just under the surface.

Fourteen

Zoey

ONCE I HAD EVERYONE calmed down, we sat and had a conversation. Trav seemed nice, though I felt like he was too good for Gill.

"Wait, so you hid not only the fact that you're gay but also the fact that you're married from your best friends? That's so messed up." Jack couldn't seem to understand Gill's reasoning.

"Yes, but I felt like I had to. I didn't think anyone would understand. My family didn't. And I wanted to protect Trav."

"You know we're not in the twentieth century anymore, right? Mack and I would have understood and been supportive. You didn't have to lie. You know Mack and I aren't like your dad." Kyro was obviously upset by the sudden appearance of his former best friend.

Gill didn't respond to Kyro's statement. I got the feeling he'd been hiding from someone other than Kyro and Mack, but I knew better than to ask. From what Kyro had just said, I guessed it was Gill's father.

"I know I have no right to ask, but how is Q? I haven't seen her while we've been hiding. I was hoping you guys would've had time to save her after I left." Oh, sure, NOW Gill was concerned with how his actions affected us.

I shook my head. "Q is fine, physically. She's dealing with some stuff right now, and you will not be bothering her. At all. I mean that. You will not speak to her. Ever." I could only imagine how pissed she would be when she saw he was on the boat. I hoped we could keep her from killing him.

Gill nodded, then looked guiltily at Trav. "Was she really hurt that badly?" Trav asked.

"She almost died. Mack saved her," I said with tears in my eyes. It was so hard to talk about Mack.

I looked at Kyro. "You should tell him." I wiped the tears as more formed.

Kyro grimaced but nodded. "Not only will you not speak to Q, but you also won't go near her. You understand?" He began.

"I get what you're saying, but I don't understand the why of it," Gill said.

"They want to protect you from me. Because there's a chance I'd kill you, just like I did Mack." I heard Q's voice and turned.

"Q, that's not what we meant at all." Kyro tried to explain.

"Yes, it is what you meant. And you all deserve to hear it from me. I killed Mack. The details don't matter. He's dead, and it was my fault. As long as you leave me alone, I won't have to kill you." Q turned and walked away. Jack decided to go after her.

"You two deal with this. I'll take care of her," he said as he walked off after her.

"What was she talking about? Did something happen to Mack?" Gill was frantic.

I wiped more tears from my cheeks, knowing I'd never get them all out. "Mack is dead. We don't know the whole story, but Q says she did it. You heard her. She won't talk about it. What she just said to you was the most she's said to anyone about it."

Gill broke down in hysterical sobs, and Trav walked over to hold him. He hadn't ever met Mack, but he cried too. It was sweet and tragic at the same time.

Against Kyro's protests, Jack and I decided to let Gill and Trav stay on the boat, at least until we hit the next port. We didn't really have a lifeboat, and it didn't seem fair to dump them in the ocean. Q said she didn't care either way and stayed in Mack's room for the next three days without talking to any of us.

I gave Trav and Gill my room after I made sure all my belongings were removed from it.

"You'll stay with me. Unless you don't want to." Kyro understood things weren't perfect between us, but he was trying to make it up to me.

"I think that'll work. I'm still not committing to anything. Thank you for understanding and for letting me stay with you." My response made both of us sad, but I wasn't sure I'd ever get over being lied to. We had been taking small steps toward getting back to the way our relationship was in the beginning. I had stayed with him for a few nights and at one point had tried to move back in with him, but I just couldn't let go of the fact that he didn't fully trust me.

FIFTEEN

Shannon

I WAS IN MY room, preparing for my appointment with the Chairman. I knew that was code for some kinky sex, and since I knew what he liked, it was just easier to be ready to deal with the abuse. I took extra time with my shower, grooming myself exactly the way he liked. The sex wasn't horrible, but it was unfulfilling. And I was fine with that. I knew how to take care of myself. I didn't need him for that.

After my shower, I spent an hour choosing just the right outfit, then fixing my hair and makeup. He may not know it yet, but tonight would be a special night. This would be the moment where I cemented our agreement and forced him to give me the powers he kept promising. If he refused, I had leverage. I had stolen some paperwork that proved he was trying to keep the magic book for himself. I could only assume his boss wouldn't be too happy about that. I wasn't above bribery and blackmail to get what I wanted.

The knock on my door startled me from my thoughts. I walked over and opened the door, irritated that someone had interrupted me.

"What is it?" I growled as I swung the door open. I was face to face with the Chairman, and he had Jeremy in tow. "I'm sorry, sir. What's wrong?" I completely changed my tone and hoped that he would let my insubordination slide. Who was I kidding? I knew I'd pay for it later.

He grabbed my arm and drug me from the room without letting me close the door. "We have to leave. Hurry." He pulled me along with him, down the hall and through the hidden door to the escape hatch. This was bad. I turned my head and looked at Jeremy as I was practically dragged through the hatch. It was nearly impossible to catch my breath at this pace.

"What happened? Why are we leaving? I don't understand." I panted as the Chairman continued to drag me to the boat waiting to take us somewhere safe.

Jeremy glared at me. "That witch is out of control. She went nuts and started charbroiling everyone. I knew it was a bad idea to force her to kill the dwarf."

"What?" I turned toward the Chairman. "You made her kill the dwarf? You know they were mates. Why would you do that?" This was low, even for him.

The Chairman growled at me, "Mind your tone. I've already let you get by with one slight today. I'll not allow another. And don't think you can question me. It was my decision to make, and I made it."

Once we were on the boat and headed away from the Pit, I kept my distance from both of them. I needed some time to process the fact I had probably just lost the only chance I had at gaining magic. My son had been in those caves, and it didn't look like anyone was making it out alive. A single tear fell from my eye. I wasn't sure if it was for me or him.

When the boat stopped, I recognized our destination. We had gone back to the main base. Which meant we'd be meeting with the Boss. That guy gave me the creeps, and I did my best to avoid him. I hoped I could continue that trend.

Before we left the boat, the Chairman stopped me. "How do I look? I have to be presentable."

I gave him a once-over with my eyes. "You look fine. This body suits you much more than the last one did."

He scrunched his nose at my comment. "I don't care for this one. I think the purple hair is a bit much. I'm stuck with it though, since the only way I can change it is to kill someone, and I have found no one else I want to be yet."

With that comment, he turned and walked toward the entrance.

As much as it creeps me out to work for a doppelganger, I'm glad he can only change his appearance by killing. It severely limits his options. Even though he acts tough, he's not. It takes a lot out of him to kill, so he doesn't do it more than once or twice a year. And after he takes weeks to recover. I had considered tracking him down and killing him the last time he transitioned, but I waited because he promised me I would have magic of my own. And he hasn't delivered yet, so I have to keep him alive until he does.

sixteen

Jack

I CHASED AFTER Q as she ran below deck. I knew she hadn't meant what she said. It was the pain talking. And since I knew a thing or two about pain, I felt like I should be the one to chase her down.

"Q, wait up. Please." I knew I'd have to approach the situation carefully or she'd bolt again.

She stopped but didn't turn around. "What is it, Jack?" She huffed the words at me, exasperation and raw emotion at the surface.

"You're not alone. I'm here if you need me. To talk, yell, whatever."

"I don't want your pity." She started walking toward her room again.

"It's not pity. It's empathy. I understand your pain. I don't pity you."

She turned at my words. I wasn't sure if she was going to talk to me or beat the shit out of me. I would have been fine with either one.

"Thank you. I'm just tired. So tired. Of hurting, of grieving, of blaming myself, and of hating myself. I can't talk about it anymore."

My heart broke at the pain she kept just enough control over. I knew it was even harder for her to hold it back. It would be so much easier to just lock herself away and hide it.

I took a chance and closed the distance between us. When she didn't swing at me, I pulled her into a hug. "It's OK to lean on people. You don't have to be strong all the time."

She relaxed in my arms for a minute, then tensed. "I know. But I don't know how much longer I can do this before I lose my mind. It plays over and over in my head every day."

I rubbed my hand up and down her back and waited for her to finish talking.

"It's like I'm being constantly punished for killing him when it was the last thing I ever wanted."

I held her against my chest as she wiped a tear from her cheek. I knew better than to say anything about it, though. It was enough that she was letting me help her this much.

"It'll get easier. I promise. And the nightmares will taper off, too."

She pulled back a bit and looked up at my face. "I didn't say anything about nightmares. How did you know?"

I smiled and patted her shoulder gently. "I've been there. I know what it looks like to be kept awake all night by bad dreams. You're not alone."

Just then, she seemed to realize that she was in my arms. She pushed me back and stepped away. Her expression was hateful, but the venom didn't reach her eyes. Sadness lived there, and I knew it would be a long while until anything else showed.

"I don't need your help. I told all of you. Just leave me alone."

She turned her back on me and continued to her room. At least I knew she had some fire left in her, even if she wasn't ready to admit it. And the small bit of herself she shared with me was enough for me to be satisfied she wouldn't be trying to hurt herself. She needed time to grieve, even if she didn't want to admit it.

I headed back on deck to see if Kyro and Zoey had made a decision on what to do with the stowaways. I was hoping she wouldn't let him throw them overboard. I couldn't handle any more guilt today. I felt as if I was almost as bad off as Q.

seventeen

Ian

I HAD BEEN RESEARCHING the location of the last pearl for weeks now and had no real leads. It seemed that Zoey and her friends were getting irritated with me, but I knew there was no way to force the information. I had to keep searching. It was unnerving they had been captured by the Order, and I was amazed they had come out of it almost unscathed.

Bay showed up with my order for the week, just in time to witness my meltdown caused by another lead falling through. She'd spent so much time with us lately that Kara and I considered her family, and she didn't bother to knock anymore. She was the only person besides Kara that was able to get through my wards on the house. The moment I noticed her in the doorway of my study was two seconds after I had thrown everything from my desk in frustration and screamed. I could do that during the day because Kara was at work, and I didn't have to worry about bothering her while she rested. Or about the lecture I would get for my tantrums.

"Wow, that was something." Bay cocked a grin at me and leaned on the doorframe, setting her backpack on the floor by her foot.

"Don't judge me, child. It has been a hell of a day," I huffed at her.

She laughed in response and started picking up papers that had been tossed in her direction. "So, what's the problem? Maybe I can help."

"I appreciate that, but unless you know where I can find the third pearl of power, I'll just have to figure it out."

She looked at me as if I'd said something funny. "Third? You know there are more than three, right?" She continued when I gave her a funny look. "And yes, I know about the pearls. Do you really think I'm just a delivery girl? C'mon, Ian."

She handed me the papers, grabbed her backpack, and took a seat across from the desk. "Which one do you need? I bet I can find it, or I can find you someone who knows where to look."

I stopped in the middle of picking up the papers, following Bay's lead. "Wait—you know about the pearls? What do you mean, there's more than three? And what kind of connections do you have that you can find them when I have exhausted every resource I have and have come up empty-handed?"

I hoped she could help, but at the same time didn't want to involve her. It wasn't fair to her if she got caught up in my mess.

"Well, you know the only way I'm going to talk is if you pay me or include me in the adventure. So, which is it?"

I could tell by her face she meant it. And I had a feeling that if I chose payment, she'd jack the price up to where I couldn't afford it anyway. "OK, you win. I'll let you in on it. Only because you're too expensive to pay. I have to warn you, it's not safe."

She grinned from ear to ear. "Awesome! A real adventure for a change. It's about time you told me what all this running I've been doing is really for."

"Don't say I didn't warn you. This is dangerous and could even be deadly."

Her expression turned from excited to annoyed. "Just tell me. What do you need the pearls for, how many, and which ones? And why is it so dangerous?"

I spent the better part of an hour explaining the whole story to her, and I have to give her credit. She was focused, attentive and asked questions in all the right places. Then she shared more information on her statement that there are more than three pearls. She explained that Poseidon had created three of them, and apparently several other gods had created sets as well. Since each pearl had a different power, a person could be virtually unstoppable if they got them all. When we were finished talking, I think both of us were a little stunned. The exchange of information was intimidating.

"Wow, that's a lot to take in. They have two of the pearls and the dodecahedron. Now we just need to find the third pearl." Bay's voice remained calm, as her face glowed with the anticipation of what was to come.

"Do you have any idea where to start or who to ask?" I still felt like this was a bad idea, but I was certain she'd never back out at this point.

Her face scrunched in thought for a bit. "I think I know a guy. I'll have to go alone, and I need to be careful about how I approach it. I can't just come right out and ask him. Let's sort out your delivery, then I'll go check it out."

She laid out each item from my list, and I checked them off. A few of them were supposed to take a week or more to obtain, and she got them within a day. I was impressed. Maybe enlisting her help wasn't such a bad idea after all. The kid definitely had connections.

"Bay, you have to promise me that you'll be careful. I can't justify sending you out on a mission like this unprotected."

She laughed, "OK, *Dad*, I promise I'll be careful. C'mon, Ian, I've been on my own since I was ten. I was smart enough to lie about my age and get this job, wasn't I? Now that I'm actually old enough to be on my own, you're gonna start trying to parent me. Geez. I'll be careful. Really. And I'll report back as soon as I have something. It could take a while."

"You make a good point. Just check in with me, please. I'll be worried. And I know Kara will beat me if she finds out I've sent you hunting intel for me."

Bay nodded as she picked up her bag and stood up. "Deal. I'll talk to you soon."

I cleaned up my mess, then sat for a while in the study and thought over what Bay had told me. It made sense that there were more than three pearls, but I hoped the three we were after were the right ones. If not, there was a chance we'd fail. I didn't want my child to live in that kind of future.

I decided I would tell Zoey about what I'd learned. I wanted to do it before Kara got home because I didn't want her to know I'd gotten Bay involved. I wasn't kidding her when I said Kara would be furious about it. I hated lying to her, but maybe I could get by with just hiding it for a while.

I picked up the book and said the incantation that triggered the pages to glow. All I could do now was wait for Zoey or one of her friends to pick up the book and respond.

A few minutes later, I heard Zoey's voice. "Ian, what's up?"

"I have some information to share." As I spoke the words, they appeared on the page.

"That's great. Everyone else is busy, but I have time to discuss it. Or do you need us all together?"

"No, it's OK, I can tell you, then you can explain it to them. I'll be available for questions tomorrow." I wasn't sure if time flowed exactly the same way through the book as it did here, but I knew that if they had questions, they would let me know.

"Awesome. So, what did you find?" Zoey seemed anxious for answers. I was anxious too, but I had a feeling our feelings didn't have the same cause.

"There are more than three pearls. From what little I've learned, there are several sets of three, and each has different powers. For now, we are still just looking for the ones I originally described. If we come across others, though, I think it's wise to collect them as well if we can."

"To keep them out of the wrong hands?" It almost wasn't a question.

"Exactly. I'll let you know when I have more information. I'm chasing down some leads now to find locations."

"Thanks. I'll let the others know. Talk to you soon." And she closed the book.

EIGHTEEN

Zoey

We walked down the paved path toward the mixed-up jungle of trees and buildings that once was Sydney. Since it was abandoned, the city had been overtaken with plants. I guess since the pollution was stopped, the plant life found a way to survive. There were vines snaking up the sides of buildings, flowers taking over fountains and coffee shops, and blades of grass popping up between bricks on the sidewalk. From what Ian had told us, we were expecting to find the next pearl somewhere in Australia. Once again, Kyro had attuned his amulet to find magic. The amulet led us to Sydney. The closer we got to the once beautiful city, the brighter the golden stone glowed. I was sure we would find a great source of magic ahead of us. Kyro watched carefully in front of us as he led us into the jungle city, while Jack all but walked backward, keeping an eye on our rear. He carried Mack's ax in honor of the sacrifice Mack had made for us to have our freedom. It wasn't easy for any of us, but we knew it was for the best, and it had been Q's idea. That left Q and me to watch the sides and listen for anything unusual.

Ky led us down streets overgrown with vines, following the glow of the amulet. We were all anxious because no part of our quest had ever been easy, so we were expecting the worst. Ky stopped short, holding up a hand for us to stop behind him. I stepped to his side and couldn't believe what I saw. On a pedestal in the middle of the courtyard ahead of us was a red pearl, roughly the size of my palm. It glowed with energy. It was too easy. Ky felt it too. It had to be a trap. Jack picked up a rock and threw it into the courtyard. Nothing happened. He took a step out into the courtyard with his ax drawn, watching his foot placement carefully to avoid any potential traps. Deciding it was safe, Q followed his lead, but where Jack headed right, she went left, stepping carefully with a fireball at the ready in her right palm. Kyro and I cautiously stepped forward, deciding without a word that we would go together straight down the middle to the pearl.

The four of us were carefully making our way in three different directions, all heading toward the pedestal holding the pearl, not trusting that there not to be an attack of any sort. We kept our guards up, even as Kyro reached for the beautiful crimson piece in front of us. "Do you think it's trapped?" Jack asked before Ky touched it.

"I don't sense anything. I think we're ok." And with that, he picked up the pearl and handed it to me. "Put it in your bag, and let's get out of here. This was too easy, and I don't like it."

I did as he asked, and we turned to leave. I caught a movement out of the corner of my eye. It looked almost like a large dog scuttling by. We hadn't seen any wildlife, though, since we arrived. "Did you see that?" I asked the others. "I'm not sure what that was, but there are more of them. They're surrounding us. Ten of them I think, though I'm not sure how I know that."

Q was already assessing the situation and ready to blast.

"Your powers are growing again. Don't attack unless they do first. It could just be animals who live here." Kyro said. He was always the levelheaded one.

We started to head back to the boat, and the creatures we had seen tightened their circle around us. They were strange-looking, similar to a beaver with a duck's bill, but much larger than anything I had studied. It was as though the duckbill platypus had morphed with a Great Dane. These were large, frightening monsters, with an angry look in their eyes. I didn't think we'd make it out of there without a fight. One of them rushed at Jack, and he swung Mack's ax down on its head. The ax went through the creature's head like a hot knife through butter. One down, nine to go. The two closest to the one Jack sliced screamed in reaction to their friend's death. They plowed forward at him, gnashing their teeth and clawing at him. Yes, they had duckbills and teeth--trust me, I was just as surprised when I saw it. Q shot a fireball at one closer to her, and it squealed as it ran off, flames following it. Kyro pulled out his blade and swung at the one in front of him, slicing into its flesh.

Jack made quick work of the two that were attacking him, though he did get bitten a couple of times. Once Kyro managed to kill the one he had attacked, there were five left. I didn't want to kill them, but I knew they had to be stopped before they killed us. "Ky, can you move them closer together with a water blast? I'm gonna try to freeze them." He nodded, then stepped a few paces over and blasted the remaining five with water, moving them toward the pedestal. I threw up my hands and tried to concentrate on freezing the water Ky was shooting. Nothing happened.

"Calm, focus. You can do this." Q was actually a pretty good coach. She was prepping another fireball to throw if I couldn't manage the ice. I took a couple of deep breaths and raised my hands slowly. I could feel the ice flow through me and out my fingers in a blast of blue. The platypus monsters were instantly encased in a block of ice. We turned and ran for the boat.

NINETEEN

Mack

AFTER WHAT SEEMED LIKE an eternity in darkness, but could easily have been mere moments, there was a bright light ahead of me. My journey to the afterlife was nothing like our histories had suggested. Other than the pain I felt when I threw myself on Quinn's sword, it didn't even feel like I was dead. I had left my body and watched the whole thing happen. I saw her lose control and vanquish those who were sent to end us, and I watched the Chairman run in fear for his life. Then this tunnel appeared, and I had been traveling down it for hours, or seconds. I couldn't be sure. Time seemed to have little meaning here. I regretted leaving Quinn and the others, but I couldn't bring myself to regret the decision to give my life to save hers. I hoped it was enough.

The tunnel came to an end, and as I entered the chamber, I couldn't help but notice the lovely woman standing next to the fire along the back wall. Instantly, I dropped to my knees.

"My lady. I hope that my service to you has been pleasing."

She turned and gestured for me to stand. "My dear one. I knew you would come. I heard your prayers, but the Fates assured me this was your path. Come, sit with me and talk."

I wasn't expecting Hestia to meet me at the end of my tunnel, but it was a huge relief that she was here. It seemed to justify and seal my faith in her. If only my brothers could see this. They'd argued we should follow Ares because his followers were sure to gain a hero's welcome upon death. Wouldn't they feel stupid?

I followed her to a sitting area not far from the fire and waited for her to sit before joining her.

"Why am I here?" I knew I needed to approach my questions with respect, both due to my faith and because it wouldn't do to piss off the gods, who were all very protective of Hestia.

"I expected questions. You have nothing to fear from me. Ask what you desire to know, and I shall answer the best I am able. You are here because you served me faithfully in your life. Though I am not a fan of violence or fighting, you reserved those for times when it was necessary and gained no enjoyment from it."

"Is Quinn all right? Did the Chairman at least keep his word to not hurt her?"

At this question, Hestia laughed. "My child. Your woman is so strong. She fought her way out of that pit and freed your friends. The Chairman, as you call him, had no chance to make a move on her at all."

I relaxed at this response. At least my sacrifice had not been in vain. My family was safe.

Hestia stared into my eyes for a moment before she spoke again. "It has been proven to me that she needs you. Her powers are out of control, and she lacks the desire to maintain what little self-control she has. As much as I enjoy your company and would keep you here with me, I would like to send you back."

Her statement caught me off guard. "What? Send me back? To the Pit? I don't understand."

Her gentle laugh broke the silence that had filled the room. "No, child. I want to send you back to her. To rein her in a bit, to protect her. You may not be aware, but she is mine. She is descended from the gods and has been gifted my power over fire. While she is not directly mine, she is mine nonetheless. There will be more required of you, but I will reveal the rest when it becomes relevant."

My jaw dropped at this. I should have realized that's why I was so drawn to Quinn, because she was so similar to Hestia. "My lady, I shall do whatever you ask of me; whatever you command. My life and my ax are yours."

She nodded. "I cannot send you back to where she is at this moment, but I can send you to a place where you can meet up with her. And as I'm certain you are aware, there will be a price."

I had studied the pantheon extensively as a child. "There always is. What will mine be?"

She looked at the floor for a moment, as if considering my question. "I cannot send you back into your original body, as it was destroyed by your love when she blew up the Pit. Also, you will not be able to seek revenge. You will only have the ability to kill if your life or the lives of your family are directly threatened."

She reached behind the chair and picked up an ax. "This will be your weapon. It is enchanted and can never be traded, sold or lost. It is bound to you."

I closed my hand around the shaft of the ax as she handed it to me. I could feel the power and connection between myself and the ax. "Very well. There is nothing objectionable in your conditions."

Hestia smiled at me. "I knew you would be the one. My champion. My hero. Prepare yourself for your return. You'll see that there are other gifts, too, that will be revealed as they are needed."

With that, there was a light so bright I had to close my eyes against it. When I opened them, I was on a small island in the middle of the ocean. There were a few trees, and a lean-to had been attached to one of them for shelter. As I looked down at the ax clutched in my hand, I noticed the change Hestia had spoken of. I wondered if Quinn would recognize me. I hoped that she would realize I was still the same person she had fallen in love with. I just had to find her to get that answer.

As much as I wanted to believe Hestia's gift had not changed me, I felt somewhat different. There were doubts in my mind that didn't exist previously. Knowing what Hestia had told me about why she was sending me back, these doubts were probably unwarranted.

There was no way to know for sure if Quinn would accept me again or if she would forgive me for what I had done.

It took me the better part of a day, while wrestling with my thoughts and fears, to build a makeshift raft so I could get back out in the water and search for my friends. I rested for a few hours, then set out on my raft with a homemade oar. I hoped I wasn't too far from wherever my love currently was.

TWENTY

Chairman

ONCE THE DWARF WAS dead, the fire mage went crazy and melted the power restraint cuffs. That was my cue to exit. I grabbed Shannon and Jeremy, and we used the teleport circle in the east wing to escape.

"I'm not looking forward to explaining this one. We lost too many men back there. How did none of you realize she would react like that? How did you not know the extent of her powers?" I was concerned that we had left Zoey behind to die, but not enough to go back for her.

Jeremy looked at me disinterestedly. "You gave me five minutes to examine each of them. How was I supposed to tell the extent of any of their powers without time for testing?"

I got a little more pissed by his disrespect than I should have, and I wrapped my hand around his throat, picking him up off the floor. Shannon stepped in, forcing me to let go of Jeremy.

"Stop. You don't want to kill him. We still need him. The project isn't done. And he's right, if you had given him enough time for testing, you would have known how powerful she was." She was forceful and logical. I had to respect that.

"What about losing Zoey? She can't have survived that mess back there." I finally voiced my concern.

Shannon laughed sarcastically. "Trust me, if I know my son at all, they got out of there before the fire mage set everything ablaze. It'll just be a matter of tracking them down."

"Then you can work on that, while Jeremy sticks with the plan and keeps at the spell." I turned to walk away.

"Are you going to tell him, or do you want us to?" Jeremy asked before I could leave.

"I'm heading there now. Hopefully, he will be in a decent mood, and I won't lose my head. Either way, the plan must continue. Find Zoey if she's alive, and finish that spell. And don't forget I'm still waiting for you to crack that book." I wasn't as confident as I sounded, but that didn't matter. I had ways to manipulate him if he tried to kill me.

I walked down the long hallway to the main chamber. Every step was harder and harder to take. The feeling of dread in my chest swelled until it almost consumed me. I slowly trudged through the door and into the chamber. I took slow deliberate steps toward the throne that he insisted on occupying.

"I wasn't expecting you today. Something has happened. Step forward and explain." His voice boomed through the chamber, echoing off the walls. He was shrouded in shadow, though the room was well lit.

The shadows seemed to emanate from him, an expression of his limitless power. None of us knew how old he was, but it was rumored he had been one of the originals. The rumors claimed he had been one of the ones who had set magic free. It was almost impossible to prove or disprove, so I didn't waste time on it.

I walked up the carpet runner to the steps below the throne. "Sir, we underestimated the fire mage. She managed to escape, and the Pit of Pierus has been destroyed. We lost many men, but I managed to save Shannon and Jeremy."

I couldn't see his face, but I could feel the rage radiating from him. "You underestimated the fire mage, or you were too stupid to know what you were dealing with?" He growled.

Before I could respond, I felt his magic reach out to me. I knew that running wasn't an option, so I tried to throw up a shield to block his magic from grabbing me. It seemed to work for a moment, but I could sense his frustration and knew I would probably pay with my life.

"You dare to try to block me? Impudent fool. You're already dead. Get your worthless face out of my sight." His voice boomed and echoed through the chamber.

I turned and ran out of the chamber. I wasn't sure what he meant when he told me I was already dead. I didn't feel any different, and I was sure I had blocked his magic from touching me. I was distracted by my thoughts and trying to figure out what he had meant.

I continued down the hall to my room. I must have dropped my shield while I was distracted. I didn't even realize the curse had hit me until my lungs started to convulse. The moment I started coughing up blood, I was certain I had finally figured out what he meant. I *was* already dead, I just had to wait for my body to catch up. There was no way to stop the curse, and I knew I wouldn't make it to Jeremy to even try.

I watched myself die in the mirror on the wall of my room. It was painful and humiliating. The skin melted from my bones. My bones turned to dust and wafted away. I knew it was an illusion caused by the curse, but somehow watching it before it actually happened was excruciating.

Twenty-one

Shannon

I HADN'T HEARD FROM the Chairman for a while, which was unusual. *Well, I'll just track him down and see if I can get any info out of him.* He was only ever in two places, so it should be fairly easy to find him.

I walked into Jeremy's lab, taking care to keep my footsteps light and not interrupt his work. Some of the things the Chairman had him working on were deadly and potentially explosive. I wasn't taking any chances.

I waited patiently until Jeremy turned around. "Have you seen the Chairman?"

He scoffed. "Not since he threatened to kill me if I didn't figure out this spell and find those escaped prisoners."

"Hmm." I turned and walked away. That meant he had to be in his room. There was no reason for him to act differently here than he had in his own hideout. There were only three places he ever went at the old hideout—the Pit, Jeremy's lab, and his bedroom. Since there wasn't a Pit here and Jeremy hadn't seen him, I headed down the hall and followed the corridor to his room.

When I was a few feet away from the door, I noticed an unmistakable smell coming from the direction I was heading. The last time I had experienced that smell was when I was forced to fake my death. This couldn't be good. I broke into a run and threw open the door as soon as I was within reach.

My eyes scanned the room for the source of the smell. It was acrid and sour, carrying the scent of death with it. Nothing in my imagination could have prepared me for what I witnessed when my eyes settled on the mound in the middle of the room.

I had expected to find the Chairman doling out his idea of justice upon whoever had offended him. Instead, I found a mound of singed and melted goop that had once been the Chairman himself. On top of that mound was a pile of dust.

I searched the room for the cause of this. I had no idea what had happened but didn't want to be caught in the Boss's crosshairs for something I didn't do. As I searched the room, I couldn't help but watch the goop mound. It was disgusting, but I couldn't seem to tear my eyes from it.

As I watched, a tiny ball of purple energy rose from the mound. It hovered above the pile and grew to almost the size of my hand. It was purple with what appeared to be flashes of white lightning inside it. I had never seen anything like it before. I was entranced by it and couldn't force myself to move when it started floating across the room towards me.

I stood perfectly still as the orb gravitated to me as though it was being pulled. I was terrified to move. I had no idea what this orb was or what it would do if it got close to me. There was a part of me that wanted to run for fear that this glowing ball of lightning was what had killed the Chairman. As much as I willed my legs to move, they refused, planted to the spot in which I stood.

It paused for a moment in front of my chest before pushing itself inside of me. The pain was excruciating, as if I was being stabbed in the chest with a blade made of lightning. I could feel the energy pulse as it entered my chest, feeling as though it was tearing me apart.

I fell to my knees and placed my forehead on the ground. Suddenly, I felt the energy pulse through me and my top half shot into the air, stretching as far as it could without making me stand up. I thought I was being ripped in half. Then suddenly the pain stopped. I could feel the power surging through my body.

I finally had what I always wanted. I knew that the goop had once been the Chairman, and now I held his power. It was like I could sense a part of him in the orb, and now it was inside me. Now that I had my powers, I had no further use for the Order. I could make it on my own. I didn't need anyone to protect me anymore. I would finally have the respect I deserved. No one would ever look at me with pity again.

I rushed quietly to my room and packed what I needed. I waited until the middle of the night and left during a shift change of the guards. No one would have stopped me anyway, but I couldn't be too careful. It was better if they didn't realize I was gone right away. Especially if the Boss could tell I ended up with the Chairman's powers.

For a moment I thought I heard an echo in my mind of the Chairman laughing. I didn't have time to worry about that, I had to move.

TWENTY-TWO

q

WE MADE IT BACK to the boat fairly easily. Zoey tended to Jack's wounds while Kyro tried to pretend he wasn't jealous. I couldn't handle any of it, so I climbed up into the crow's nest to get away from all of them. I knew if I stayed down on the deck, they would end up asking how I was doing, and trying to help me deal with Mack's death. I wasn't ready for that yet and didn't know if I ever would be. And I refused to cry in front of any of them.

It wasn't fair. We'd only had a few weeks, and now that minuscule amount of time had to last me for the rest of my life. Maybe if I was lucky, we'd get to go up against the Chairman again, and he'd kill me this time. That would be way better than this hole inside of me. It was more likely, though, that I would rip out his heart and feed it to him because of my anger. I was so angry.

I was angry with myself for letting Mack die. For not fighting harder to get us out of there before we were taken to the Pit. For letting myself fall in love with him, after telling myself for years that nothing good could ever come of falling in love. I sat in the crow's nest, emotions spilling over, and finally let myself grieve. The tears ran until there were no more. I was empty and hollow inside. He'd been gone for just over a week now, and I wasn't sure how much more I could take.

I decided I would just spend the night in the crow's nest since there was less chance of having to deal with anyone up here. I couldn't take watching them pity me. Maybe I would just leave. I was sure the boss wouldn't object to me coming out of the field. After all, she was the one who kept telling me my obsession with the Chairman would get me killed. Maybe she's right.

I knew we would have to go into port again soon because supplies were running low. I would just gather what I needed and disappear. They could finish the mission without me. After all, they had the dodeca and pearls now. Ian would give them the location for the spell he'd been working on, and they would finish the quest. Everything would be fixed. Except for my heart. I knew that would never be the same again. I cried myself to sleep knowing nothing would ever be the same again.

I woke with a start in the middle of the night, kicking off the blanket I hadn't brought up with me. The nightmare had come again. It took me a minute to realize where I was. That minute of panic was pure torture. It was a relief to realize I was in the crow's nest, where the others wouldn't have been able to hear me. I hated that nightmare, but I'd had it every night since Mack died. Since I'd killed him. And I knew I deserved it, even if it was horrible.

I deserved so much worse than a dream that made me relive that moment over and over. It wasn't fair that I was alive and he wasn't. Fate could be so cruel. Oh, great, now I was one of those people who blamed fate for my choices. It didn't matter, because I was the only one who would ever know that thought had crossed my mind. I pulled the blanket back over me, then I managed to cry myself to sleep after sitting there for a while.

I had been right about heading to port. We had headed northwest from Australia after securing the final pearl. I acted as normal as I could for the two weeks it took to get to Africa. Kyro decided that was as good a place as any to port for a few days to get supplies and figure out where we needed to go next.

I wrote a note to Zoey and slipped away while they were occupied with getting the boat settled into port. Once I had a temporary place to stay, I would call James and see how difficult it would be to come out of the field permanently. Or maybe I would just disappear. It didn't really matter to me if they liked it or not. I was done. I'd lost too much, and I wasn't taking the chance of getting attached to anyone else. If they really thought Zoey and Kyro needed help, they could send someone else. I wasn't going back.

I hiked for about four hours. Since I had a head start, I figured I'd take advantage of it and get as far as I could before I started looking for a place to stay. Because I was trained for this type of travel, I made it from the tip of South Africa to Botswana before I took a break. I didn't want to stay there; it was too close to where the boat was docked. I rested for an hour or so and ate before I started hiking again. Within another four hours, I had made it to a small village in Zimbabwe.

I decided this would be far enough, at least for now. I knew I would need to keep going, but I hadn't decided where. This would be as good a place as any to stop for a while. It was a small village, and I figured if I asked around, there may be a place to rent or a tent to buy. Either was fine with me. I just needed to be away from everyone I knew. I just needed to be me. And to try to heal.

I asked a villager about lodging and got redirected to the clan chief, Zarlen. His hut was in the center of the town. I marched myself up to him.

"Greetings, guest. I am Zarlen. What brings you to our village?" He seemed gruff, but most men who seemed that way were pushovers, so I wasn't worried.

I stared him in the eyes as I responded. "I need a place to stay for a while. I need to be in a place where I'm not known or bothered."

He nodded knowingly. "You have felt a loss. You have come to the right place to heal. My people will welcome you. We will not interfere with your grief, but we will protect you from the outside."

"Thank you. I have no problem with working to earn my keep. Or I can pay for lodging. Whatever you prefer."

"We will find you a job here. What would you like us to call you? As you are hiding from someone, or perhaps just the pain, you may wish for something other than your name. We shall respect that."

That was a relief. I didn't think I could take anyone calling me Q anymore. I wasn't sure what I wanted to be called. Mack had taken to calling me Quinn after we got together, so I knew it would sting to hear that every day. Maybe that's what I needed. To let the pain run its course and try to move on.

"You can call me Quinn. Which is funny, because it's my name, and I've never gone by it." I said with a half-hearted chuckle.

He smiled at me, as though he could see right through everything I wasn't telling him. "It's nice to meet you, Quinn. I'll have Meileah see to a hut for you. I'd like you to consider what you can do to help the village, and we can discuss it in a few days. You will take that time to rest and grieve, then we will talk about your place here. You're welcome to tell me your problems, though I suspect you won't."

I nodded. "Thank you. I really appreciate that. You're right, I won't. I know talking about it might help, but I have to heal from this in my own way. I'll be fine, I just needed to get away from all the things that remind me of what happened. I hope you don't think I'm being rude." I wiped the tear from my eyes.

Zarlen stepped forward and hugged me. It was surprising, but it felt so nice to be held. "It's all right, Quinn. You don't have to be strong all the time. And it's all right to not talk about it. Just know that you are welcome here and we will treat you like a part of our clan."

Within a few days, I had settled into my new life in this village. I learned that the locals called the village Asha, which as they told me, means life or hope. I thought it was pretty fitting. It took a couple of weeks to stop looking over my shoulder expecting Zoey or Kyro to come looking for me. I could only guess that they understood my reasons for leaving and respected my need for healing.

The day to day living in the village turned out to be fairly easy. Asha wasn't a rich community, at least not by society's standards. But they were the most accepting, caring people I'd ever met. The village elders went out of their way to make sure I was included. If I had to guess, I would say that was Zarlen's doing. His people respected him, and he showed himself to be stern but fair.

I spent a lot of time with Meileah, taking care of the elders and protecting the village while the hunters were out on the hunt. They went out for days at a time, and most of them were considered the protectors of the village as well. With them out on a hunt, the village was almost defenseless. Zarlen always stayed back to make sure there was at least one person who could defend those who were more vulnerable.

At first, I assumed I was asked to help Meileah because I was a woman. The hunters were all men, so it made sense that I wouldn't be included in that tradition. It didn't take long for Meileah to slip and tell me that Zarlen had requested I stay back and help with defenses. I wondered if that meant he trusted me or that he wanted to keep an eye on me because he didn't trust me. Either way, I did what I could to help out.

Meileah liked to braid my hair, so most days I let her. She was the closest to my age in the village. It felt good to drop the bitchy exterior I'd carried around and just be whoever I wanted.

"You're thinking again. That can't be good." Mei liked to tease me when I got too serious.

"You're right. Sometimes I have to otherwise I'll go crazy." I gave her a half-hearted grin.

She sat behind me weaving braids through my hair. "You should tell me about him. It might help."

I froze. "What makes you think I was thinking about a guy?"

She laughed, and it was both hearty and genuine. "Oh, Quinn. Grief like yours can only be over a child or a man. And we've spent enough time together for me to know you're not a mother."

I shrugged. "You're right, I don't have kids. My job was too dangerous for that."

"You just tried to change the subject. Who is he? What did he do that was so horrible that you refuse to even speak his name?"

I felt the tears and fought to keep them out of my voice. "His name was Mack, and he saved me." I knew the tears would win if we kept talking. I wasn't sure I cared anymore.

"He saved you, and now you try to forget him? That doesn't make sense. I don't mean to pry, but please. You know you can tell me anything." Mei sounded hurt that I didn't want to talk.

"OK, I'll tell you. I don't want anyone else to find out. And I don't want you to look at me differently for what I'm about to say. Promise me."

I turned my head to look at her. She met my eyes with her own and nodded her head. I trusted she wouldn't speak a word to anyone about this.

"Mack and I were part of a quest to save the world. We were working with some others to gather magic objects for a wizard. He and I ended up falling in love. It was crazy and scary and wonderful all at once." I paused as the tears started to run down my cheeks.

Mei continued braiding small sections of my hair as I talked.

"I wanted us to grow old together. It wasn't meant to be. We ended up in a bad situation, and..." I couldn't bring myself to say it. The tears fell faster.

Mei wrapped her arms around my shoulders and put her cheek against mine. "It's all right, love. You can tell me."

"I killed him. I didn't want to, and I would have happily died to save him. He wouldn't let me. He made the choice without thinking about how it would ruin me. I love him so much, and I hate him for that. It's hard to explain, and I don't think I can relive that again." I cried harder, unable to continue.

"Oh, love. I'm so sorry. I'm sure you didn't actually kill him. It just seemed that way at the time. It's OK to cry. I'm here for you." She was gentle and reassuring, everything I didn't deserve.

I calmed down a bit. "He used to call me that. I appreciate you saying all of that, but I did kill him. It was the sword in my hand that was buried in his chest. And I can't take it back. I would give anything to trade places with him."

She didn't offer any platitudes and didn't look at me with pity. She looked at me with respect and held me while I cried it out. Once all the tears had fallen, I felt surprisingly better.

"Thank you. For listening, and for being my friend." I smiled at her and hugged her close.

She finished braiding my hair, and we continued with our day as planned. I was relieved she didn't bring it up again or try to get me to talk when I got quiet.

I took some time by myself down by the river, just sitting there watching the water flow and thinking about the good times with Mack.

TWENTY-THREE

Kyro

AFTER GATHERING SUPPLIES IN South Africa, Zoey and I met Jack back in the boat. He had been dealing with repairs and upkeep of the boat, taking over for Mack the best he could. I knew he wasn't trying to replace my friend, but it was still hard to count on him the way I had Mack. We waited a while for Q to return from wherever she had gone. By dark, I began to wonder if she was coming back. I didn't say anything to Zoey because I didn't want to scare her if I was wrong.

I was in the galley cooking our dinner when Zoey ran in, holding a letter. I guessed the contents before she explained. "A letter from Q?" She nodded somberly.

"Ky, she's gone. She's not coming with us and doesn't want us to look for her. What are we gonna do? We have to go get her, to make her come with us. " She seemed distraught at the thought of Q out there somewhere alone.

"No. We have to respect her wishes. She'll come back when she's ready. We can't exactly kidnap her and force her to come with us. She needs time to deal with Mack's death." I agreed with her that it would be better if Q came with us, but couldn't agree that kidnapping was the best course of action.

"But Ky, she's out there all alone. I can't just go on like she was never here. I can't pretend Mack didn't exist either. This whole situation sucks. Why can't Ian just bring him back? We have to go after her and make her see we're her family, and we want to take care of her." Zoey would not let that idea go.

"Zo, I know you're worried about her, and I know you love her, but we can't chase her down. She knows we're here if she needs us. It's not fair to her to force her to be around us when we remind her of him. It has to be killing her. Especially since she was the one who killed him. I know it wasn't her fault, and I don't blame her for what happened. But he's gone, and she has to deal with how she feels about that. We can't do it for her. I'm sure we'll see her again soon."

I wasn't sure what I would do if I couldn't convince her to drop the idea of chasing Q all over Africa. For all we knew, she found a boat and headed home to Spain. Or back to the Resistance and off on another mission. I needed to convince Zoey that continuing with Ian's quest was the best thing for everyone.

Zoey looked defeated. "Fine, I'll give her a few days. If we don't hear from her soon, I'm coming back here and searching for her. And I'll do it with or without you. Got it?"

The fire and determination coming off her were enticing. I briefly wondered if seducing her would be enough of a distraction, but the pissed off glare she shot at me before she stomped off shot that idea down instantly.

Once the stomping stopped, and our bedroom door slammed, I headed up on deck to see if I could find Jack. I would have to give Zoey room to cool off. I just hoped this mood didn't last too long. I hated feeling like she was angry with me, even though I was sure this was my fault. Maybe we should go after Q and drag her back. I kind of wished Q and Mack had done that to me when I took off. If they had, though, I may have never found Zoey again.

Jack was on deck in the training area with Mateo. They were practice sparring, which was something we all needed to get back in the habit of doing. There was no telling what was coming next for us. I seamlessly inserted myself into their fight. I tackled Mateo and pinned him to the wood. He flipped me over and jumped to his feet. Then Jack tried to creep up behind me, but I turned on him just before he had the chance to reach out. I swung a leg out and knocked his feet out from under him. He hit the deck with a thud, then rolled, got to his feet and lunged at me. I had a feeling we may end up fighting for real after Zoey told him how I refused to chase after Q. If it came to that, I'd deal with it. I had to keep this mission on task. It was getting harder to do with people dying and running off.

I was distracted by my thoughts, and Jack managed to knock me off balance. My head bounced off the wood of the deck when I went down. Instinctively, my hands came up to ward off the pain. He must have realized that he actually hurt me because he stopped.

"Kyro? Are you OK? I'm sorry man, I just got a little carried away." He held a hand out to help me back to my feet. I cautiously accepted his help.

Once I was on my feet, I turned on him. "Are you sure that was just you getting carried away? Or did you hear Zoey and I fighting and decide you needed to protect her again? I need to know what your real motives are for coming back with her. This mystery crap has gone on long enough." I realized it was stupid and petty, and that the whole thing was just me being mad at myself for upsetting her. That coupled with the fact I was still jealous of him, and here I was, embarrassing myself in front of Mateo by blowing up about nothing.

Mateo tried to step in. "Ky, take a minute. He wasn't trying to hurt you. Look at him. He's twice your size at least. If he wanted to hurt you, it'd be a lot worse than a bump on the head." He stepped up to me and put both hands on my chest. I knew he wasn't trying to start anything with me. He was starting to use his calming powers on me, and it was probably a good thing. I was in a mood to fight. Maybe Q wasn't the only one who needed to deal with their feelings about Mack's death.

"Mat, I know you're right. Thank you. I'm not even mad at you for using your powers against me." I patted him on the shoulder and then turned to Jack. "I owe you an apology. I'm sorry. You've obviously been through a lot protecting her, and I'm accusing you of having ulterior motives like a jealous schoolboy. It's not fair of me, and I swear I'm working on it. I wouldn't blame you if you decked me."

Jack laughed. "Nah, man, if I did that, I'd have to deal with Zoey. It's not worth it. Besides, I understand. It's a weird situation. Add to that the fact that one of your best friends was just killed, and the other one already betrayed you, and it's pretty easy to see why you'd have trouble trusting me. I haven't done anything to earn it yet. Give me time, I will."

I looked at him. His words astonished me. "You don't have to earn my trust. Zoey thinks the world of you, and that's enough for me. I agree we need to get to know each other better, and I should probably spend some time dealing with Mack's loss. Maybe I'll go talk to Zoey and see if I can fix this."

I turned to walk away, and Jack grabbed my arm, turning me back to face him again. "I'm not going to get between your argument, but if it helps, I agree with you about chasing after Q. It'll just make her run further. We all need time to grieve and prepare for whatever comes next. If you want, I can talk to her for you."

I smiled at him, genuinely this time. "I appreciate that. This is my mess, and I need to clean it up myself. If I need you to back me up, I'll let you both know." With that, I walked away to find Zoey and try to get myself out of the hole I'd dug with her earlier.

twenty-four

Mack

I SAILED ON THE raft for a few days before I caught up to Kyro's boat. It was heading back towards Spain from the southern tip of Africa. I managed to flag them down, and they threw me a rope. Imagine my surprise when Gill's was the first face I saw.

"What are you doing here?" I asked as soon as I had boarded the boat. I drew my fist back and planned to deck him.

He held his hands up and looked confused. "Woah, buddy. We're sailing in the ocean. What are you doing here?"

I cocked an eyebrow at him, almost mirroring his expression. It took me a minute to realize that he didn't recognize me. *Geez, Mack, how's he gonna know that Hestia put you in a different body?* I laughed at that realization.

His expression changed, and I was sure he thought I'd lost my mind. Maybe I had. Imagine seeing a stranger who looked like he was about to punch you just start laughing like a crazy man. I probably should have decked him the second I saw him. He almost killed Quinn, after all.

"Where's Zoey?" I wanted to ask for Kyro, but I didn't think he'd believe I knew Kyro but Gill didn't know me.

"Oh, you know Zoey? Hang on, I'll get her. Stay here." His expression changed again, and I saw a hint of distrust. To be fair, I wouldn't trust me either. Some strange man gets picked up in the middle of the ocean and asks for my friend's girlfriend—that would throw up so many red flags.

He left me on the deck while he went below to get someone, though I'd bet it wouldn't be Zoey. I paced on the deck while he was gone, trying to figure out how I'd tell them what had happened. I was most anxious about seeing Quinn.

Gill came back with Jack and Kyro, but no girls. I couldn't blame him. I would have done the same thing.

"Oh, good, Gill got you guys. I have so much to tell you. Where are the girls?" I blurted out without thinking.

"Do we know you?" Kyro asked. He scrunched up his face as he looked at me closer.

"Wait, how'd you know my name? I didn't tell you that." Gill sputtered.

Jack looked me up and down, then walked over, bent down, and put his face right in mine. We stood there eye to eye for a minute. A huge smile spread across his face. "Mack? How is this possible?"

I laughed. "How is it that you knew when they didn't? Those two have been my best friends since I was a wee lad."

Jack picked me up in a bear hug. "They said you died. Yet here you are. How?"

I hugged him back until he put me down. "Hestia brought me back. She told me a little bit about what happened, but not much. I was hoping you guys and the girls could fill me in on what I missed."

Kyro looked like he was in shock. Gill's expression was almost identical. I looked between the three of them, and nobody spoke.

"Maybe you can start with why the traitor is back? And how you kept Quinn from killing him on sight?" I asked.

"Well, he kind of stowed away when we escaped. And he's trying really hard to make up for everything he did wrong. Also, his husband made a very convincing argument for us to not kill him." Kyro explained.

I turned to Gill. "Husband? Did you get married? That's awesome! When did this happen? I can't wait to meet him. Where is he? And I guess if Quinn didn't kill you, then you're OK."

"Mack, there's something else." Jack started.

I looked at his suddenly serious expression. "What is it? Did something happen?"

"Q took off when we docked in South Africa. They wouldn't let me go after her." Zoey stepped out onto the deck. She had apparently been standing on the stairs just inside the door to head below.

She looked me up and down, then launched herself into my arms. "I'm so glad you're back. Now we can go get her, and our family will be whole again."

"I'm not even sure she'll still want me. I mean, I'm not exactly my usual handsome self. To be honest, I haven't even seen what I look like now. I wasn't worried about it before." I suddenly felt self-conscious.

"Oh, Mack, you're just as handsome as you were before. You're just...taller now. And your hair. I never would have pictured you with white hair. It looks good though." Zoey was sweet to try and make me feel better.

I lived my life as a dwarf and had gotten used to being short and stocky. This new body was lean and tall. Being reunited with my family allowed me to understand just how different I was now. Standing next to Zoey, I towered over her by almost a foot, making me six foot two at least. My beard was still full but was trimmed short, and my hair barely touched my shoulders. I could tell from my arms that I was just as tanned as I had been before, but that seemed to be the only thing I got to keep from my previous life.

******

I got settled back in my room while the others prepared the boat for a trip back to Africa. I was nervous about seeing Quinn again and hoped she wasn't too mad at me. I did what I had to, and I would do it again if it meant saving her life.

I spent some time staring at myself in the mirror after my shower. This body was so strange to me. I wasn't used to being tall, and the white hair would be a big adjustment. My face hasn't changed that much, but it was still a stranger staring back at me. It appeared that my eyes were the only thing other than skin color that had transferred to the new body. The pale blue eyes staring back at me were comforting, but I wasn't sure I'd ever get used to seeing them in this body.

I knew as soon as Kyro turned the boat around. I felt it in my soul. It was like I was being drawn back to Quinn, and it felt like going home. As scared as I was to face her, I knew I had to find her. I wasn't complete without her. I would just have to convince her she still needed me too.

Once I was dressed in the clothes Kyro loaned me and had gotten more used to the face staring back at me from the mirror, I went to find Jack. I had to find out how he'd recognized me when no one else did. I might need to use that info when I found Quinn. I found him on deck, staring out at the ocean.

"Jack. Can we talk?" I didn't want to bother him, but I needed to know.

He looked at me and smiled. "Sure, Mack, what do you need?"

"I need to know how you knew it was me. No one else could tell, and I don't even sound like myself anymore." I wasn't sure he'd even be able to explain it, but I was hopeful.

He smiled wider. "It's the eyes. Your eyes are the same as they were before. Anyone who's paid attention should be able to tell. The others were caught off guard, that's all."

"Do you think she'll be mad?" I wondered aloud, even though I knew the answer.

"Wow, even I know that's a dumb question. She's gonna be so pissed. She'll be happy too, once you make her realize it really is you." He chuckled at his own answer.

I nodded because he was right. "Do you think she'll still want me? I mean, there's nothing wrong with this body, it's just not me. You know?"

He clapped his hand on my back. "Mack, it is you. This *IS* you now. You're right that you're different, but you're also still *you*. She'll still want you, as long as she lets herself take the chance. It'll be OK, Mack. Don't worry about it. We're all here for you."

"Thanks." I walked off to get ready to chase down the love of my life and convince her I'm the man she fell in love with.

TWENTY-FIVE

QUINN

I'D SPENT THE BETTER part of a month here in the village of Asha. It was mostly peaceful and very quiet. Mei and I had grown close, and she was the only person I'd shared anything about Mack with.

She would ask me questions sometimes about him, not to bring up the pain, but so she could learn more about him. I described to her what he looked like, his mannerisms, the way he talked, and I ended up telling her almost everything. There were a few more personal details I left out because they were between Mack and myself.

I had been summoned to Zarlen's hut for the first time since we had met. I had talked to him a few times, but a summons seemed to mean something different here. I was a little nervous as I approached the door. I jumped in surprise when Mei opened it before I could knock. Her cheeks turned pink, and she ducked her head as she left.

Her actions had me suspicious as I entered, but I wasn't going into this with any expectations. I had removed myself from my friends' lives for a reason, and that reason had led me here. I walked into the main chamber, where Zarlen was seated in the center of the room.

"You wanted to see me?" I asked casually, though my insides were not as calm as my exterior. I was good at putting up this front. I'd had years of practice.

He nodded and gestured for me to sit on a pillow on the floor to his right. I didn't really want to, but I did because I had no reason to disrespect him.

"What's this about?" I asked as I sat down.

He looked at me thoughtfully. "Mei has shared your troubles with me. I can see that angers you. This village does not keep secrets, and if you choose to be a part of it, you'll have to live with that fact."

I was beyond angry. I was pissed. Everything I had shared with Mei would be common knowledge for the village. I was not OK with that. Maybe instead of settling in, I'd be moving on.

"Maybe I won't choose to be a part of it. And maybe you shouldn't teach your village to lie. She promised me she wouldn't tell anyone what I told her. Anger is mild compared to what I'm feeling right now." I could feel the flames building inside of me. If I didn't get it under control, I'd end up burning down the entire village. I knew Zarlen wouldn't be able to stop me.

"This isn't what I summoned you for. It was simply an explanation for the look you gave Mei on her way out." He seemed pretty calm for a guy who could die at any moment.

"Then what did you summon me for?" I didn't hide the contempt in my voice.

"The traders have been down to the port. A boat has come in, and people are asking about someone fitting your description. I wanted to let you know that your friends have decided to find you after all."

Shit. Could this get any worse? This guy knows I killed the man I loved, and now I have to decide between acting like I don't care if the whole village knows or leaving. Either way, I needed to avoid my friends.

"I see. Well, I guess I'll gather my things and be on my way. I have no desire to talk to them, and I no longer have any desire to stay here. Your 'peaceful' village has deceived me for the last time. Thank you for your hospitality when I needed it." I walked out of the hut and into the woods, turning in the direction of my hut. I would gather what few belongings I had and go live in the wild on my own.

I made it to a clearing in the woods before my powers took over and I was engulfed in flames. I wasn't sure if it was anger or grief that had done it. I was angry and grieving for so much these days. I stopped in the clearing and sat down, waiting for the flames to die down. I closed my eyes for a moment, and when I opened them, I swore I saw Mack for a moment.

I shook my head, trying to clear my vision. The flames receded, and I was myself again. I looked up one more time and saw a tall, lean man with white hair walking through the woods towards me. There was something eerily familiar about that walk and that man. I was certain I'd never seen him before. I got to my feet quickly and created a fireball in my palm.

"Put that away, love, you'll not be frying me today." He kept walking, obviously not scared of me at all. And he had used Mack's nickname for me. That wasn't too odd since Mei had done the same. It was always odd to hear Mack's words in other people's voices.

"I don't know you, and I'll decide if or when to put my fire away." Even as I said the words, my heart screamed that they were lies. The flames in my palm went out as though they had a mind of their own. It was like the closer this guy got to me, the closer I wanted him to be.

He laughed as the flames went out. "Your words say one thing, but your body says another. You used to be so good at lying, love. What happened?"

He stopped about three feet from me and just stood there staring at me. I looked at him curiously. I could almost swear I knew him from somewhere, though I had no idea that I'd ever seen him before.

"Do I know you? Why do you seem so familiar?" I tilted my head to the left and stepped closer to him.

He laughed. "I've heard it's something about my eyes. You wanna take a look?"

I stepped closer, as if I didn't have a choice. His voice was musical and sucked me in. I found myself face to face with this stranger, who was about an inch shorter than me. I stared into his eyes, tilting my head from side to side slowly, trying to figure out where I knew them from.

He gently reached up and tucked a strand of hair behind my ear next to the scar from Gill's attack and Mack's stitches. "I'm guessing this is fully healed now?"

At that moment, looking into his eyes, hearing his words, it hit me like a ton of bricks. "Mack?" Tears streamed down my face. He nodded, and I grabbed his face with both hands and kissed him hard.

I slowly pulled back from the kiss, looked him in the eyes, and shoved him on his ass. What right did he have to come back? How could he put me through that?

"What the fuck, Mack? I killed you. You made me kill you. I don't understand what's happening right now." I held my hands up in front of me as he got back to his feet.

"It's OK, love. I promise. Quinn, please, just look at me. I chose to die so you could live. Hestia sent me back to you. She needs you, and she says you need me. I know *I need you*. I know you're pissed. I understand. *Please*." He was so damned handsome when he made logical arguments.

I shook my head. "How? How could you leave me? I would have happily died with you that day." Tears streamed down my face, and I let them. At this moment, I didn't care if that made me weak. He would see the pain he had caused me.

TWENTY-SIX

Mack

I DON'T KNOW WHAT I expected to happen when I found her. I do know that whatever it was, it wasn't her breaking down into a crying mess after kissing me and then knocking me on my ass. To be fair, the kissing and knocking me down were pretty much a given. I knew she'd be relieved to see me and pissed. I couldn't handle her being sad. After her outburst, she turned away from me.

I knew she hated pity, so I wasn't going to give her any. "Please, love, just give me a chance. We'll take it slow. Although the living situation on the boat is a bit crazy right now. I'll gladly sleep on the deck every night if it gets you back."

She turned and looked at me. "You think I'll come back? You really think just because you came back and said you need me that I'll come running? You don't know me as well as I thought." She turned again and started walking.

"Why don't you tell me what upset you so much that you turned fully to fire? You don't want to talk about us, that's fine. You don't have to be alone." I didn't want to, because it would hurt, but I'd bait her into anger if it made her stay and talk to me. I'd take every bit of her pain as my own if it got me another moment in her presence. Yeah, I have it bad for her.

She stopped but didn't turn around. "It was you. I've worked really hard here to keep anyone from learning my weakness. They managed it anyway. I can't stay here. I can't go with you. I'm pretty much lost now." She didn't start walking again. I could feel that I was wearing her down.

"Then why not come with me? Let me watch your back for you. I can't promise to always keep you safe, but I've already proven I'd give my life for you. That should count for something."

She started walking again. I couldn't just stand there and let her go, so I followed. She stopped again when we got to a hut that was settled out here in the woods. It was beautiful and simple, just the way I'd begun to imagine our life together.

"I have to get my stuff. Not that I have much. Then we can go back to the boat. Don't think everything will be back to normal because it won't. I'm not sure I will ever be able to go through that again." She spoke quietly, and my heart broke at the pain in her words.

"If that's all you can give me, I'll take it. I'd rather have you—your heart, your body, your soul—but I'll settle for just knowing you're safe."

I spoke as quietly as she had and with almost as much pain in my voice. She turned to find me standing too close, and for a moment her mouth smiled, though it didn't reach her eyes. I leaned a bit closer and kissed her gently. She wrapped her arms around me and tangled her hands in my hair. I pulled her closer and deepened the kiss. I wasn't giving her passion for this one, I was showing her love. She responded with the same.

I pulled back first, holding her arms down so she couldn't hit me again. "I know you're not ready to forgive me. And I'll accept that...for now. But you can't punch me every time we kiss. That'll just lead to wrestling, which will lead to...other things. And I know you're not ready for that. So, we'll take it slow."

She nodded with tears in her eyes and laid her head on my chest. Her arms wrapped around my waist to my back. We stood there for a minute just holding each other. When she pulled away, the sadness had faded a bit, and she seemed more like her usual self. She gathered the few items she had brought with her, and we headed back towards the boat.

"Do you need to tell anyone here you're leaving?" I wondered if she'd made friends or had anyone she cared for here.

She shook her head. "No. These people were nice enough to take me in when I needed it, but then they betrayed my trust, so I don't owe them anything."

She surprised me by taking my hand and weaving her fingers with mine. It was just like before, and I knew it wouldn't last. After a few minutes, she seemed to realize what she had done and tried to pull her hand free. I gave it a squeeze. She looked at me and smiled. It was a start. I'd take what she felt like she could give for now. The next time she tried to pull her hand away, I let her.

We made it back to the boat before the others, and I got Quinn settled back in our room. "I'll stay up on deck at night until you're ready for me to come back to our room. I'm not rushing you or pushing you. Take as much time as you need. I'm here when you're ready."

She smiled at me, and this time I could see it in her eyes too. Just as I was about to leave her to go find the others, she walked over and wrapped her arms around me again. I held her for a minute or so.

"Thank you," she whispered.

"For what?" I asked.

"For not leaving me there. For not leaving me alone. For coming back to me." She spoke into my chest, then pulled back a little and kissed me again. It was sweet and full of emotion.

"You're welcome, although I'm not sure my motives are completely selfless. I have to go find the others now and get some supplies. Will you be OK here, or do you want to come with me?" I was a little scared that if she left again, she'd never come back, but I knew I couldn't keep her locked up.

"I'll stay. I want a shower and a nap. Honestly, this day has been pretty rough. Come see me when you get back?" She looked at me hopefully, her arms still wrapped around me.

I smiled at her with tears in my eyes. "Of course. Whatever you want. I won't be gone long." I kissed her cheek and went to find the others.

TWENTY-SEVEN

KYRO

ZOEY, JACK, MACK AND I went into town once the boat was in port. We asked a few people about Q, but no one seemed to have seen her. Mack went off on his own after a while. He told us not to worry, and he'd check in soon.

After a couple of hours searching around town, we decided to head a little further out and check a couple of villages that we'd heard about while we were asking around about Q. Zoey asked Jack to stick with us, and he agreed. I took that to mean she was still angry with me over the whole thing. We headed east to look for one of the villages.

"We've been walking for an hour and haven't come across a village yet. I think we went the wrong way." Jack was getting irritated at the lack of results. To be honest, I was too. It would just be easier to head back to the boat and see what we could come up with.

"We're not giving up. I don't care how long it takes; we're going to find her. Mack didn't come back from the dead just so we could wuss out in finding his girl." Zoey was pissed all right. I was pretty sure I'd be paying for this one for a while.

"OK, so we'll keep going, but let's try another direction." I thought my suggestion was good, but I got dirty looks from both of them. I shook my head and walked off towards the town we'd just come from. There was no reason to fight about it. We'd either find her or we wouldn't.

I was going to head back to town and see if maybe we'd gone the wrong way. There was a part of me that hated leaving Zoey alone with Jack, but I had to show her I trusted her somehow. When I was about halfway back to town, I heard something and stopped. I turned around slowly and found myself face to face with a native girl.

"Hi. Were you following me?" I wasn't sure but thought I had seen her in town.

She nodded. "I know the girl you're looking for. I can take you to her if you want. She's pretty messed up emotionally and may not want to see you."

"Can you wait here for a minute? I need to go get my friends. Please."

She nodded again, and I ran in the direction Zoey and Jack had been heading. "Hey, guys, where are you? I found someone who knows where Q is." I yelled as I ran. I heard them before I saw them.

"I get that you're mad at him, but you really need to chill. He's doing the best he can. Just give him a chance to make it up to you." Jack was obviously defending me. I wasn't sure how I felt about that, but it was better than trying to steal my girl.

"I know. And I want to move ahead with our relationship, but I just keep circling back to the fact he didn't trust me, and then with the whole Q thing, he wouldn't listen. It's so frustrating." She sounded defeated, and I never wanted that for her.

As much as I wanted to listen to the rest of this conversation, I felt guilty for eavesdropping as it was. "Hey! Zoey, Jack! Where are you guys?" I yelled again, knowing they were just around the next couple of trees.

They heard me and called back to me. "Come on, we need to get back to the girl I ran into. She's going to take us to Q. Ah, shit. I didn't even think to ask her name. I hope she's still there." Now that I'd clued them in, I started running back the other way.

I wanted to fix things with Zoey, but I also knew we needed to find Q. I couldn't let our best chance to find her get away just because I'm being selfish. I glanced back at Zoey and Jack, and they were following me. Their conversation had been halted for now because of my interruption.

The three of us ran up the path until we came upon the girl, standing in the exact spot I had left her.

"Thank you for waiting. I'm sorry. Can you take us to her now?" I fought to catch my breath as I spit out the words.

She nodded. "My name is Mei. I'll take you to my village and show you where your friend has been staying. I hope she will talk to you. Her pain is great. She needs her family."

"Thank you, Mei. I'm Zoey, this is Jack, and this is Kyro. I'm sorry he forgot his manners and didn't introduce himself. We've all been so worked up about finding Q that I think we've all forgotten how to act." Zoey stepped in. I was glad she did because this whole thing really did have me messed up.

"It's fine. I understand. Let's go." Mei headed down a path to the west, and we followed her.

We trudged in silence for a while, then Mei stopped us in the middle of the path. "My village, Asha, is just ahead. Your friend's hut is just outside the main circle, out in the woods. It's this way." She turned east and headed into the woods.

We came upon a small hut just past a clearing. It was quiet and appeared to be deserted. "This is it. I'm not sure if she's here right now. She had a meeting with the village chieftain earlier, and he said she was upset when she left." Mei excused herself and walked back the way we had come.

Jack took point in checking the hut. He was concerned because it was too quiet. Sure enough, Q was not in the hut. It looked like someone had cleared it out as well. There was nothing there to indicate she was planning to come back. We were basically back to square one.

TWENTY-EIGHT

Zoey

WE SEARCHED ALL AROUND the hut for any clue as to which way Q went or if she went willingly. There was nothing. I was feeling defeated, even more so given that Kyro would probably feel like he was right about leaving her alone.

"OK, she's not here. Let's head back to the boat. Maybe Mack had better luck than we did." I hated giving up, but there was only so much a person could do in a day.

Kyro walked over to stand in front of me. He took both of my hands in his. He used our entwined hands to lift my chin so I was looking at him. "Are you sure?" He asked as he placed a tender kiss on my lips.

I nodded, blinking back the tears that were threatening to fall. There was no point in delaying the inevitable. We had to face the fact Q didn't want to be found. "I'm sure. Let's just go home." Given Kyro's expression, I was sure I looked as downtrodden as I felt.

We started down the path back to town. No one was speaking. Jack was fidgety because awkward silences make him crazy. Comfortable silence was one thing, but awkward was completely different.

"So, did you two make up?" He asked to break the silence.

Kyro looked at me expectantly, as though he had put Jack up to asking. Since he'd been walking beside me sulkily for the past half hour, I was pretty sure he hadn't put Jack up to it. It was nice that they were getting along now though.

"Mostly," I responded with a shrug and took Kyro's hand in mine. It would be nice to get back to normal. Of course, we'd have to figure out what that was first. I had decided earlier today that I was going to try to forget about Kyro hiding the first pearl from me, and not trusting me, because I wanted this to work.

It would be like a clean slate, and we'd move forward together. I just hadn't decided if I was going to tell him or not. At some point, I'd either have to, or he'd figure it out.

As I was thinking about our relationship, things got quiet again, and I heard crunching from ahead of us on the path. I looked at Jack, then Kyro, and I could tell from the looks on their faces that they had heard it too.

"What was that?" I asked.

"I'm not sure, but I'm gonna split off and see if I can find out." And with that, Jack disappeared silently into the woods.

Before I could respond, there was a yelp, and I knew Jack had ambushed the person or animal responsible for the noise. Kyro and I could hear the whole thing as it happened.

"Oh, shit! I'm so sorry. I didn't mean to tackle you. I'm just not used to the new look yet. Are you OK?" Kyro and I rounded a tree and found Mack with Jack sprawled on top of him.

Mack laughed. "I'm fine. Just get off me. Really, I'm OK. Just let me up." He kept laughing as Jack picked himself up.

Kyro held a hand out to assist Mack to his feet. "We didn't find her, man. I'm sorry."

Mack smirked. "That's why I came to find you guys. I found her. She's on the boat. I'd have been here sooner, but I had to buy some clothes. I can't wear any of my old stuff, and I can't keep borrowing Kyro's. I'm gonna have to forge new armor and everything."

Kyro laughed. "That's great! Not about the clothes and armor, but about Q. Let's go home." He took my hand, and the four of us headed back to the boat.

twenty-nine

Quinn

I TOOK A SHOWER, running the water as hot as I could stand. There were so many things running through my mind. I stayed under the spray until it ran cold, then used my fire magic to warm it and stay under it longer. It was probably the longest shower I'd ever taken. By the time I was finished, I was wiped. I dried off and got dressed, then laid down on the bed. I was exhausted, emotionally and physically drained from the events of the day.

I fell asleep easily, and at first, slept dreamlessly. I wondered if that was because I knew Mack had come back. I still didn't know all the details, but I was sure there had been a price for it. Magic always came with a price, especially when it dealt with life and death. My parents had made sure I understood that.

I knew the instant the nightmare started. It was the same every time. I was standing there, in the Pit with Mack next to me. One moment we're talking, the next moment my sword is thrust hilt deep into his chest. This time was different because once I stabbed him, he morphed into the body he has now. His eyes opened and he looked at me pleadingly.

I sat up in bed, screaming as I woke up covered in sweat. I drew the covers up to my chest and tried to breathe. The door flew open, and Mack was standing there.

"Are you all right, love? I heard you scream." He ran over to the bed and took me into his arms.

I laid my head on his shoulder and cried. I was broken now and didn't think I'd be myself again. I sat there in his arms, crying against his shoulder until there were no more tears. He held me and rubbed my back, pressing kisses to the top of my head.

He didn't try to placate me or pity me. He just held me and let me get it all out.

"I'm sorry. It was just a bad dream. I'm fine, really. I just feel silly for crying like that." I pressed a kiss to his cheek and laid my head back on his shoulder. I was even more tired now than I had been before my nap, if that was possible.

"No apologies. If you need to cry, I'll hold you. If you have a bad dream, you can tell me about it. If you don't want to tell me, that's OK too. I have a feeling I know what this one was about, though." He sounded confident and sad.

"What do you think it was then?" I asked, wondering if I was really that transparent.

"It was about my death and how it happened. You blame yourself for it when it was my own fault. I chose that, and it wasn't fair to you. I'm sorry."

"How did you know?" I tripped over the words.

He slid a hand under my chin and lifted my head so our eyes could meet.

"The pain in that scream. There was no way it could be anything else. I'm sorry for causing you pain like that and for leaving you alone to deal with it. I will never willingly leave you again. I promise."

I leaned in and kissed him gently. "I know. I won't let you leave me." He grinned at my statement.

"Good. I didn't want to anyway. Does that mean you want me to stay here with you? Or do I still need to find a place to sleep?" It was so sweet of him to offer, but I knew if he was anywhere but beside me, I'd never get any sleep for worrying about him.

"I want you to stay. I'm still upset, and angry, and confused. I don't want to be alone anymore. And I don't want just anyone, I want you." I knew he would understand what I meant by all of that, and he would give me the space I needed to heal. Mack and I held each other for a while longer, then he got up and walked across the room.

"The others are worried about you. Do you want to see them?" He asked with his hand on the door.

I shook my head. "I do, but not tonight. I just want to rest. Where are you going?"

He grinned at me. "I'll be right back. I'm going to get some food. I'll let the others know you're not up for company right now. It'll be OK, love."

******

It wasn't that I didn't trust him to go get food and come right back, but I was tired of being locked away from everything. About five minutes after he left, I decided to follow him. I was completely silent, so I could turn and run if I didn't think I could handle people.

I stopped right outside the galley door, suddenly anxious about my plan. These were my friends; I had no reason to be scared. But I did abandon them after Mack died. I wouldn't blame them if they hated me now. I turned my ear toward the opening, listening to the conversation.

"Do you think she's OK?" Zoey sounded concerned.

"Yeah, I just think the shock of me coming back was a lot to process. I'm actually surprised she took it as well as she did. I don't think my own mum would have taken it so well."

"It's hard for all of us, but we're getting used to it. I think mostly we're just glad to have you back." Jack said softly.

"That's true, but none of us are in love with him. It has to be harder for her." Kyro jumped into the conversation.

I wasn't sure what I had expected, but it wasn't understanding and concern. I thought they'd all be pissed I had run away. At least it wasn't pitying. I wouldn't be able to handle that. I felt myself tearing up again and ran back to our room. I just wasn't ready to see everyone yet. I needed a while longer to get my emotions in check.

I decided to use my private time to check in with James. Once I was back in the room, I quietly closed the door and called via the secure connection on my comm device. It barely took two rings for James to answer.

"Is everything OK? Where have you been?" He sounded scared.

"I think it is now. I'm sorry I ran off like that. I know I should have talked to you instead of sending a message. I'm back with Zoey and the others now." Apologies were hard for me, and it looked like I'd be dealing with them for a while.

James was the most understanding person I knew, but even he had limits. Apparently, I had found them. "I can't believe you would do that to me. I'm so pissed at you; I can't even think straight."

I knew him well enough to know he was going to hang up. "Don't hang up. Please. Let me explain."

"I'm listening." Wow, he was pissed.

"When we got captured by the Chairman, he separated all of us except for me and Mack. He sent us to the Pit, and it's a long story, but I killed Mack." My voice caught in the middle.

"What? You'd never hurt him."

"Exactly. That's why I was so messed up over it. A goddess brought him back. He looks different, but it's him. I'm kinda messed up over that too, but I'm glad he's back. I couldn't take everyone feeling bad for me and looking at me with pity in their eyes. So, I ran off. Mack tracked me down. And I'm back now." I waited for James to respond.

It took a few minutes of silence before I started to worry that he'd hung up anyway.

"Are you still there?"

"Yeah, I'm here. That story is crazy. Which is how I know it's true because you don't tell crazy stories. OK, I forgive you. Just don't ever do anything like that again." James growled and then hung up. I guess he was still mad. And I knew I deserved that.

THIrTY

Mack

QUINN WAS ASLEEP WHEN I made it back to our room with food. To be fair, I had been gone longer than I had intended. Everyone had so many questions. It was hard to walk away without trying to answer. After I had answered as many as I could, I gathered the food and headed back to our room.

I was going to ask her what made her turn around at the door to the galley instead of coming in, but I wasn't going to wake her up to find out. She wouldn't even realize I knew she was there.

It was almost like I had the ability to sense her now. The most interesting sensation came over me when I got close to her, and it faded the further away I was. Since I liked the feeling, I wanted to make sure we weren't separated again.

I set the tray of food down on the table, then got ready for bed. I kept trying to figure out how I would convince her to marry me, but couldn't come up with a good way to ask. I would have to forge a ring, though, and that would take time. I wasn't about to ask without a ring. I needed a few days to design it, then pick the right metal and gemstone. Then it would take a few days to forge it, if I could find a way to distract her so I had some privacy.

The way I saw it, all of that would take me the better part of a month, and that was if I could work on it every day. That would give her time to get used to my new face. I think we both needed that. We still had to complete Zoey's mission and get the pearls and dodeca to the location for Ian's spell to work. So, my proposal dilemma would have to wait.

After everything we've been through, I didn't think it would hurt to give things a little while. Maybe I'd talk it over with Kyro and see if he had any ideas. It seemed logical he and Zoey would be heading in that same direction.

I was just about to climb in bed beside Quinn when she sat up and started screaming. I ran to her and pulled her into my arms. Just then, the door swung open. Zoey and Kyro ran in ready for battle.

"It's OK. She just has nightmares sometimes. Nothing to worry about." I said to them while rocking Quinn.

I turned my face to her ear and whispered to her. "It's all right, love, I'm here. Remember? I came back to you. It's all going to be fine. Just breathe."

She relaxed a little. It seemed as though she didn't even wake up. I wasn't sure how she could sleep through her own screams. She sighed in her sleep and relaxed even more into my arms.

Zoey looked concerned. "Are you sure it's just a nightmare? You don't think the Chairman is astrally pulling her away, do you? I mean, he did it to me."

Kyro nodded. "Maybe Zoey should astral project and check on her?"

"Maybe. Can you take me with you?" I didn't mind Zoey checking on Quinn, but I think if I could go in and calm her down, it might be better.

Zoey looked at me thoughtfully. "I can try." She sat on the bed next to us and put her hand on top of one of mine. "Close your eyes, relax, focus on Q, and take some deep, slow breaths. I'll see if I can pull you in with me."

I did as she asked, and the next thing I knew, we were standing side by side next to the bleachers at the Pit. Quinn was in the center of the ring, and I was being brought out to stand next to her. It was exactly as that had happened before my death.

I knew what was coming next if I didn't do something. "Stay here," I said to Zoey, then ran towards Quinn.

"Quinn! Look at me. I'm right here. This is a dream. It's not real. Everything is fine now." I called to her as I ran. It was strange to be in my old body again, but I could tell from my vantage point that I was a couple of feet shorter than I was before we entered the dream. I wasn't sure if that was Quinn's doing, or my own.

She turned her head towards me and looked at me quizzically. "Mack? What are you doing here? This is my nightmare, not yours."

"I know, love, but we came to make sure you're all right. You started screaming in your sleep, then just stopped. We were all worried." I stepped up to her and took her hands in mine.

As soon as I touched her, the dream faded away. Quinn, Zoey and I were standing in a white void.

"What happened?" Quinn asked, looking around as if she was lost.

"I don't know, this is strange," I responded.

Zoey smiled. "It's OK. You broke the nightmare. I can't guarantee it will stay away forever, but it's gone for tonight."

Quinn breathed a sigh of relief. I hoped Zoey was right. I hated seeing Quinn tortured by that nightmare.

"We need to go now. Mack will be there if you need him." Zoey said to Quinn as she leaned over to hug my love.

THIRTY-ONE

Trav

THE DAY TO DAY activities on the boat were fairly straightforward. Every morning, we trained. Every evening, we studied. The middle of the day was mine to do with as I chose. Gill was assigned more menial chores to keep him busy. I didn't think having Jack watch him was a big deal, since he wasn't doing anything out of line anyway. I could tell he was upset that I agreed with Kyro on that being necessary, but I needed to have some time to myself and couldn't with him following me around watching every move I made.

Gill being busy gave me time in the afternoons to work on spells and practice to make sure I could control the powers I would need to be helpful here. I wasn't a healer by trade, but since that was what this group needed, it was what I would do. My powers were different from anyone else I knew. Most people couldn't change what the powers did.

If you were gifted with combat magic, you could fight. If you were gifted with creative magic, you could create. If you were gifted with healing magic, you could heal. I had a strange combination of the three. The more time I spent with Zoey, the more certain I was that she had the same kind of magic, though her element was water, where mine was earth.

Mack was thrilled that I was able to grow fresh plants on the boat. There was no need to purchase fruits or vegetables when we docked anymore. I could grow what we needed for as long as I was here. It was nice to have a useful job, too. I spent so much of my life thinking I couldn't do anything helpful that I had almost convinced myself it was true.

After a few days on the boat, I had begun to be seasick. I had never traveled by boat before, and while I enjoyed the experience, it was pretty rough on me.

It seemed like Zoey had decided instantly that she liked me. When I was sick, she would bring me tea and cookies, then sit with me for a while until I felt better. We talked about a lot of things that I didn't expect to be discussing with anyone.

"So, you think I have some sort of multi-magic? What does that even mean?" Of course, she was curious when I finally explained my theory to her.

I put down the brush I had been running through her midnight locks, letting her turn to look at me. I enjoyed brushing her hair, and she didn't seem to mind letting me do it, so it became part of our daily routine. "OK, so I'm going to tell you stuff that Gill doesn't even know, but I need to know that you won't tell him. I'm not exactly hiding it; I just haven't told him yet."

She looked at me as if I'd just escaped from a nuthouse, which made sense. It wasn't a good idea to hide anything from your spouse, and I would be the first one to tell you exactly that, but here I am, not telling Gill the basic truth about who I am and what I can do.

"I have it too. I can control earth, shape it, move it, change it. I also have healing abilities, can move items with my mind, and sometimes I can see pieces of the future. Growing up was hard. I learned really quickly that hiding most of it was the best way to cope." I kept my voice low in case Gill happened to be listening at the door.

"You have multiple different powers? That's so awesome. How did you learn to control them?"

"Well, to be honest, I'm still learning. In the beginning, my parents were my best teachers. I somehow got half my powers from my dad and the other half from my mom. Most people only get powers from one parent or the other. I'm not sure exactly how it happened, but it did, and I think that's what happened to you as well."

"I don't think either of my parents has powers. I'm not even sure if my dad is still alive, honestly. They both work, or worked, for the Patrol, and he went undercover in the Order. No one has seen or heard from him since, and it's been years."

She wiped a tear from the corner of her eye, and I felt horrible for bringing up a bad memory.

"I'm sorry, I didn't mean to bring it up. I didn't know. They must have powers, otherwise, you wouldn't. I've studied the genetics behind it for years. There has only been one time in history when it didn't happen that way. At least with humans. Maybe with your species, it's different. I really don't know."

"It's OK, Trav. I know you weren't trying to hurt me. And maybe you're right. Maybe they hid their powers from me the way you're hiding most of yours from Gill. No judgment. Really. I don't think it's a good idea, but ultimately it's your relationship and has to be your decision."

"Thanks. Maybe I can help you work on controlling your powers if you want?"

She grinned at me. "That would be fantastic! We can start as soon as Kyro and I get back from our next mission. Ian thinks he found a lead on another artifact or pearl. We're not sure which, but either one is helpful at this point."

Zoey gave me a huge hug, then took off to take care of her afternoon responsibilities. That left me to practice my magic for a while until time for group study.

Zoey

MY BREATH CAME IN gasps as my head broke the surface of the water. Ky had warned me it would be a long swim. I finally understood why he had asked me to stay behind, as well as why the others had agreed without argument to remain on the boat. I was stubborn and insisted I could handle it.

I hoped that determination was enough to keep me alive. I couldn't let him do it for me. This was my mission and I had to be the one to complete it. It was hard enough to convince Jack to let me go. He wanted me to stay behind and let Kyro do it on his own.

My lungs burned from the air hitting them after holding my breath for so long. I glanced blindly around the underground cavern, looking for any indication that Ky had made it before I did. He had to be here. He was much faster in the water, especially with his tail.

It was so dark. I couldn't see anything but inky black surrounding me. I shuddered as I felt a cool breeze waft over my face. I was suddenly chilled to the bone. Which way would lead out of the water? There was no way to tell in the darkness that enveloped me.

I treaded water, debating if calling out to Kyro was safe. I knew there were dangers around every corner, even underwater. "Ugh, Ky, where are you?" I muttered to myself.

Suddenly I saw a faint blue glow heading toward me. The blue globule of light bobbed up and down, as though it was swimming in my direction. The glowing sphere got larger the closer it came.

I expected it to be Kyro, with his amulet glowing to lead him to me, but instead it was an enormous angler fish with a huge blue light hanging over its head. Well, at least that decision was made for me. I frantically tried to swim away from the giant beast, barely clearing its gaping jaws, kicking my legs and swinging my arms wildly to move through the water.

In my attempt to escape, I slammed into something solid that felt somewhat human. "Kyro?" I whispered, terrified it may not be him.

"Zoey? Are you OK?" He whispered in response, with his mouth against my ear. Now I was out of breath for reasons other than the exertion of swimming for so long. He ran his hand up my arm and rested it on my cheek. Then he pressed his lips to mine, so gently.

The warmth started at my lips and spread throughout my body. I was fully warmed in an instant. I opened my eyes to a purple glow around my legs beneath the water. At once, my legs morphed into a beautiful purple mermaid tail. I had a tail where my feet had just been!

"What did you do to me?" I asked in a hushed voice.

"I didn't," he breathed, "I mean, I guess I must have, but it wasn't like I was trying to. I was just so relieved to see you. I thought you were fish food, and I'd never see you again."

He pressed his lips to mine again, gently like before. This time, my skin illuminated, and I was somehow emitting a blue glow, lighting up the area like a lantern in the dark.

"Well, that's new," Kyro exclaimed in a hushed tone.

"I have no idea what's happening. Why am I glowing?" I couldn't wrap my thoughts around what had just happened.

"Let's just try to figure out which way leads to shore. We have an artifact to find." Kyro took my hand and led me south, directly across from the direction we had entered the underwater cavern. After swimming for what felt like miles, we saw the edge of the water lapping against the shore.

I wondered if I would be able to change back the way Ky could once we reached land. We made it to the edge, and he stepped out of the water, reaching a hand out to help me up. The moment I touched his hand, crippling pain shot down my tail. It felt as though my tail had been ripped in half. I looked down, and that's almost what it looked like watching the change happen.

"I'm sorry. I know it hurts. It'll happen faster next time—if there is a next time." Ky tried to offer comfort, though he had just been through the same thing.

"Is it like that every time?" I knew the answer without him even muttering a word. It was written all over his face. I nodded, and we began to look around for the marker that would let us know which way we needed to go.

My glow had begun to fade, which was comforting, except that soon we'd be in the dark again. We had to act fast. "This way." I saw the marker and pointed toward the direction it led.

We turned a corner and ran into a man, sitting on a rock. Ky and I were both pretty skeptical at this point since everything we had run into had tried to kill us recently.

The man waved and called out to us. "Hello there. I've been waiting for you." Kyro had his hand on his dagger, and I realized I had been just about to do the same.

"It's all right, you won't need the blades. I'm here to help. It's my job to protect the item you've come to claim. I just need you to answer a riddle, then I'll give it to you."

Ky and I exchanged suspicious looks, then walked slowly over to the man. "We have to answer a riddle? Then you'll give us this item? That sounds too easy to be the truth."

I wasn't convinced he would keep his end of the bargain, but I was sure Ky and I could take him if we had to fight.

"So, what's this riddle?" Kyro asked before I had a chance. I took a good look at the man while he paused.

He was older, with gray hair sprouting from his head and face in all directions. He looked as though he hadn't bathed in ages, even though he was sitting a few feet from the water. He smelled as though it had been even longer. He was thin and somewhat sickly looking. His voice was strong, and his hands didn't shake when he moved them to run over his hair, smoothing it as if he was feeling self-conscious about his appearance.

"Well, it's a bit of trivia, perhaps. Maybe riddle wasn't the right word for it, but anyway, if you answer the question correctly, I'll give you the item." His voice was strong, but he stammered through, stalling a bit.

"What if we answer wrong?" I wanted to know exactly what I was getting into dealing with this gentleman.

"Let's just hope you get it right. I'm not allowed to tell you, because you may decide to leave without trying." He seemed to be getting irritated.

"Very well, give us the question." Ky was getting impatient as well.

"Fine, here's the question. Then you'll have one minute to come up with the correct answer, but whatever answer you give first will count as your answer, so be careful."

He hesitated again, this time it seemed for added dramatic pause. "What item did the evil queen use to poison the princess with the hair of jet and skin white as snow?"

Kyro looked at me with a puzzled, concerned expression. I grinned back at him. "I know this story. The item was a poisoned apple. I've read it so many times over the years."

I gave the old man a cocky grin. "So, where's my prize?"

He bowed his head, obviously disappointed that I had answered correctly. "I didn't think you could answer it. It's been so long since we've had books. I thought all the old stories were gone. Ah, well, a promise, and all." He reached in his jacket pocket and pulled out a sphere wrapped in a piece of cloth. He paused before placing it in my outstretched hand.

I didn't even bother to check it; I knew from the last one that it had to be one of the artifacts. I nodded to Kyro, and we started to walk away. "Thank you," I said over my shoulder to the old man.

He nodded, then crumpled to the floor. I ran back to him, but it was too late. He was dead, and his body began to turn to ash in front of our eyes.

Kyro grabbed my arm and pulled me toward the water. "We need to leave. Now." I didn't argue, securing the pearl in the bag we had brought with us. We waded back into the water, and Kyro's legs once again became a tail. I looked at him expectantly, because mine did not change. He shrugged, and I waded out further toward him.

"I guess I'm gonna have to make this work, then." With that, we began to swim back toward our exit. Once we hit about the midway point, my legs were aching, and my lungs were burning from trying to keep up with Kyro. When he noticed, he stopped and waited for me to catch up.

"Do you need me to pull you?" He offered.

"I'm fine, just can't keep up with you. Maybe if you kiss me again, I'll change?" I figured it was worth a try, as that was how it had happened before. He leaned over and his lips touched mine gently.

In an instant, I felt the now-familiar warmth that turned my legs into a tail earlier. When I looked down, once again, I was a mermaid.

"I guess I should have thought of that earlier," he said sheepishly.

"I know. Me too." At least I would be able to make it back to the boat now without too much trouble.

THIRTY-THREE

Jack

I KNEW SOMETHING WAS wrong when Elena called me out of the blue. For a while, we had been communicating daily, but it was suspected that those calls were what tipped the Order off to our location. We had agreed that calls would be reserved for weekly check-ins, and anything in between would be emergency only. Our weekly check-in had been two days ago.

"What's wrong?"

"We need to talk. It's important. Are you alone?" Elena sounded freaked out, which wasn't like her. She had always been calm and collected.

I looked around me. Kyro and Zoey were swimming with Mateo beside the boat. Mack and Q were sparring in the training area. It appeared the only issue I could have with privacy was Gill and Trav.

"Give me a sec." I headed down below deck, planning to find them and make sure I had some privacy.

I walked down past the galley, and when I glanced inside, Gill and Trav were in there. It looked like they were making dinner. I could easily go to my room and have this conversation. I casually strolled down the hall to my room, went inside, and locked the door behind me. I activated the silencing bubble Q had created. She understood that sometimes I needed to have delicate conversations with Elena. Or maybe she thought we were having phone sex. It didn't matter to me as long as I had privacy.

"OK, I'm alone now, and the bubble is up. What is going on?"

"You might want to sit down for this," she began cautiously.

I sat on my bed. I had a feeling this was going to be bad. "That good, huh? All right, shoot."

"I found some files and papers in Mama Bear's office. Do you remember how we suspected there was a mole in our operation? Well, from what I just found, it looks like it was her. I don't know what to do."

I couldn't believe it. How could Mama Bear be working with us and against us at the same time? Especially when one of us was her own daughter?

"Are you sure? I've known her for most of my life, and I can't see her betraying her own daughter like that."

"The evidence is pretty damning. She's apparently been feeding our locations and plans to the Order for months now. I don't know if I can turn her in for it. I don't want to ruin what we have. And Zoey is my friend." She sounded like she was about to break down.

"If the evidence is real, we have to turn her in. Can you send me the files first so I can look at them? I just have to be sure they weren't faked."

"I appreciate the second set of eyes. I don't know how I'll handle it if we have to turn her in. And I don't know how I'll keep this to myself, but I know I have to. Thank you, Jack."

"No problem. Just don't say anything to anyone until we're sure. If it comes to that, I'll talk to Zoey and make sure she knows we investigated first. I'll get back to you as soon as I've reviewed the files."

The call was disconnected, and within moments I had the files in question on my comm device. I spent the next hour going over documents detailing our movements and missions over the last few months. Everything that had helped the Order capture us was sitting in front of me. She was right, the evidence was damning.

I had to figure out how to talk to Zoey about this. How do you tell someone that her mother is the reason we all got locked up? How do you tell someone that her mother is the reason her friend died? I mean, yeah, he was brought back, but we all still deal with the grief from the time period when he was gone. This was not going to end well.

I tried to find anything in the documents that would prove they were planted or faked. I knew Elena wouldn't do that, but if there was a mole, it was possible they could have planted evidence to frame Mama Bear. Every document had originated from Mama Bear's device or computer. There was no way any of it had been planted or faked. I spent hours trying to find a way to prove they had been, to no avail.

I messaged Elena and told her we'd discuss the documents tomorrow. I needed to sleep on this and figure out how to explain it all to Zoey. I had a feeling this was going to be bad.

After isolating myself from everyone and studying the documents Elena sent me, I couldn't argue their authenticity. I stayed up way too late, then got up way too early and poured over them again. If they had been faked, I would have figured it out. The only explanation was that Mama Bear was guilty. And if I turned her in, I would be forced to testify. I would be the one to ruin my best friend's life.

That thought stayed with me through much of the morning as I showered and searched through the documents again. The more I reviewed them, the more I learned about the "secret" organization I had been working for. I thought Mama Bear had recruited me to work for the Resistance. Turns out, I was wrong. The Resistance didn't even really exist. Not in the way we all thought anyway.

The organization itself was real, but it wasn't working against the Order and the Patrol. It was being controlled by the Patrol. The

Resistance might as well have been a special ops section of the Patrol. I wondered how Q would feel when she found out.

Given her hatred for the Patrol and the Order, I figured that would be a fun conversation as well. At least I had documentation to back up my claims. It was disheartening to know I would be ruining not only Zoey's life, but Q's as well. To be fair, these documents had already turned my life on its side. Everything I thought I knew was a lie. Everyone I had trusted there had lied to me as well.

Then there were the documents showing that members of the Patrol were under the thumb of the Order. That may have been the most disturbing part. There was a list of the Patrol and Resistance members who were actually working for the Order. It looked like it had been a slow process, with a couple of double agents being recruited into the Resistance, then more being recruited into the Patrol, until both organizations were mostly the Order. All that fighting and never getting anywhere finally made sense.

I had to give Mama Bear credit; she had manufactured a fantastic cover for her illegal dealings. The Patrol controlling the Resistance also explained why she was able to pull off taking Zoey and me from Calliope, then releasing us. That part had never really sat well with me. I felt like such an idiot for not seeing what she was doing right under our noses. All those years of following her orders, for what? What had I been a party to?

What had I done thinking I was protecting Zoey when in reality I was working for the Order? The whole thing was confusing and outrageous. I couldn't put it off any longer, I needed to talk to Q and Zoey. Then I had to call Elena back and move forward with what had to be done.

THIRTY-FOUR

Zoey

I HADN'T SEEN JACK since yesterday afternoon and was actually starting to worry. I knew he had to be on the boat, but it wasn't like him to hide unless he was working on a project. I checked the training area on deck for him, but there was no sign he'd been up there recently. I headed down to the galley, but he wasn't there either.

I ran into Trav on my way out of the galley. "Have you seen Jack?" I asked hopefully.

He shook his head. "Not since yesterday afternoon. I saw him peek in the galley while Gill and I were starting to prep dinner. I thought it was weird he didn't eat last night, but I don't know where he went."

I nodded and walked off in the direction of Jack's room. That was the only place he could be, although it was not like him to stay in bed all day. He was usually up early and busy all day. I stopped outside his door, and a feeling of dread washed over me. I raised my hand to knock, hesitated, then lowered it. Maybe I was overreacting. There were a million reasons why Jack could be locked away in his room.

I shook my head to clear my thoughts, then raised my fist to the door again. I knocked loudly. It didn't matter why he locked himself away, it wasn't healthy. He at least needed to eat.

"Jack? Are you in there?" I called before trying the door. Of course, it was locked. Why wouldn't it be? Lucky for me, I had been working with Ian on spells and power control. I told him lockpicking would be a handy skill to have.

I felt the power push from my fingertips and extend into the lock. I closed my eyes and worked on moving the tumblers into place. At the moment I felt the final tumbler fall into place, the door jerked open, and I was face to face with Jack.

"Oh, hi." I jumped and squeaked out the greeting, my face turning purple from embarrassment at being caught red handed.

"Zoey, what are you doing here?" Jack seemed anything but happy to see me.

I could swear that was a look of panic on his face. I pushed the door open and went inside, turning to look at Jack as I did. For a minute, I really thought he was going to bolt. There wasn't really anywhere to hide while the boat was in open waters. His attitude was perplexing.

"Jack, what's wrong? You've been locked away for almost a whole day. That's not like you." I walked back to the door and closed it before he had a chance to run.

He shook his head and walked over to the bed. "I'm fine, really, I just needed some time to think." He flopped down on the bed.

"I don't get it. You can't tell me what's going on? I've known you almost my whole life, and you suddenly can't be honest with me? What the fuck, Jack?" Every part of me wanted to give up and run, but I couldn't abandon him like that. Something was wrong and he needed my help.

He shook his head again, then rested it in his hands with his elbows on his knees. "It's not like that and you know it. I was just trying to make sure before I brought it to you. I don't even know where to start. You're my best friend. I just had to be sure, OK?" He didn't look up from the spot on the floor that he was staring at.

"I have no idea what you're talking about. You had to be sure? OK. About what? Just tell me. It can't be that bad. You're my best friend too. That should mean something." I pushed hard to get him to open up.

"Fine. Are you sure you want to know? Then I'll just tell you. I have proof that someone has been feeding intel to the Order. Actual documents that implicate this person. I made sure they weren't faked or planted. They originated on this person's personal devices. I know who it is and how they did it." He still refused to move, sitting perfectly still.

I walked over and sat next to him, leaning down and twisting so I could see his face. "You know who it is and have proof, that's great. We can turn them in and let the Patrol take care of it. What's the problem?"

There were tears in his eyes as they met mine. He gave up on hiding and sat up to face me. It hurt me to see him like this. I put my hand on his arm and gave him a little smile.

He leaned over and kissed me. For a moment, I relaxed into it, and then I realized that Jack was kissing me. I pulled away from him and put my hand on his chest.

"What was that?" I asked. I couldn't believe he had just done that.

Tears streamed down his face as he looked at me. "I love you, Zoey. I need you to know that. I'm sorry, I shouldn't have kissed you. I just didn't want to have any regrets. You have to know that I would never do anything to hurt you." My heart was breaking as I stared into his eyes.

"Jack, it sounds like you're saying goodbye. Please tell me what you're talking about. You can't just tell me you know who is responsible then kiss me and not explain." I was starting to freak out inside.

He nodded and wiped his face with the back of his hand. "The documents that were sent to the Order were created on the same device. They were all made under the same account. I hate that I have to tell you this." He just stopped talking and stared at me.

"You're killing me. Who is it? We've been searching for the mole for a while. If you know, you have to tell me."

"It was your mom, Zo. She's the mole. And I have to turn her in. I realize you'll probably never be able to forgive me. I don't know if

I'll ever forgive me either. You and I both know it's the right thing to do." Tears ran down his face again, matching the ones streaming down mine.

"That can't be right, Jack. Mama would never put us in danger. There's no way." I wished that I sounded more convinced than I was. How could my own mother sell us out like that? It wasn't possible.

"I spent half the night and all morning trying to figure out how it could be any other way, but I can't. The documents originated from her devices and under her codes. She's the one, Zo. It was her fault we were captured. It was her fault Mack died."

"That's hardly fair, Jack. Besides, Mack is back now. That doesn't change the pain we all went through, I know, but he's here now. There has to be another explanation. Mama wouldn't do this. She must have been framed."

I turned to storm out of his room, but he caught my arm and pulled me back. He wrapped his arms around me and held me close for a minute. I couldn't help but break down and cry. This hurt me so badly. I was being forced to choose between my mother and my best friend.

Losing Jack was going to be painful, but losing Mama might kill me. I'd suffered so much loss already. I hugged him tightly, then pushed my way out of Jack's arms.

"You do what you have to, but don't expect us to be OK after. And you're right—I may never forgive you. I just can't be around you right now. We're supposed to stop for supplies tomorrow. I think you should leave when the boat docks." I walked to the door and opened it.

"If that's what you need, Zo, that's what I'll do. I meant what I said—I love you." The emotion in his voice almost broke me.

I walked out and closed the door behind me. "I love you, too," I whispered softly. I ran down the hall to our room and spent the next couple of hours lying on the bed crying.

THIRTY-FIVE

KYRO

IT HAD BEEN A week since we had docked for supplies in Brazil. Jack had announced five minutes before we docked that he was leaving as soon as we stopped the boat.

He refused to tell us why, and he didn't bother to tell Zoey good-bye. Since he left, she refused to even speak his name or answer any questions about what had happened. I could see the hurt in her eyes any time someone said his name.

It had been hard for me to accept that he cared for her, but it was even harder for me to see how much she cared for him. I hoped whatever had come between them wouldn't be a force to tear us apart.

We had been trying to get Zoey to understand the need to be proactive. Mack, Q and I had been talking since Jack left and had decided it would be safer to split up. Zoey was fully against the idea. She got angry every time we brought it up.

With the Order closing in on us again, I had to make Zoey mad by bringing up the topic she hated.

"We're going to have to split up if we want to hide from the Order."

She growled at me angrily. "I don't want to split up. It's not safe for us to be apart."

Mack jumped in to help me out. "We're not going to go four different ways. Nobody is going to be alone. We just need to make it more of a challenge for them to find us."

She growled at him in response, too, as she stepped forward. Q grabbed Zoey's hand and stopped her from attacking Mack. "Zo, just listen to them. We have to at least consider that splitting up is the best chance we have to get away from the Order."

Zoey's face sank in defeat. "I don't like it."

"I know, but it won't be forever, just long enough to get them off our backs. Then we'll all meet back up. I promise." I tried once again to convince her. It just made sense.

Mack chimed in, "You don't have to like it, you just have to let us do it. I didn't see you making a big deal when Jack took off."

"And you've known *him* way longer than you've known *us*, so it seems like that would have been more of an issue than this," Q interjected.

"I don't want to talk about him. Just let it go. Please. I'll do whatever you guys want me to, just stop asking me about him." Zoey wouldn't even say Jack's name anymore. Something big must have happened between them. With her refusing to talk about it and him taking off suddenly, there was no way for us to find out.

"OK, it's decided then. Mack and Q, you two will take off when we port tomorrow. Don't tell us where you're heading, but make sure you have the necklace I gave you. It'll allow communication if either group gets in trouble. Zoey and I will make our way north to start."

It wouldn't be a good idea for either group to know where the other was heading, so we'd keep that between the couples for now. I hoped at some point we would all be able to settle down near each other, but there was no guarantee.

I had already arranged with Trav and Gill for them to head out as well. We all needed to be as far away from each other as we safely could right now. Hopefully there would be a chance for us all to reunite after the Order had been dealt with.

THIRTY-SIX

Jack

WITH MAMA BEAR BEING arrested and Elena taking her place in charge of the Patrol, it was an easy decision to go back to headquarters with her. I didn't feel good about turning Zoey's mom in, but the proof was there. She was guilty. It made sense that the Patrol would just promote Elena, then let her choose her second. The same thing had happened when Mama Bear was promoted. I just had no idea who her second was until after she'd kidnapped Zoey and myself from Calliope.

We'd spent weeks in meetings and depositions going over the evidence while Mama Bear swore she didn't release any info to the Order. Because of my tech background, I got to be the one to argue against her. It killed me inside.

Elena stepped in and took over, and it seemed like things were getting better. The Order wasn't getting our intel (that we knew of), and Zoey was safe. That was the most important part. Even if she never spoke to me again, I had to keep her safe.

"Baby, where'd you go? Come back to bed," Elena called to me softly. She had been sleeping soundly when I got up to use the bathroom. I found myself staring out the window instead of climbing back into bed with her. I had so many things going through my mind with the hearings and upcoming trial. I wasn't sure I could force myself to testify against Mama Bear, no matter what she had done.

Elena walked up behind me and wrapped her arms around my waist. "You know sulking about it won't make it go away. You're doing the right thing."

"I know. I just wish it wasn't me doing it."

"You know why I can't testify. Carter would remove me from my position if he knew I discovered the documents and didn't go straight to him. And we don't want that, right?" She sounded hurt that I had even mentioned not wanting to testify.

"I know, and you're right. Carter is a vindictive asshole who would use everything against you, even though you had no part in it."

I knew she was right, but still had that small part of myself that hoped that Mama Bear had been framed. It was like a strange puzzle my brain wouldn't give up on. I was like a dog with a bone. Something was wrong with the whole thing, and I couldn't quite pin it down.

"Come on, let's go back to bed." Elena was insistent, but I knew sleep would avoid me the rest of the night.

"You go ahead. I'm going to the gym for a jog. It'll help clear my head and relax me enough to go back to sleep. I'll see you in a bit." I leaned down and kissed her forehead, then grabbed my gym bag from the hall closet. A workout and a jog were just what I needed.

I couldn't get rid of the feeling I was being watched. I slowed my pace heading to the gym and listened closely to my surroundings. I couldn't hear anything out of place. It had to be the guilt from betraying Zoey that had me imagining things. I had almost convinced myself that it was my imagination and nothing else by the time I made it to the gym.

I settled into my workout routine pretty easily, letting my mind wander as my body was pushed to its limits. I was so focused on the routine that I almost missed the high-pitched whining noise that was coming from the vent above me. The more I thought about it, the more I realized the noise was familiar to me. It was like I'd been hearing it for so long that I almost didn't notice it.

At first, the noise was just annoying, but then I noticed it was getting louder. It seemed like whatever was making the noise was getting closer. I moved over to the row of treadmills on the opposite side of the room. The noise seemed to be quieter over here, then suddenly it got louder again.

I walked back to the rowing machines I had been next to when I first heard the noise. Again, it seemed to follow me. No matter where I went into this room, that noise followed. At this point, I was feeling a bit paranoid and decided to check it out. I climbed up on the top of one of the leg press machines and popped a ceiling tile out.

I stuck my head through the opening and saw a small android on wheels. It was about a foot tall and close to the same around. The noise seemed to be the engine that was motoring it around. I stretched my arm through the opening in the ceiling and grabbed it. I pulled it down with me as I climbed off the leg press.

I disabled the power to the android, then started taking it apart to inspect it. The good thing was that this droid was just for recon. So, at best, someone was spying on me. At worst, I was a target and my life was in danger.

I guess maybe my suspicions were right. Maybe Mama Bear was framed. Or she had operatives working for her and had sent them after me. It didn't really matter either way, but I wanted to know who was after me. Were they just watching my every move, or was there something more sinister planned? I had no idea, but I vowed to find out.

THIRTY-seven

Trav

Before everyone split up, Gill and I spent our days taking care of whatever Kyro and the others needed. I was grateful they let us stay. Gill seemed distant at times, but I think that was because he found out about my powers. It was a difficult discussion, but I tried to make him understand that I didn't hide them to be cruel.

He didn't understand the pressure that I was raised under. I had been expected to control my powers and use them to fight for those who were unable to fight, whether it was against the Resistance, or the Order, or the Patrol. There was no way I was going back there, so it didn't matter anymore.

Zoey and I became fast friends, and I even felt like Quinn liked me. I understood her feelings toward my husband, and while I didn't agree with his methods, I could sympathize with the reasons behind his actions.

I knew she could too. That was why she hadn't fought when the others decided to let us stay. If someone had taken Mack and threatened him, she would have done the exact same thing. And I would have backed her up on it. Any of us would.

Gill tried to get me to train with him using my magic, but I refused. I couldn't let him see the extent of my powers. I knew he meant well, but he also had a jealous streak, and I wouldn't put it past him to try and control or take my powers from me if he felt like he could do more with them.

I was tired of being controlled and tired of being manipulated. So instead, I trained with the girls and Mateo. I read and studied with Kyro and Mack, trying to figure out where the other pearl was and how to combine their powers once we had all three.

I kept my magic practice to the few hours a day when Gill was occupied with other things. Kyro had decided that each of us needed to have responsibilities on the boat, which made sense to me because he seemed to be the one paying for everything. I didn't mind a little laundry to keep a roof over my head.

Because of his past, Gill got the shit jobs, meaning he had to clean the deck, the galley, and spend two hours a day up in the crow's nest scouting for trouble. I really think the last one was to give me a break from him because I was able to get my chores done in the time Gill spent in the galley and on deck.

The more time I spent with this group, the more I felt like I had been brought here for a reason. I just hadn't figured out exactly what my purpose was yet.

I spent some extra time with Zoey when Jack took off. It seemed odd, but she wasn't as upset as I had expected. They seemed really close. I wanted to ask her about it, but she was shutting down and pushing everyone who brought it up away from her. I wanted her to know she didn't have to go through it alone, so I never asked.

I wasn't a fan of being on a boat for an extended period of time, so I spent as much time below deck as possible. Which meant Gill hovered. He was concerned about me getting sick and wanted to do everything he could to prevent it. It was sweet and annoying at the same time.

THIRTY-EIGHT

Jack

I WAS BEGINNING TO wonder why I had come back to the Patrol. I probably would have been better off heading to the small village where Q had hidden from us. At least there I wouldn't be shipped back to Calliope to do shit jobs because no one else wanted to do them.

I wasn't seeing any of the accused favoritism, either. I got nothing out of my girlfriend being the Commander. But of course, the board listened to Carter over me. That dick had a way of manipulating the situation to get what he wanted. And right now, he wanted Elena.

Maybe not sexually, though I was pretty sure he'd start putting the moves on her before I even made it back to Calliope. He wanted access to her, to manipulate her into letting him have more money for his experiments and side missions. I guess he saw me as a threat, which was good. And bad.

Honestly, I wasn't even that upset about being shipped away from Elena. Something was off about her lately, and I couldn't quite pin it down. So I would take this relocation as a way of following what I know would be Mama Bear's suggestion.

"Take a step back and look at the evidence. That's the easiest way to figure out what's causing the problem."

I couldn't count how many times she told me that while we were growing up, and even after. I was pretty good at figuring things out, but sometimes I got caught up in the details and missed something bigger. That was my greatest struggle in school, and it carried over into my career.

So I would take a step back, or rather a few thousand miles away, and see if I could figure it all out. I'd also be able to continue to investigate Stephen's murder, which has bothered me more than I would have expected. I mean, I barely knew him, but I felt responsible for his death.

With everything that had happened, I never did get to question Marlene. I'd have to make it a point once I got settled to pay the security department a visit. Fortunately, I was being reassigned to Calliope permanently, so it wouldn't be a difficult thing to do. At least I was going to get my old job back.

I missed being the Head of Engineering, although if I'm being honest, I missed Zoey more. I hated the way we left things, and I was seriously pissed at myself for screwing things up by pushing my feelings at her. I should have kept my lips to myself and my mouth shut. I wanted her to believe me that I didn't want to turn her mom in. I didn't have a choice. If anyone else had done it, there would have been no way I could have protected Zoey or the others.

Elena didn't come back to our room the entire time I was packing to leave. After thinking about it, I hadn't actually seen her in a couple of days. She'd been up before me and had come in after I was asleep. If it wasn't for the fact that I had woken up at three AM and saw her, I would have thought she was staying somewhere else.

It didn't matter anyway. We'd spent more time apart than together since our relationship began. If it was meant to last, it would. I wasn't planning on doing anything else to ruin it. I'd already done enough, and I wasn't sure if she'd find out or not. I just knew I wouldn't be the one to tell her. If Zoey ratted me out, I wouldn't deny it. Maybe a part of me secretly hoped she would call Elena and tell her everything.

When it was time to board the shuttle and I still hadn't seen Elena, I sent her a simple text. I wasn't going to force her to say goodbye if she had no interest in it.

Shuttle is leaving now. I guess you're too busy to say goodbye. See ya soon.

There was no response, but I really didn't expect one. I was beginning to wonder if she and Carter were working together on this. It seemed odd that she wouldn't fight to keep me here, but I didn't even have time to think about it until I was on the shuttle.

I watched the planet I had become attached to fade in the distance as the shuttle returned me to the only home I'd ever known. I knew this would be a struggle for life or death, and I was determined to live. I had to find a way to clear Mama Bear and make all of this up to Zoey.

THIRTY-NINE

Zoey

I HATED THE IDEA of splitting up. I felt so much safer when we were all together and working as a team. I knew we'd be harder for the Order to find this way, but I hated it. And I didn't hesitate to tell Kyro exactly that on a daily basis since we'd split from our group. I was being childish, but I didn't care. It hurt me that none of them took my feelings into consideration when they made this decision, and even when I objected, they overruled me.

We had been holed up in a tiny apartment in the attic of an abandoned building for two weeks at this point, and I was going stir crazy. I wanted to do something, anything. All we could do was sit in this apartment and hide.

"How much longer do we have to stay here? I miss the boat. And our friends." I wasn't above whining to get my way. I'd been pacing the room for half an hour, taking a break from our research.

Kyro shook his head at me and responded without looking up from his book. "We have had this conversation every day since we left. You know we have to stay away until we can close the rift. And since Ian isn't being too helpful on that front right now, we're stuck in hiding."

"Ugh. I just want to go home. I don't even want to be the chosen one. Can't we just go somewhere off the map and live normal lives?" I had almost reached the point of begging. I was desperate to be finished with all of this.

Kyro stopped reading the book he was holding. "Do you mean that? Do you want to give up? That's not like you. I know this is hard, but you've never talked about giving up."

Tears shone in my eyes when I turned to face him. "I don't want to give up. I don't want to spend the rest of my life running either. We need to either face this head-on or quit and go live our lives. I'm tired of looking over my shoulder, waiting for the next horrible thing to happen to me or you or our friends."

"I understand that and totally agree. I want nothing more than to be out on the water again. I miss it. But I have to keep you safe, and we have to figure out how to use these items to close the rift. To do that, we have to find the rift first. Maybe we should try talking to Ian again."

I flopped on the floor next to the stack of books I had been reading before my fit. I flicked my wrist at the journal, and it opened. "The only good thing about being locked up like this is that I've gained better control over some of my powers."

Kyro chuckled, "That's true. You are the reason we had to leave the last hideout. If you hadn't caught the place on fire, we could have stayed there longer."

"Hey! That's not fair. It wasn't my fault! I didn't see that the target was set up so close to those hay bales." He'd been teasing me about this since we got here.

"It's OK. Just stay calm and focus. Try to get Ian to respond."

I knew Kyro was concerned because Ian hadn't responded to us since we decided to split the group. I wondered if he knew that we'd done it and if that was why he didn't answer.

I laid my left hand on the book and pushed a bit of power into it. "Ian, we need to talk to you. Please. Are you OK?"

We waited for a few minutes with no response.

"Maybe something has happened to him. Should we use the teleport pearl to go check on him?"

"Zo, you know we can't control the jump. You, Mack and Trav tried. There's no way to know it would drop you where you wanted to be. It's not safe. We can try again later."

I knew it wasn't the best idea, but I was tempted to use the teleport pearl and try anyway. Our isolation time hadn't been completely in vain. We had figured out exactly what each pearl did and learned that the dodeca was the key to combining the powers to close the rift. And since we'd learned that there were more than three pearls of power, we knew there was an added urgency to our quest.

If the Order managed to find three pearls of their own and another of the combining artifacts, we'd be in serious trouble. It was hard to coordinate efforts when the group wasn't together, though.

"Should we go out and try to find another artifact? Those sailors thought there was something down by the docks. It would give you a chance to get close to the water again for a bit. And if we can find it, the Order won't have it." I was pushing to leave the safest place we'd been in weeks. I had to have lost my mind.

I couldn't believe Kyro agreed with me. He'd been arguing for days that we needed to stay hidden, but I had finally worn him down. "We should go. We have to be careful and try to stay hidden. Got it?"

I nodded my agreement, and we gathered what we would need. Kyro helped me load everything else into my haversack, and he put a spell on it to make it look empty to anyone but us. We snuck out of the building onto the fire escape, then climbed down to the ground. Our breaths puffed in tiny clouds in front of us as we walked toward the dock. I pulled my jacket closed against the chill in the air. The street was empty until we got closer to the docks.

We didn't talk on the way to the docks, instead keeping a lookout for anyone who might be following us. I didn't notice anything that looked strange. Once we got within a block of the docks, we saw more people heading to and from the boats. The docks were bustling with workers loading and unloading boats, running around in crazy patterns that somehow worked for them. One boat carried fish, freshly caught from the bay. Another had crates of some sort, probably dry goods.

The boat we were looking for should be unloading barrels of whiskey or loading empty barrels if we missed the unloading. We slowed our steps and found some crates to duck behind. Kyro pulled me into an embrace, making it look as though we were simply stealing a moment for ourselves. It would be less obvious we were looking for something and would give us a moment to make sure we weren't being followed.

He caught me off guard by actually pressing his lips to mine. My breath hitched, and I sighed as he deepened the kiss. I wrapped my arms around his neck and ran my fingers through his hair. He groaned as he pulled his face away from mine, and I kept my fingers tangled in his hair, rubbing his scalp. "Can't we just go back to the safe house and be alone?" His voice was raw with need.

"We agreed it would be better to find the next artifact. What if it's a pearl, and the Order gets it because we were more interested in each other than in protecting the world?" I hated being the voice of reason, but I knew we would never forgive ourselves if we failed this mission, even if I had just wanted to abandon it.

Kyro nodded, leaning in to kiss me again. "Did you see anyone following us?" He whispered in my ear after he kissed me. I shook my head in response. I hadn't seen anyone who looked particularly interested in us or what we were doing.

FOrTY

Mack

QUINN AND I HEADED toward the highlands when our group split. We figured camping was the best way to make sure we didn't get caught. We started in Scotland and worked our way through Ireland. Quinn figured we could double back and hit different spots to keep from being tracked. If our scents were everywhere, it would be harder for anyone to figure out which trail was the right one.

It would also give us some time together to just be us. I hoped I could help her heal from the trauma of my death and resurrection. I know she still felt guilty and blamed herself for everything. I just wanted my Quinn back. I felt bad I couldn't give her the Mack she had before. So many things had changed, but I knew our feelings weren't one of them.

She mostly kept her comm device turned off except to check in with James or to check on Trav. Kyro had refused a comm device to protect Zoey. I wondered if he had even told her about that conversation with Quinn. We didn't think it was a good idea to be out without one, but he insisted. I hoped they were doing OK, but we had no way to tell.

Trav and Gill had settled in Northern Africa in a little village where they could live on the outskirts, more or less in the jungle. It was good to know they were safe.

I had spent a lot of time camping with my father as a kid. It turns out my love had done a fair bit of survival training. Seems to me we were meant to go on this adventure together. It was nice to be staying with someone who knew how to build a fire, make a lean-to, and could even hunt for dinner.

Most days we made a game of it, finding a camping spot, setting up camp, taking care of the necessities. Then when we were settled around the campfire eating, we'd tell stories. Mine were mostly about my childhood, and Quinn's were mostly about her training with the Resistance. She didn't have much to say about her parents or her life before the Resistance found her.

I found that I could get more information out of her by not asking than I could by prodding. The first few nights, I had asked her about her parents and her family life. She gave vague responses, then shut down for the rest of the night. When I just told her stories without asking about her family, she'd let little details slip in response.

So far, I learned that she's always had long hair and that her mother used to brush it for her when she was little. She was made to keep it in braids as well, which is why she mostly wears it loose now. And a few days ago, she made a comment that implied she had a brother, but I wouldn't dare ask about it. I'd wait and see if I can coax it out of her.

After a few days of camping, I was convinced we were being followed. There were signs of it all around our campsite when we returned from hunting our dinner.

Quinn laid our rabbits next to the fire pit to be cleaned, then walked to the tent to get her skinning knife.

"Wait, love, I think someone is here." I grabbed Quinn's arm and pulled her away from the tent.

"What? Where?" She looked around, confused.

I pointed to the tracks that were all around the campsite. "Those weren't there earlier."

"Damn, how did I miss that?" She instantly made a fireball in her hand and took a defensive stance.

"Let's hold off on charring anyone just yet. Maybe it's someone camping like us. We have to find them first, then decide if they're a threat."

Quinn nodded, then we started creeping around the campsite, checking anywhere a person could hide. There was no sign of anyone, except for the footprints that didn't belong to us. The only place left to check was the tent.

"Tent," She whispered to me as we crept forward. "You take the back; I'll go in the front."

I did as she asked and circled around to the back of the tent to cover that exit. I heard a gasp from inside the tent, pulled out my ax and rushed in the back. "Are you OK, love?"

Standing there, a fireball in her hand, she nodded. Her eyes never left the cot in the corner. There was a rust-colored fox laying in our cot, fast asleep.

"It has to be a shifter. There's no way for the fox to get in here without leaving tracks, and there are no humans in our camp." Quinn didn't move her gaze as she spoke. There was something about the way she looked at the fox that seemed odd, like she was looking at a memory or something.

"So, what do you want to do with it? Wake it up or just wait?" I looked at her expectantly, letting her take point on this. I'd never come across a shifter before, so I wasn't really sure what to expect.

Quinn snuffed out the fireball, then walked over to the cot and grabbed the fox. She wrapped one hand around the animal's muzzle so it couldn't bite, and the other arm around its chest so it couldn't escape. She had it pinned when it woke. The animal's eyes held a panic I'd only seen in those sentenced to death. It was terrified of us.

Suddenly, it started to twitch and convulse. "Love, what's it doing? Is it OK?"

She held tight to the beast as it jerked more violently. "It's trying to shift. If I can't hold on, be ready with your ax."

It was strange and awe-inspiring to watch an animal turn into a person. It was also disturbing that my love was suddenly standing there holding a naked man. He must have realized there was no way to escape because as soon as his shift was complete, he stilled.

He was just an inch or so shorter than Quinn, with the same shade of fiery hair and similar features. Was it possible they were related? Even the build of their frames was similar, as was the face they were both making.

Quinn stilled as well, her limbs tightening. Recognition crossed her face, and she shoved the man at me.

"Put some damn pants on, Sebastian. You're lucky I didn't blast first. Dad would be pissed if you got yourself killed so easily."

"Well, hello to you too, sis." His voice sounded so much like hers that it was unreal. He slowly pulled on a pair of pants from a bag that was sitting next to the cot.

"Would it be possible to get an introduction?" I didn't want to intrude on whatever this was, but I desperately wanted to know.

Quinn looked at me, and something akin to embarrassment crossed her face. "Mack, this is Sebastian. Sebastian, this is Mack." She turned, picked up her skinning knife, and walked out of the tent.

I held out a hand to shake, and Sebastian took it. "Nice to meet you." I was polite and decided I'd withhold judgment on this guy until I knew the whole story. It was obvious there was some tension here.

"You too. I see my sister hasn't changed. She's still a vicious bitch. At least she's alive." A sadness crossed his face with the last words. He turned toward the opening of the tent as he spoke, then turned back to me. "I mean no disrespect, but if you're in love with her, you're so screwed. She's a mess. I really hope you can take care of her."

I looked at him curiously. "Is it that obvious?" I laughed as I spoke. Of course, it was that obvious. It was written all over my face that I love her.

He laughed with me. "Do you think you can get her to talk to me? It took weeks to track her down, and it's kind of important."

I nodded. "I can try. If she refuses, I can try some other methods. I can't promise anything."

Forty-one

Kyro

I DIDN'T WANT TO scare Zoey, but I was pretty sure we were being followed. When I asked her, she said she hadn't seen anyone. I would just have to keep an eye out and hope I was being paranoid. This whole situation was enough to make any of us paranoid, really.

I pulled her into an embrace on the docks and ducked us behind some crates. It didn't seem like anyone reacted. Maybe the looks we were getting were just because aliens weren't that common in this area. A guy can hope.

We figured out our game plan through whispers and set off to find the next artifact. It seemed odd to me that Ian had suddenly realized there were other ways he could fix the rift than just the pearls. Or maybe he had other plans in mind for the spoils of this mission. I still wasn't quite sure I trusted him.

The way Zoey's face lit up when she talked to him was enough to keep me from speaking my mind. I couldn't crush her like that. She had been through enough already. If he was lying to us, I would make it my mission to find a way to hunt him down for it. I'm pretty sure I could talk my father into helping.

I was letting my thoughts distract me. I needed to stay focused so we didn't get ambushed. We tracked the artifact to the last boat at the end of the dock. Of course, that's where it would be because that was the most inconvenient place for us to go. There would be no way to sneak up, so we would have to disguise ourselves and hope for the best.

I pulled Zoey behind some crates again so I could talk to her. "We need disguises. We'll never make it onboard like this."

"I agree. Do you think we could get a couple of those cloaks?" She pointed at a guy who was pushing a cart of crates up to the boat. I took a good look at the cloak.

"Oh, no. This is bad. Zoey, that cloak has a patch with a lyre on it. That's the symbol for the Order. We need to leave. Now." I could feel panic taking hold of me as I tried to calm myself. I needed to stay levelheaded to protect Zoey. There was no way I could keep her safe if I let myself freak out.

She shook her head. "We just need disguises. We can recover the artifact and be out of there before they even know. Let's take a bit and regroup." She grabbed my hand and pulled me away from the docks. I reluctantly followed, hoping I could talk her out of this.

We headed back toward our safe house, but in a different direction than we had gone before. There was a small market on this side of the docks that we hadn't seen before. Zoey pulled me toward one of the tents.

"Look, we can find something to wear here." She pulled me into the tent and started looking at cloaks and pants. Her enthusiasm was sort of contagious. I couldn't believe I was actually starting to think we could do this.

"I guess if we found something similar in color, we might be able to sneak by them without being noticed."

We found cloaks and pants that looked similar to what the Order was wearing to interact with the boat. I still wasn't convinced this was a good idea, but I knew Zoey was set on it.

"If anything looks or feels off, we bolt. Got it?"

"You've said that five times in the last three minutes, Kyro. It's going to be fine. We're going to wheel a cart in, find the artifact, and then we'll bolt." Her confidence amazed me. I couldn't believe I'd let her talk me into this.

We waited at a safe distance from the boat, watching the men or women who were coming and going. It would do no good to walk on the boat if we had no idea what the people who were supposed to be here were acting like.

After watching for a while, it seemed like they were just walking on board. We didn't see anyone asking for documentation or any kind of clearance, so we decided to just wing it.

I pulled the hood of my cloak down as low over my face as I could, then started walking forward. Zoey waited a few moments, then followed my lead, pulling her cloak down the same way I did to cover herself as much as possible. She pulled on a pair of gloves and added a scarf for good measure. If I didn't know it was her, I would have thought it was one of the random guards we'd seen all day.

We made it up the ramp and onto the boat without so much as a sideways glance from anyone. Zoey had agreed to follow me because my amulet would alert me when we got close to the artifact. I strolled casually across the deck, glancing around as if I was checking to make sure the right number of crates had been loaded.

A guard stopped me. "What are you doing?"

Oh, shit. We may be busted.

"I'm counting to make sure my guys brought all the crates. It looks like there are a few missing." I tried to sound gruff so he wouldn't recognize my voice, just in case he was one of the guards from the Pit.

"The rest are down below in the cargo hold. Check down there before you start knocking guys off for not doing their job." I ran into the one guy who wasn't all "kill first, ask questions later." Nice. I glanced over my shoulder at Zoey and saw her wiping down walls and windows with a rag. *Shew, I thought for sure she'd try to intervene. Good job, Zo.*

I nodded. "Oh, good. I'll check down there for the missing crates. Thanks, man."

"Just trying to keep the peace. Dude came over earlier and took out half the crew for something stupid. I didn't tell you that." And he walked away, leaving me to check the rest of the crates before heading down to the cargo hold.

Once we were below deck, I motioned for Zoey to catch up to me. It wouldn't be as suspicious for us to be walking together down here. We continued down the corridor to the cargo hold without running into anyone. Once we were inside, my amulet started to get warm, indicating we were close to the artifact.

"It's here somewhere. We just have to figure out where and then get to it before we get caught."

Zoey nodded, waiting for me to tell her which crates to check. I pointed to a couple of them close to her, and she started pulling lids off. I turned to check a couple in front of me.

A few minutes passed with us digging through these four crates. Then I heard Zoey gasp. I turned to see her holding a cube that was just about the size of the dodeca. "I can feel the magic pulse through it. This has to be what we were looking for."

She handed it to me, and I felt a rush of power hit me. "I think you're right. Now we need to get out of here."

I tucked the cube into Zoey's haversack and tucked it back under my cloak. "We need to be cautious but walk with purpose. If anyone stops us, we counted the crates, and there are four that are missing. We have to go track down the guy who brought them and find out why."

Zoey nodded at my instruction and waited for me to walk past her so she could follow me.

FORTY-TWO

Zoey

WE MADE IT OFF the boat with no issues. Apparently the one guy who stopped us was the only one who really cared what went on there. It was nice, but it scared me. *Was their lack of concern because the Order would kill anyone for doing exactly what we just did?*

We kept our voices low as we ducked around a corner to remove the disguises we'd used. Kyro tucked the cloaks, pants, scarf, and gloves into the haversack, then put it back on. We strolled casually through the open-air market, even though our hearts were racing, and I wanted nothing more than to run. Kyro made it a point to stop at different tents and shop as if we hadn't just stolen a priceless magical artifact from an organization that already wanted to kill us. It was unnerving.

"Do you think our place is safe?" I whispered to Kyro as we looked at silk scarves.

He held up a beautiful scarf with a tiger lily print. "This one suits you. I think I'll get it for you." Then he leaned in to kiss my cheek and whispered in my ear, "Not at all. I think we need to leave as soon as possible."

I nodded and followed him as he walked to the merchant to bargain for the scarf. The process fascinated me, as I had never experienced anything like it on Calliope. Up there, the prices were set, and if you didn't pay full price, you didn't get the item. The process of the market on the space station was really simplistic, but this bartering looked like fun. Maybe when all of this was over, I would try it out myself.

Once Kyro had bargained for the scarf, we started to head out of the market. I noticed the guys following us before he did. "Ky, don't look now, but I think we have company. About 20 yards behind us, on the left. Those same two guys have been following us since we entered the market."

Kyro was very casual about it but managed to sneak a peek at our tail. "Shit. Are you sure there were two of them?"

I nodded slightly but didn't turn, instead deciding to focus on the path ahead of us. "Yeah, there were two of them. One wearing a black cloak and the other in a brown leather jacket with a baseball-style hat."

Kyro grabbed my hand and started walking a little faster. He was trying to get out of there without being obvious to anyone but our tail, who I'm sure by now knew we were on to them. He leaned close and whispered in my ear. "The only guy following us is wearing a brown jacket and a hat. The other guy must have gone for reinforcements."

This was bad. "What if this is a trap? What if we're being steered into an ambush?" I tried to keep the panic out of my voice, but I wasn't sure if I managed.

"It's OK, Zo, we'll figure this out. We're not going to go where he steers. We're going to make him think we are, then we're going to cut off in another direction."

We were heading west out of the market, and it seemed like our tail was going to keep following us. He stayed far enough back that most people probably wouldn't have noticed him, but we were pretty much used to being followed, so for us he stuck out like a sore thumb.

When we got about a half a mile away from the market, it was harder for him to hide he was tailing us. The guy had guts, though, because he didn't act as if it bothered him to be following strangers. The trees were starting to become denser the further west we headed. There was a chance we'd have cover in just a little while.

"OK, he's had time to tell his back up that we're heading west. We're going to duck behind some trees and cut north to get away from him. Just follow my lead." Kyro had been weighing our options and decided north was the best way to go. It looked like the trees were closer together in that direction, so I agreed with him.

I followed his lead and into the trees we went. It was slow going, and I was pretty sure that guy was still following us. Kyro had us weaving between trees to make the path harder to follow. I grabbed his arm and stopped him.

"I heard something." I wasn't sure what it was but needed us to stop for a minute so I could figure it out.

Kyro stopped and turned toward me. "What is it?" He kept his voice as low as possible.

"There are more of them now. He must have had groups meeting him in different places so they'd be covered no matter which direction we went."

I distinctly heard three different groups of footfalls heading from different directions around us. We were surrounded.

There was nowhere to run, and no way for us to escape. "You remember how you told me we had a better chance of hiding from the Order if we weren't all together?"

Kyro looked at me in disbelief. I was certain he knew exactly what I was about to say. "No. We aren't doing it," he started, but I cut him off with a kiss before he could finish the thought.

"It's OK, I'm going to lead them southeast, and you're going to go northwest. I'll circle back around and meet you. It'll be fine."

"What if it's not? What if they catch you? Or what if they realize it's a trick, and split up to chase us both? We're stronger together."

"Kyro, we have to. You and I both know we can't let them get the pearls or artifacts. Take the bag and run northwest. If I don't meet you in ten minutes, leave without me. I promise, it's going to be fine, just trust me."

I pulled him in for another kiss, then took off running southeast making as much noise as I could. I glanced over my shoulder to see him duck behind some bushes to wait for the coast to be clear. That was the last I would see of him for a while. I could hear the Order chasing me. I just hoped I had pulled their attention away from Kyro and that they were all chasing me instead of him. Otherwise, my plan was all for nothing.

I kept running until I ran out of tree cover. There was nowhere else to go but back toward the market. I headed that way with the intent to circle around and meet Kyro on the other side of the woods. I got about thirty feet before I was tackled to the ground. My hands and feet were bound, and I was gagged.

Well, that didn't end up as planned. I hope Kyro got away. Just keep running, Ky.

Forty-Three

Bea

Sitting in a cell, knowing that your life hangs in the balance, is a difficult thing to deal with. Especially when you've been there before. I wasn't a stranger to difficult situations. I was twelve when my parents were murdered and I was sold to a man who was simply referred to as "The Boss."

The Boss kept me in a cage, as he did with the other girls he had "saved" from life as orphans. It seemed odd to me at first, but as the days turned into weeks, and the weeks turned into months, things started to make more sense. He had selected girls who were just coming into their fertility as women. His plan was to impregnate each of us and raise his army to power by fathering them. It was a sick and twisted plan.

I remembered hearing the screams of the other girls when the Boss would visit them in the middle of the night. After a few weeks of isolation, the guards realized I wasn't losing my will to fight. One of the guards told me that my interactions with them were to prepare me for the Boss. I was terrified of what that meant and kept fighting anytime they got close.

I was lucky to be a late bloomer, as that gave me more time to figure out exactly what was going on in this compound. The Boss wouldn't touch me until I had officially become a woman, so as long as my monthly cycle was delayed, I was safe. It seemed as though he had done quite a bit of research into the mating and breeding of several races. There were girls from every planet I'd heard of and several I hadn't.

The most difficult decision I ever made was to love my child, although her beginning wasn't at all what I wanted it to be. She could not be blamed for how I was treated, nor for how she was conceived. There was no way to know for sure who her father was or if she would have powers. I prayed every day that the Boss wasn't her father, because I couldn't stand it if that were true.

All I could do now was try my best to protect her and find a way to keep her from him. That's how I met Dmitri. He came into my life as my guard, meant to keep me in a cage. He became so much more than that.

He was the only one who treated me as a person instead of an object. It didn't take long for me to fall in love with him. Of course, Dmitri may have been the only person I wasn't forced to have sex within the entire compound. After the first week, I stopped keeping track of how many times a day it happened, or which minion the Boss had decided to share me with. From what I gathered, he had been the first, but had some strange tastes and had insisted I be drugged so I wouldn't fight.

Over the months after it was discovered that I was with child, Dmitri and I hatched our escape plan. He had powers and could use them to shield us while we talked. Even the Boss couldn't break his shield, so I knew we were safe. Even if we weren't, I would have given everything to be close to him. He was the kindest person I had ever met. No one in the compound knew about Dmitri's powers and for good reason. The Boss had made it clear that anyone who could be considered a threat would be disposed of and detailed how it would happen. The one they called Boss was a cruel and vicious killer with a taste for torture. I knew for certain if the plan didn't work, we would both wish for death.

Once Dmitri had figured out the guard schedule of the entire compound, we were able to plan the escape to the minute. There was a four-minute window during which a path would be free of guards. If we could move quickly enough, with the help of his magic, Dmitri and I could be free.

We planned and plotted for weeks before finding the perfect moment. Unfortunately, it wasn't meant to be. I went into labor before we could even try to escape. I remember the entire thing like it was yesterday.

I knew the time was near. The pale blue skin of my belly was stretched taut, with whitish tiger stripes appearing where it had grown too quickly, showing that the skin had strained to not rip open. The pains were coming more quickly, and I felt the gush as my water broke. The baby was coming now. I knew there was no way to stop it, though I had wished foolishly to birth my child at home or, at the very least, in a medical unit. Being a captive didn't allow for me to make those kinds of decisions. And I was certain those holding me captive did not much care for what I preferred.

If they had, I wouldn't be in this dark, damp cell, with a rough straw pallet to sleep on. The only thing they allowed me was an actual bathroom. It occurred to me that there had to be a reason they wanted me to be able to remain clean. I wondered if it was truly me that they wanted or the baby I carried. I knew it was my child but wished it had just been me. I tried to breathe through the pain as my mind went to work formulating a plan to protect my precious child.

I decided the bathroom was the safest place to give birth to the young one. I gathered what I could to help with this task. After placing towels in the tub, I climbed in and laid on them, waiting for what was next. I hoped that I was able to do this on my own. The moment came to push, and all of my focus moved to force this tiny being down the path to birth. I took a deep breath, bearing down and pushing as hard as I could. After a short break to breathe, I went through the motions three more times, until the little one came out. The tiny blue bundle, covered in afterbirth, took a sharp breath in but didn't cry. It was as though the child sensed its mother's fear and understood the need to keep quiet. Tears of joy fell from my eyes, then tears of sadness that my love was not here for this magical moment.

We would have to change our plan and find a way to get my daughter out of here, even if I had to stay. Her safety was the only thing that mattered. I waited patiently for Dmitri to come back to me.

FOrTY-FOur

Shannon

AFTER I ABSORBED THE Chairman's power, I felt like I was high on adrenaline. I knew I had to act fast to get out of there. I ran from his room as quickly as I could without getting caught. I had no idea if I could disguise the fact I had powers now, or how to do it if I had the ability. I was in my room packing what few things I had when I heard his voice.

Go back and get the amulet.

"What? Who's there?" I asked out loud.

Go back to my room and get the amulet from my dresser. It will cloak and protect us.

Suddenly I realized I was hearing the voice inside my head. Not only that, but I knew exactly who it belonged to. "How is this possible? I watched you die and absorbed your power."

A great many things are possible that have been considered impossible. My body is gone, but my spirit holds onto my power.

"So, I'm stuck with you? Will I at least be able to use the power? Shit. Now, what am I going to do?"

I don't care that you possess my power. I have no idea why I'm with you. I will help you obtain your freedom. All I ask is that you repay the favor when the time comes.

I probably should have thought it through more, but at that moment, it was a good deal. "Deal. Now get me out of here."

First the amulet, then the escape.

I did as he asked, realizing that having his experience to guide me wouldn't be a bad thing when it came to learning how to use his powers. If I worked it right, I would be able to use him the way he'd used me all these years.

Once I had the amulet and a few other items he decided would be helpful, I threw my backpack on and snuck out through the escape tunnels below the compound. He claimed the amulet would hide me from the Boss, and I had no choice but to trust him, at least for now.

Forty-Five

Quinn

My brother showing up at our campsite wasn't exactly in my plans. I hadn't even told Mack about my family yet and didn't really want to, but here comes Sebastian to ruin everything. Part of me wanted to kick his ass for showing up out of the blue, and part of me wanted to hug him close and tell him that I love him. But our family wasn't really that kind of people.

Our mother was loving enough until it got her killed. And our father was a hateful taskmaster who only cared about what he could get out of us. He taught us at home until we were old enough to attend a finishing school that would teach us about magic and how to use our powers as weapons. He's the reason I joined the Resistance. It was my only way out.

I knew I should ask what Sebastian wanted, but I didn't care enough to do so. He'd corner me and want to talk anyway, so I'd find out soon enough. I wondered what he was talking to Mack about in the tent, but since I'd stormed out, I couldn't just walk back in like nothing happened.

So, I set to work skinning the rabbits that Mack and I had caught. I hoped there would be enough meat to feed the three of us since Sebastian had a habit of hanging around even if he wasn't wanted. Once I had the rabbits skinned and prepped, I made the fire and started cooking. When the rabbits were roasting, I sat down and waited.

It didn't take long for Mack to sit down beside me. Just like my twin to send someone else to do his dirty work for him. *That little bastard.* I wouldn't be able to tell Mack, not without explaining exactly why I want nothing to do with my brother. *Evil genius.* I was actually a bit impressed he managed to sway Mack that easily.

"Fine, I'll talk to him." I didn't even give Mack a chance to spout off whatever bullshit Sebastian had given him.

Mack looked surprised. "That was way too easy. What's going on here? Can you tell me?"

I shook my head. "I'd rather not. I know I'll have to. It's a really long story that starts with an overly strict borderline abusive father and ends with his favorite child getting anything he wanted."

"OK, that's a start. We can talk more about it later. For now, he says it's important. I have to know, which one of you is older? You look so much alike, it's hard to tell."

I smiled at him. "I'm older by two full minutes—fraternal twins, though we look enough alike that people always mistook us as identical when we were babies. It's why my mother insisted I keep the long hair. Too many people thought I was a boy, which is what our father wanted anyway."

"I thought you may be twins. I'm sorry about your dad. That's tough to deal with. We don't have to talk any more about it if you don't want to. Just talk to your brother and see what he wants. I can stay or give you some privacy. It's your call."

I looked over at Mack and took his hand. "I can't promise to explain it all, and I don't know what you'll hear, but I'd like you to stay while Sebastian and I talk."

He nodded, then got up to go get my brother. I hoped this wasn't another plea from father for me to come home and give up the Resistance. I expected him to give up on that a long time ago.

They came out to the fire from the tent and sat down. Sebastian sat on my right, and Mack took a seat right beside me on my left. They both stared at me for a few minutes with no one speaking.

"Well, Bas, what is it?" I wasn't sure if he'd get upset that I used his nickname or not. It had been years since I'd seen him.

He smiled briefly, then his expression turned serious. "It's Dad, Quinny," he said, returning the favor of using a childhood nickname.

"What does he want this time? I've already told him I'm not coming back. I won't be used by him for his purposes. I don't care if marrying Todd will help the business or not. I won't do it."

"He's dead, Quinny. I've spent the past few weeks trying to track you down to tell you. The service was small and tasteful, and the lawyer already took care of the will. You get half of everything."

"Wait, what? What happened to him? And what do you mean, I get half? He told me I was cut from the will when I left. Why would he change that?"

"He was killed. We know who did it, but since they're protected by the Order, there's nothing we can do about it. And yeah, he said a lot of things that weren't true. Like when he told us Mom died."

"The Order killed him? Why? Are you saying Mom's not dead? Bas, what the actual fuck is going on here?"

"Mom went into hiding when Dad started working with the Order. Then he tried to screw his partner over and cut him out of a deal, so the guy had the Order kill him. Now that he's dead, we're in the clear as long as we don't expose his connections to the Order. I can get you in touch with her if you want."

"I don't know how to handle this. I don't know how to process any of it. Father is gone, Mom is alive. The connection to the Order. I'm gonna need some time with this one. I just can't right now, Bas."

He stood up, grabbed my hand and pulled me to my feet and into a hug. "I know, sis. It's OK. There's no more pressure. I thought you deserved to know. That's all."

I hugged him so tight, I expected him to break in half. Instead, he hugged me back just as tightly.

"How did you find me?" I finally thought to ask the most important question.

He grinned at me sheepishly. "Twin connection and fox tracking. It wasn't that hard. I did hear the Order has been hunting you for a while with no success. So, I really expected it to take a lot longer to find you."

I wasn't sure if I could trust my brother or not. I was even more skeptical since he told me our father was working for the Order. He was my brother, and this wouldn't be the first time I had let our family connection cause me personal problems.

Once the rabbits were cooked, we shared the meager rations as a tiny family. It was almost quaint. The overlying distrust kept inching in, and I couldn't quite relax. Bas decided he'd stay the night with us when Mack offered. We had a second tent that he could borrow, and Mack helped him set it up.

All in all, it was a nice visit. We sat around the campfire and talked late into the night. I fell asleep almost as soon as my head hit the pillow on our cot. Mack held me all night, and I woke feeling more rested than I had in a while.

Of course, Bas had taken off in the middle of the night, leaving me a note with a comm device link and a promise to get in touch with me soon. I had a feeling I'd be on guard for a while after this. If Bas could find me, maybe it wouldn't be too hard for the Order to track me down either.

FOrTY-SIX

Zoey

THE BOSS SAT ON a throne; his face mostly obscured by the shadows. "Ah, the chosen one arrives. Bring her to me." His deep voice bellowed the command at his minions. His voice grated on my brain like nails on a chalkboard. I shuddered as I felt the large hand wrap around my left bicep forcefully, and the beast of a man who had been holding me captive began to drag me to the front of this chamber. I tried to break free, but with my hands bound behind my back there wasn't much I could do. Digging in my heels failed and resulted in a tug so hard I hit the floor face first, feeling my shoulder wrench from its socket. Feeling the trickle of blood run down my upper lip from my right nostril, I tried to fight back anyway, though I knew it was useless. It didn't help that my captor was almost three times my weight and close to double my height. I wanted to scream, but the cloth that was meticulously tied around my head holding my mouth open was preventing that as well. I had no choice but to go where I was being led.

As I was dragged closer to him, I could see the shadows weren't the only things obscuring him from view. He was wearing a long robe with a hood pulled down to shade his face. In addition, it appeared as though he was wearing some kind of mask over the bottom half of his face. I had a feeling it was magical, as it shimmered in the dim light of the chamber, almost glowing in the near darkness. Once I was directly in front of him, my arm was released, and with a hard shove, I was on my knees. I jumped back to my feet, headbutting the monstrous underling who had tried to rip my arm off. He swatted me back down with one giant mitt, and I groaned upon hitting the floor.

"Enough!" the voice bellowed. The beast-man ducked his head in shame and backed away quickly, leaving me on the floor looking up at my host. He held his left hand out toward me. I did my best not to flinch, thinking he was reaching out to me. With a flick of his wrist, the rag in my mouth vanished, allowing me to speak for the first time in what seemed like days. "What do you want with me?" I panted, trying to catch my breath from the tussle with his guard while adjusting to having control of my own jaw again. I was certain I already knew the answer and hoped someone would be able to rescue me before I met my end. At this point, that thought was pretty pointless, since this man had already caused the deaths of everyone I loved. All I could do was bide my time and fight when given the chance.

"You really don't know, do you?" he asked, his voice raspy from raising it earlier. "I want the power, and you're going to give it to me. Or you will meet the same fate as the others who have tried to deny me." Well, at least I was right about one thing. He wanted the pearls, or the dodeca, probably both. I knew I couldn't turn them over to him, especially since I didn't have them.

"And I thought you were smarter than that. I gave you too much credit," I retorted. "I don't have the items you want, and even if I did, I wouldn't give them to you anyway." It wasn't easy to appear tough when I was facing my own demise.

"Have I not taken enough from you? Do you truly have no fear of me? Of what I can do to you?" His words caused a shiver to run down my back, but I managed to fight off my physical reaction.

I masked myself with determination and responded with venom. "You think you've beaten me, but you haven't. I'll never give you what you want, and I'll fight until my last breath to keep you from getting it. Of course, you could just kill me now, but you can't find it without me." I wasn't sure if I believed myself, but that didn't matter. As long as he believed me, I had a chance.

Apparently, he bought it because his goons took me back to my cell and threw me inside. At least I had some time by myself.

And as for him taking everything from me and killing everyone I loved, who knew if it was the truth. It was what they kept telling me to keep me in line once they managed to capture me. At first, I was convinced it was true, but the longer I was here, the less I believed anything these assholes told me.

I hated that Kyro and I got separated, but it was the only way to keep him safe. And since he had the items this dick was looking for, it was better that I didn't know where Kyro was.

All I knew about Mack and Q was that they had headed south. I had no way to know where they ended up, and I was glad for it.

Then there was Jack. I couldn't think about that right now. There was too much at stake.

At this point, I'd even be happy to see Gill, although everyone knew I liked Trav way better. We had dropped them off in Africa, at the village where I had first met Gill and Mack. They were better off being kept out of all of this. I had already decided I would keep saying I had no idea where any of them were until I believed it myself. So far it was working.

FOΓTY-seven

Bea

I KNEW THERE WAS no way I was going to get out of this alive. My focus had turned from proving my innocence to saving my daughter and her friends. It hadn't taken me long in solitary before I realized exactly who had set me up. I had no proof, so it wouldn't help me any to try and make accusations.

I waited a few weeks, then took a chance. They took me to a conference room every day to question me and try to force a confession. The Patrol was good at using different agents for each interrogation. They were feeling me out to see what it would take to make me confess.

I was surprised to see they hadn't sent Jack to break me yet. I was expecting it, so I guess they were saving it as a last resort. What I wasn't expecting was for Elena to waltz through the door like she owned the place. The door slammed and the two of us were alone. She tapped some buttons on her watch before stomping over to me.

"Are you ready to confess?" Elena began with an attitude. I guess she decided her best option was to start tough and see if I broke.

I shook my head, "What am I supposed to confess? I didn't do anything."

She scowled, "We both know why you're here. If you confess, I'll get them to go easier on you."

I laughed, "You and I both know you did this. You framed me. And you turned off the cameras because you knew I'd figure it out."

Concern flashed across her face, then a smirk took its place. "So, you figured it out. You can't prove it. You should just confess. Things will be so much easier for you if you do."

I didn't believe her for a second. "I'm not worried. Jack will figure it out, and he will find the proof to get me out of here. Then you'll be the one going on trial." My words held a confidence that I didn't quite feel. I hoped my bravado was enough to fool her.

"Jack won't be figuring anything out. He's been reassigned back to Calliope and won't be here to get in the way. And if he does stick his nose in my business, I'll take care of it." She smiled sweetly as if she hadn't just threatened one of my children. Jack may not be blood, but I'd had a hand in raising him, which made him mine.

"How did you arrange that?" I wondered aloud.

Elena laughed. "I have more connections than you realize. I've been after your job since you selected me as your second. I honestly can't believe you never suspected me of anything before this. It's too late now. I've done it. I'm the boss now."

"So, I was right. It was you. You logged into my accounts and created those documents. Why? Why would you want to frame me? Why would you work for the Order?"

She glared at me without responding. I knew she wasn't going to answer my questions, but I was hopeful she would decide to boast to me. It wouldn't do me any good to know, but for some reason, I wanted her to tell me.

I pushed further. "You're scared to tell me? Do you think someone will believe me when I tell them you are the one who framed me? Does that worry you?"

She narrowed her eyes. "I'm not scared of you. You're nothing. You're less than nothing. There is nothing you could say to make them believe you. No one will go against me now. I've got you exactly where I want you."

"You're scared to tell me who you're working for." I planned to keep taunting her until she lost her temper and blurted out the answer.

She darted across the room and grabbed a handful of my hair. I had definitely made her angry. She growled in my ear.

"I'm not scared of anything. I'm also not stupid. I'm not telling you my secrets. No one would believe you anyway. Apparently, you missed the documents where you tried to take a hit out on me to get me out of your way."

The smirk on her face as she spoke proved what I had been afraid of. Elena was crazy. Whether it was for power or just mental illness didn't matter. I couldn't figure out how she made it through the screening process for the Patrol. The corruption may go higher than I thought.

"You used me the whole time you were working for me? You were just here to set me up so you could take over? You can't win. My daughter won't let you." I probably shouldn't keep goading her, but I couldn't help myself at this point. I knew she'd kill me the first chance she had, so I might as well go down fighting.

The mention of Zoey sparked a jealous rage in Elena's eyes. Her hand shot out and connected with my cheek.

"Shut your whore mouth. Your bitch daughter couldn't fight her way out of a paper bag. Jack is the only reason she is still alive, but I've eliminated that factor. He's on his way back to Calliope, remember?"

I didn't flinch when her hand made contact. My tongue flicked out and wiped the blood off my lip where it split. I refused to react to her insults of myself or Zoey. I wouldn't give her the satisfaction of a response.

Elena released my hair with a shove, turned and walked out the door.

A few minutes later a guard came in and took me back to my cell. I hadn't expected the director to get involved, so it shocked me when he walked into my cell as the guard walked out.

"Director. To what do I owe this honor?" I knew sarcasm wasn't going to get me out of this, but after my run-in with Elena, I didn't have much hope for escape at all.

The director leaned cautiously against the wall, just out of view of the camera that was trained on me. He kept his voice low to avoid anyone overhearing our conversation. "I think we can help each other. I know you didn't do what they're accusing you of, but I can't get you out of here just yet. I need more evidence."

His words gave me hope, but at the same time, I knew I would be putting myself at risk again. "What do you need me to do?"

He nodded. "I thought you'd be up for it. I need you to tell one of the guards you're ready to confess."

"What? You want me to confess to something I didn't do? I don't know how that will help you get whatever evidence you need."

He cocked an eyebrow at me. "I don't want you to actually confess. I want you to get in a room with her and see what you can get out of it. Of course, it won't be easy and will require wearing a wire. Are you up for it?"

"Definitely. I have to ask, what made you realize I'm not guilty?"

"Well, when she started transferring anyone who even hinted at your innocence, it was a red flag. When she transferred Jack off-planet it confirmed my suspicions. I don't have anything to connect her to the documents or accusations against you, because she convinced Jack to review them and turn you in. Unless I can get him to testify, or you can get her on tape confessing, we're stuck."

I nodded. "Do you have the wire? I can set it up today."

The director shook his head. "You'll need to wait a few days to avoid any suspicion. I don't want her to realize you're still working for me. Normally I'd send you right back in, but I think this one will take more time because she knows our usual procedures."

"Understood."

He pulled a small package from his pocket and slid it to the floor, just out of view of the camera. As he turned to leave, he caught my eye again and nodded once more. I waited until he was gone and the door was closed again to retrieve the wire, making it look as though I was simply sitting on the floor. I was certain he had jammed the audio recording when he entered. I knew he would never risk having a meeting like this if we could get caught by the person we were after.

FORTY-EIGHT

KYRO

ONCE I MADE IT back to the boat, I did a scrying spell to activate each of the necklaces. It would be nearly impossible to find the others without the tracking ability of the necklaces I had made for everyone. Even with them, there was no guarantee I would find anyone in time to save Zoey. I had to start somewhere. There was no time to waste. I needed to find the others and get to Zoey fast.

It had taken me the better part of a week to track down Mack and Q. I wasn't upset with them about it, but I knew that Zoey's life was in danger. And that her chances of making it were slim to none if we couldn't find where they'd taken her.

I knew why she surrendered, but I didn't like it. She gave me her bag and led the goons in the opposite direction. I blamed myself for not being vigilant or paying enough attention to our surroundings. I was hoping to take her back to my home, to show her the caverns and propose to her beside the underground waterfall. That wasn't going to happen now, but I still hoped for someday, and that would have to be enough. I had to find her.

I could still see her face when she shoved the bag at me. That image haunted my dreams since we were separated. I could still taste her kiss, the urgency of it, along with underlying passion and sadness. If that was the last time that I saw her, I would never forgive myself. I shouldn't have let her go, but she was right, it was the best option to keep the book and pearls away from the Chairman and whoever he was working for.

As soon as I got out of the cave, I started looking for Mack. I knew wherever he was, Q would be there, and I needed them both. It was unfortunate that Gill and Trav had decided to hide as well. I could have used their help. It took way too long to find Mack, and I didn't want to risk Zoey's safety any longer.

Before the necklaces were activated, I turned the boat towards Ireland. I think it may have been a sixth sense that led me to follow Mack's trail without even knowing for sure. Fortunately, Zoey and I had been near the Canary Islands, so it wouldn't take too long to get to the others. I just hoped we could find her before it was too late. I pushed the boat with every bit of power I could. I reserved enough to prevent exhaustion, but just barely. I couldn't afford to take any chances or waste any more time. Once the necklaces were activated, my hunch was proven to be correct.

Using my powers, it only took a couple of days to get to Ireland. Tracking Mack and Q down once I was there proved to be a bit more challenging. I loaded up my gear and started hiking, following the illumination of the necklace I wore while tapping into its connection with the one Mack wore. I walked and climbed for hours, heading in the direction the necklace led me. It was all I could do to keep exhaustion at bay; if I didn't find them soon, I'd fall over from it and be lost.

When I was almost ready to give up and head back to the boat, I stumbled across signs of a campground. It appeared deserted. I crept carefully into the camp, watching the area for any sign that my friends were nearby. The necklace was flashing quickly, indicating they were close. I carefully made my way across the campground to the trees on the north side. I made sure to keep my eyes searching for traps. We couldn't be too careful, especially when there were people out to kill us.

As much attention as I was paying, I still didn't expect the full-body tackle that happened once I reached the tree line. It was a tangle of limbs as we rolled back into the center of camp. When he pinned me, Mack finally looked at who he captured.

"Kyro! What the hell, man?" He started, then continued before I could respond, "Where's Zoey? Wait, is everything OK?" He finally climbed off my chest so I could answer.

"They got her. I have no idea where they took her, but she saved my life by distracting them. We have to find her." My voice cracked when I spoke, and I barely contained my tears. This wasn't the time to break down. I had to push forward and find her.

Q stepped out from behind a tree, where she'd been listening to the whole exchange. "Slow down. The Order got her?" I nodded and she continued. "Then we need a plan. We can't just run off after her without knowing exactly what we're doing. Let's pack up and head back to the boat."

She walked off to one of the tents that was set up in the campground. Mack and I exchanged a glance and followed her.

"I know it sounds weird, but this is actually a good thing." Mack chuckled as he spoke.

"How?"

"This is the closest she's been to herself since I died." He motioned to Q, who was a woman on a mission.

Forty-Nine

Quinn

Mack didn't realize that even in my frenzied prep state, I could hear everything he and Kyro were saying. And he wasn't wrong. This was the most like myself I had felt in a long time. I had a mission and could focus on that instead of focusing on how much of a mess I was. I knew he blamed himself for my current issues but it wasn't his fault. Killing someone changes a person.

I still had nightmares almost every night, even with him lying beside me. For the most part, I was able to fight them, but there were some nights when I still woke up screaming and covered in sweat from watching it happen all over again. Those nights were the worst because I could never get back to sleep. I would have to pretend to be asleep so Mack would settle back in and go back to sleep himself. Then when I was sure he was sleeping, I would just lie there and stare at him. It was so strange getting used to him in the new body.

None of that mattered right now. The only thing I needed to focus on was finding Zoey and rescuing her. That gave me the freedom to be the old Q again. Focused, determined, single-minded. It was nice to have a break from the emotions I fought to keep under control.

Once I had everything packed that we would need, the three of us headed back to Kyro's boat. As we settled back into the familiar routine, I realized that I needed this. I needed to have a purpose, a reason to keep moving forward. I wanted to see this finished, and the first step was finding Zoey. We gathered in the galley to discuss our plan over dinner.

"So, you activated her necklace, too, right?"

Kyro glanced from Mack to me as he considered his answer. "I did, but there wasn't any response. I'm worried about what that could mean."

I slammed my fist into the table. "Don't even think that. All it means is that they're keeping her in a place that blocks the magic of the necklace. We just need to focus."

Kyro nodded, "You're right. She's going to be fine. We just have to find her. I'm just anxious because I couldn't keep her from being taken again."

"I get that. Freaking out about it and panicking right now is not the best way to handle those feelings. What options do we have for finding her if the necklace isn't working?"

Mack leaned back in his chair a bit. "Can't you scry on her? Or does that work along the same lines as the necklace?"

"That's a great idea. We can't know if it will work unless we try it, right? Kyro, get what you need, and we can help you scry." I didn't even care that I was being super bossy. This wasn't about me or whose feelings I hurt. This was about finding Zoey.

Kyro left to gather the supplies for scrying. I could feel Mack's eyes on me, though he never said a word. I knew he wanted to, but wouldn't for fear of hurting me again.

"You might as well say it," I snapped without turning to look at him.

"What?" He asked, sounding confused.

I turned slowly to face him. "You might as well say what you're thinking instead of holding it in and pretending like it's nothing."

"Don't you think you were a little hard on him? He's doing his best to find her. This isn't easy on any of us." His eyes, filled with concern, met mine. I had expected disdain or pity. I should have known I would get neither from him.

I nodded, turning my eyes toward the ground. "I was. It's what he needed to snap him back to focus. He can't find her if he's scared something has happened. We need to take it one step at a time."

FIFTY

Mack

ONCE KYRO FINISHED SCRYING, we set a course for Zoey's location. I had a strange sense of deja vu that I just couldn't kick. I wasn't sure what had caused it, but I made sure I was paying attention to everything. We couldn't afford any delays or interruptions.

Kyro focused on pushing the boat as much as he could with his water abilities. Quinn and I would have to force him to rest so he wouldn't exhaust himself before we got to our destination. We would need him at full strength and completely focused. A few hours into our journey, we caught a good wind, and I made Kyro go below to rest for a while.

Once he was below deck, I decided to talk to Quinn about what had happened earlier.

"Are you OK, love?" I began as we watched the water expectantly. I couldn't shake the thought that we were in danger.

She shifted her eyes from the waves to me. "I am. What are you actually asking me?"

Ah, she always could see through me. "You were a bit rough with Kyro earlier. I wanted to find out why, but I didn't figure you'd just tell me." I chuckled as I responded.

Her eyes narrowed. "Of course, you think this is funny. I wasn't that hard on him. He needed a push and I gave it to him. That's all."

I took her hand in mine. "I know you're anxious about finding her. We are too. You were a bit inconsiderate of his feelings, and that's not like you."

"How would you know what's like me? We haven't even known each other for a year. And you were dead for a few weeks, so there's that. Maybe I'm just that much of a bitch. Maybe that's why I was so hard on him earlier. Had you considered that? Are you prepared to deal with that, or are you leaving me too?" She turned to walk away, but I grabbed her arm and pulled her back. I had to admit, it was easier to do now that we were closer in height, but I had the same fears she did. Maybe this was her way of telling me she didn't care for this body.

I tilted her head so her eyes met mine. "Are you scared I'm going to leave?"

She nodded in response.

"Oh, love, I would never willingly leave you. I was scared you'd decide you didn't like the new me, even though the only thing that changed was my body. We should have talked about this sooner. Can you ever forgive me?"

She leaned closer and pressed her lips to mine just for a moment. "I can, but only if you can forgive me. I haven't fully dealt with your death and return, and to be honest, I'm not really sure how to process it all. It's like you're back but you're not. And don't get me wrong, this body is really attractive. It just feels a bit like I'm cheating on my Mack."

I pulled her closer and kissed her a bit harder. "Love, you could never cheat on your Mack. I'm right here. No matter what I look like. I can't change this body, but honestly, it's just a shell that houses my soul. And that belongs to you."

I wiped the tears from her eyes and kissed her tenderly. In an instant, the kiss deepened as our passions mingled. Quinn wrapped her arms around me, letting her hands explore as our mouths tangled.

I fisted one hand in her hair and trailed kisses down her throat. Her soft moan was all the encouragement I needed. My free hand roamed around her waist and cupped her ass as I pulled her closer. I felt like I would never get enough of her.

I held her for a while longer, then she pulled away. I raised an eyebrow at her, asking if she was OK without words.

"I need to go make sure he knows I wasn't trying to be a bitch. He needs to know we'll find her no matter what." She grinned sheepishly at me.

"It's fine, love. You don't have to apologize or admit that I might have been right. I'll let it slide this time."

I kissed her hand and gave it a squeeze before letting her go. I watched as she walked to the door that led below deck.

After I was sure she had gone downstairs, I pulled the small velvet-covered box from my pocket and opened it. I hoped Quinn would appreciate the deep red garnet set in silver filigree that I had worked so hard to create. And that I could choose the right time to give it to her. With any luck, we would rescue Zoey and be engaged by tomorrow.

I closed the box and put it back in my pocket. *I'm not going to count on it being that easy, though. Mama always told me anything worth having was worth working hard for.* "I think our girl Quinn is definitely worth it, Mama. I wish you could have met her." I spoke to my mother as if she was standing next to me, knowing that her spirit had been gone for a long time.

I shook off the emotions that were threatening to overtake me and kept a vigilant watch on the water while Quinn and Kyro were talking.

FIFTY-ONE

Kyro

I WAS SURPRISED WHEN a knock at my door while I was sleeping turned out to be Q. "What's wrong?"

She looked somewhat embarrassed as she responded. "I owe you an apology."

I was confused. "What for?"

"I was really harsh earlier, and it wasn't fair to you. I'm sorry."

I smiled at her. "It's not a big deal. I know you're just worried about finding Zoey. Don't stress over it."

"Are you sure? Mack was pretty well convinced that I stomped all over your feelings. I didn't want that to be the case."

"Not at all. I'm tougher than he gives me credit for. Besides, I don't care what anyone says to me as long as we find her and she's OK."

She nodded and pulled me into a hug. "We'll find her, and she'll be fine. I promise."

The closer we got to Zoey's location, the more familiar our surroundings looked. It took me a while to figure it out. I could tell something was bothering Mack and Q as well, but I wasn't able to figure it out.

An island formed in the distance, and my heart sank. I had hoped to never see this place again. And I could only imagine how it would affect Q. Maybe she and Mack could wait on the boat and I'd go in alone to rescue Zoey. Of course, that was a reckless idea, and I didn't think it could possibly work.

My pulse started racing the closer we came to the island. Once we were close enough for me to be sure of our location, I called out to Mack to drop sails so the boat would stop.

"What is it, Kyro? Why are we stopping here?" Mack questioned me as he and Q walked over to where I was staring at the island that had almost taken our lives, and had taken his. I turned toward them just as the realization crossed Q's face. I watched as her expression contorted with grief and anger.

"She can't be here," Q said, as though she could make it so with her words.

I laid my hand on her arm. "This is where the scry led us. I can sense her necklace now. She's in there."

Her eyes met mine, then darted to Mack, who still wasn't sure what was happening.

"It'll be OK. We're all together, and we're going to go get her." Even with my reassurance, I could sense her hesitation and unease.

"What is it? What am I missing?" Mack was still trying to connect the dots.

I pointed at the island. "That's where the Pit is. Or what's left of it anyway. And that's where Zoey is being held. We have to go get her."

"Oh, well I can see why you're both hesitant to go back there. I am too, but I left a different way, so I wouldn't recognize the entrance." Mack tried to play it off as a joke, but I got the impression he actually understood the way Q and I were feeling.

Once we got past the initial shock of being back at the Pit, we set about making our plan. It would have been easier if we'd known where she was being kept exactly, but honestly, I think we were getting used to nothing being easy. As we were leaving the first time, Q and I had noticed the exits that would serve as entrances this time around.

With our plan in place, we decided to move forward carefully. We entered from the east, just as the sun was setting. I used a touch of magic to create a soft glow that could be mistaken for a deep-sea fish., After hiding the boat around the other side of the island where there were no entrances into the caves, we used that small bit of light to sneak into the cave through the shallow water.

Much to Mack's dismay, Q and I decided the most effective way to find Zoey was for us to split up. Each of us would head in a different direction, and I rigged our necklaces to ping a notification to the others if one of us found her.

Mack headed off toward the Pit itself, while Q took off toward the mines where I had been held. I made a beeline for the rooms where Zoey had been kept when we were here before. I knew it was unlikely that they would put her in the same place, but it was as good of a place to start as any.

I crept down the hall carefully, expecting the place to be crawling with guards, but there were none. I slowly pushed the door open to Zoey's former prison, but it was empty as well. I closed the door behind me just in case someone came along, and then I inspected the room.

I found a secret door on the west wall. It took me a few minutes to find the loose brick in the wall that triggered the door to open. The door clicked and swung open as soon as the brick was pressed. I said a silent prayer to my father and walked through, careful to stay low and pay attention in case there were traps.

I stayed close to the wall, moving slowly to make sure I had plenty of room and time to check each area for traps. It was a good thing too, because first I almost fell into a pit of spikes, and then I almost tripped the trigger wire of a crossbow pointed at me from above.

The wall was cold and felt like packed mud, though it was dark and hard to see for sure. The darkness extended around me like a blanket. The contrast of the soft glow of my necklace made it appear that much darker. It seemed like I was following this hallway lower and lower. I was beginning to wonder if it would ever end. Just then I saw a door. I crouched down and crept toward it slowly. Standing in front of the door, I turned and examined my surroundings. There were no windows or other doors around, and there didn't appear to be anyone nearby.

I turned my attention to the door itself. It looked to be wooden, thick and well-made. There were intricate metal details in the hinges and kickplate. It had a handle and a lock. I carefully wiggled the doorknob. It turned easily in my hand. This might have been too easy.

I wasn't sure if luck was on my side or if this was a trap. I had hidden the book, the pearls, the dodecahedron, and the other artifacts in a secret compartment on the boat that only Zoey and I knew about, so I didn't have to worry about that. If the Order was holding her, it was only a matter of time before they started torturing her, or worse. And I couldn't bear that. I also knew that giving them the book and magical items wasn't an option.

Part of me wished that Mack and Q had come this way with me, but I knew that as soon as I found Zoey, the necklaces would glow and they would be led to where we were. And it might have been harder to miss the traps if it had been three of us heading down. *Oh, the traps! I need to take care of those so they don't get caught.*

I stopped where I was and forced an image of each trap into my mind. I sent a bolt of water to trip the crossbow wire, and another to fill the pit of spikes. I hoped that what I had been able to do was enough to keep my friends safe, but I didn't have time to worry about it. Zoey's life was in danger. I had to find her.

FIFTY-TWO

Quinn

I HAD SECOND THOUGHTS the moment I stepped away from Mack and Kyro, but finding Zoey was more important than my fears. I headed toward the mines where Kyro had been held. As I got closer, I heard voices ahead of me. I ducked into a doorway outside the mine entrance.

I pressed my back against the door and looked around the room. It was obviously a bedroom, from the bedroll in the corner and the clothes hanging in the closet area. Luckily the room was empty, so I was safe...for now. I pressed my ear to the door and listened. The voices were getting closer.

They stopped right outside the door. *This is it. I'm busted. How many voices are there? Can I take them all out?* I wasn't sure that I could. After what happened when Mack died, I didn't trust myself to not lose control. Maybe losing control wouldn't be so bad. If I just let go, I know I can take out the entire complex. *Do I really want to risk my friends like that?* I had only used my fire twice since that day, and I couldn't remember how I had managed to control it. My emotions were so raw from being here, that I was certain I wouldn't be able to keep myself in check. I would have to find another way. Lucky for me, I was trained by the best.

I pressed my ear to the door again. The voices were moving again. It sounded like they were going away from the entrance of the mines, back in the direction I had come from. I waited a few more minutes before carefully inching the door open and looking outside. The hallway appeared to be empty. This was my chance.

I quietly pushed the door open just enough for me to slip out of the room and into the hallway, closing it behind me. Keeping close to the wall, I crept to the mine entrance. I knew Zoey probably wasn't being held here, but I wanted to check it out anyway. I continued forward in the darkness until I came close to a lantern on the wall. I heard footsteps again, but this time I had no place to hide. All I could do is stay in the darkness and hope whatever was coming didn't see me.

I crouched down and pressed against the wall. I felt something shift behind me. The wall opened just enough for me to slip inside. I looked from the opening to the darkness where I could hear the footsteps getting closer. A split-second decision had me diving into the opening in the wall. I hoped there weren't more guards on the other side.

Fortunately, I ducked through the opening just in time to see the guards who had been standing there exit the room. I decided it would be better to head in the opposite direction, just to make sure I didn't have any issues with the guards.

I turned down the hallway and followed it, careful to keep an eye out for traps. I knew this place wasn't safe, even when we were here before. I came up behind a guard heading down a dimly lit hallway, and I followed him. He passed through a secret door, and I took a chance. It wasn't trapped, and it opened easily. I crept through it and found myself in a new corridor.

It was dark, but I could easily conjure a tiny bit of fire to light my way. It took so much concentration to keep it under my control that I lost the guard I'd been following, which wasn't surprising. There were three different directions laid out in front of me, and I had no idea which was the right one.

I heard what sounded like a splash of water off to my left, and curiosity got the better of me. I followed the sound and came upon a pit full of water. *That's a strange thing to find here.* I kept walking, dropping the bit of fire I had been using for light and climbing up divots in the mud wall to work my way around the water. A few feet later, I came across some crossbow bolts stuck in the wall and the floor.

I searched around and discovered the crossbows and what looked like triggers that had been tripped. I felt like I was headed in the right direction. I kept moving forward, following the trail of triggered traps until I almost ran right into Kyro.

"Hey, I found you. I thought you were checking out Zoey's old room here."

"Q, I'm so relieved that it's you. I heard footsteps and thought I was getting caught too. I found a secret passage that led me down here. I thought you were in the mine."

"Secret passage. Thanks for tripping all the traps back there. That made it so much easier to catch up to you."

"No problem. Now let's find Zoey and get out of here. This place is horrible."

I nodded in agreement, then fell in behind him. He was carefully working his way down the hall, checking any doors we came across. Part of me wished Mack was here, but another part decided I would probably handle being here better with him not standing beside me. It was a strange back and forth pull.

We continued down the hallway, with Kyro watching in front of us, and me keeping an eye behind us so no one could sneak up on us. Our system was working pretty well when we came to a three-way intersection, and suddenly there was a noise down the corridor we weren't watching. Kyro and I both braced for combat, knowing this could be where it all ends.

"Well, what are the two of you doing down here?" Mack asked, popping out of the dark.

"You scared the shit out of us. At least we know she's not down that hall. Let's keep going." Kyro continued forward, leaving Mack and me to catch up.

"Secret passage?" I whispered.

"Secret passage," Mack responded quietly.

At least now we knew there were multiple ways out of here if we could just find Zoey. The three of us made it through the maze of corridors quickly. It was a lot easier to navigate with all of us than it would have been for one of us.

"Looks like this is the end of the line," Kyro said when we hit a dead end.

"Yeah, so now what?" I asked, looking from him to Mack.

Mack stepped forward and started inspecting the wall. It appeared to be blocks of mud, which was different than any of the other walls we'd seen. "I think there's a secret passage here too." He pushed a couple of the blocks in the wall, and it started to move.

Kyro gave him a high five. "Great job, man!"

Mack nodded his thanks and we continued through the opening. There was another corridor in front of us, but we could barely see because there was no light. "Do you want me to light it up?" I offered.

"Can you do just a tiny, dim light?" Kyro whispered.

I did as he asked, then gestured to the tiny bit of light coming from my left hand. He nodded and smiled at me. We continued down the corridor, noticing the cells on either side. Most were empty, but a few held prisoners.

"Do you see her?" Kyro asked. He had started checking the right side of the hall, while Mack checked the left. I stayed in the middle with the light so they could both see. I couldn't hold concentration and look for her, so I decided it was better to just be the light source.

Mack gestured for me to bring the light closer. "Zoey, is that you?" He whispered softly at a lump laying on the floor of one cell.

Kyro grabbed the bars of the cell to try and get a better look. I stepped up behind him and pushed my left arm through the bars to give him a bit more light.

"I think it's her, but she's not conscious. Can we pick the lock and get in there?" Kyro sounded desperate.

Fortunately, Mack had a talent for opening locks. He set to work on the lock and after a few fumbles, was able to get the door open. Kyro rushed in and scooped Zoey up. I brought the light closer to make sure it was her.

The cuts and bruises on her face and body couldn't mask her identity. We'd found Zoey, although she was knocked unconscious, and there was no way to tell if she'd recover. For now, finding her was enough. We just had to get out of here without getting caught.

We made our way carefully back the way we had come, with only a couple of near misses. Each of us had come a different way into these tunnels, so it took a minute to decide which way we should go back.

"It seemed like it took me less time to get to you two than it took you to get together." Mack wanted to exit through the Pit.

I wasn't sure I could handle being near the Pit again. My nightmares were still an every night occurrence. "Can't we go back through the mines? I think it's closer to the exit."

Kyro shifted Zoey in his arms. "I don't think we can stay in these tight corridors that long. We need more room. We'll have to go out through the Pit."

I nodded, glad for the dim light, so they couldn't see my defeated expression. I really hoped I could keep it together once we got near the Pit. I didn't want to be there. It was physically painful. There was no way to explain it so that Mack and Kyro could understand though, so I just stopped talking and followed them.

FIFTY-THREE

Zoey

I MUST HAVE BEEN dreaming because when I woke up, I was in Kyro's arms. Since I knew I was being held captive by the Order, it had to be a dream. I sighed anyway and snuggled closer to him. It was so realistic that I thought I could feel his body heat, and it was almost as if I could hear his heartbeat.

The moment I snuggled closer, Kyro spoke. "Zoey, are you OK? Please be OK. I can't handle this. I'm so sorry I left you. I should have stayed with you. We could have fought them off together."

"Wait, this isn't a dream? You're really here?" I sat up and looked around the dimly lit corridor. Mack and Q were here with Kyro. *It's not a dream. They're here to rescue me!*

Kyro hugged me tightly for a moment. "Yes, we're really here. We're getting you out of here. We have to move quickly. Can you walk? Better yet, can you run?"

"I think so. I'm willing to try." Kyro nodded at my response and set me on my feet.

I followed Kyro as he crept behind the others to an opening in the wall. We each crawled through it and into an empty room. "The Pit is just through there; we can go around it to the left. Once we're around it, the exit is about fifty feet ahead." Mack instructed us quietly.

I didn't miss the look on Q's face but didn't mention it, because I could tell she was barely holding it together. Instead, I decided to try to distract her. "Q, my legs aren't as strong as I thought. Can you help me so the guys can focus on making sure our exit is clear?"

The look on her face was thanks enough to let me know she needed the distraction. "Sure. What do you need me to do?"

"Just stay close and keep an eye on me, please?"

She nodded in agreement, and we followed the guys out into the area around the Pit. I shuddered when I saw where I'd been forced to watch countless fights without knowing what was really happening. It made me feel sick to know what Q and Mack had gone through there.

We moved quickly, hoping no one would be near the Pit to catch us. Just as we headed around the left side of the arena, there were footsteps. Q and I froze.

"Ah, so nice of you to join me. This will be fun." I would have known that hoarse voice anywhere. It was him. The one the Order called Boss. I had taken to calling him Big Bad in my head during my short time here. I thought of him as being kind of like the Big Bad Wolf from the folk tales.

When he stepped out of the shadows, I was finally able to get a good look at him. The hood of his cloak was pulled back, and his face was no longer hidden. He was tall, six-foot-three at least. He had shoulder-length wavy auburn hair and golden-brown eyes. In any other circumstance, I would have thought he was handsome. After everything he'd done to my family, I knew he was a monster. I wanted to kill him for all of it.

"You can't. You aren't strong enough." He responded out loud to my thoughts. This wasn't good. If he could read thoughts, there was no way we could get the upper hand.

"You don't know how strong we are." I retorted.

His laugh scrunched his face in a way that made him look even more evil than his actions had proven. "I know everything. I can read your minds. I know you've had help from one of my old friends. This will not end the way you want."

"Your old friend? Who are you talking about? We don't know any of your friends, and we for sure didn't get help from any of them." I was confused but hoped that by keeping him talking, I was giving the others time to come up with a plan.

"I was there the night your wizard friend opened the rift and received my powers at the same time that he did."

A realization hit me. This was one of Ian's friends who was there the night Ian opened the rift. Which one? I had to think about it...I know Ian told me what powers each of them got, but I just couldn't remember.

"You're one of Ian's friends? How are you still alive? There's no way that's possible."

"Magic, my dear girl. I spent my life acquiring magic to make me immortal. Did Ian really think he was the only one who got multiple powers?"

Wait, Ian has multiple powers? He only told me about seeing the future. What the hell? "What do you mean? Ian doesn't have multiple powers."

I kept wracking my brain for this guy's name. *Trent! That's it!*

He nodded as he responded. "Oh, my dear, sweet, naive girl. Of course, he does. Why else would he want you to close the portal? He wants to take your magic away and keep his own."

I wasn't sure if what Trent said was right, but even so, closing the rift or portal or whatever it was would take his power away as well. I knew we had to try. And if that meant giving up my powers, that's what I would do. I glanced behind him to see Kyro and Mack with a chain and a pair of the power blocking cuffs. I knew I needed to keep Trent busy for a few moments more so they could attack.

"You seem to have forgotten, my dear Zoey, I can read your mind. I know what your friends are planning, and it will never work. I'm too powerful."

Shit. I can't believe I forgot that. Now we're screwed. Or were we?

"No, Kyro, don't! It's too risky!" I shouted, hoping he would get my hidden meaning while keeping my thoughts on what Trent would do if he caught Kyro.

It was enough to get Trent to turn around. I saw that Mack and Kyro were ready with the cuffs. Q and I exchanged a glance, and then we both opened up our magic on Trent. We knew that we couldn't seriously injure him, but our plan was never that anyway. Q and I managed to catch him off guard and push him forward into the magic chains the guys had. Kyro and Mack were able to slap the power blocking cuffs on his wrists. I just hoped they would hold long enough for us to get away from here.

Once the guys were sure Trent was secure, we ran like crazy to get out of the compound. We could hear his screams and curses following us, even when we made it back to the boat. I was terrified. There was no way we could escape him. He would just keep coming after us. I kept expecting the worst, but it never came.

Kyro tried to comfort me, "Our trap will hold him for a while. It's OK. We're safe for now."

"We need to focus on the mission. Kyro's right. Maybe we can get to the rift and close it before he catches up to us." Q backed him up, pushing me to agree.

We headed below deck to plan out what was supposed to be the finale to our mission. We needed to close that rift.

Now that we were all back together and had finally incapacitated Trent, we had to act quickly to set the spell in motion. Our cage wouldn't hold him for long, and once he got out, we'd all be in danger.

We needed to get to the right coordinates and combine the pearls with the dodeca to activate the powers. I knew that we hadn't stopped The Order; we had just slowed them down. There wasn't much time to finish this.

"This is our only chance. And we're not even sure how to combine the pearls with the dodeca. How do we know this will even work?" Mack spoke the words that were in all of our heads.

I stared at the ocean as I responded. "We just have to believe that we can do it. We can't give up now. There's too much at stake."

Kyro walked up behind me and wrapped an arm around my waist. "You're right. We have a short amount of time to get to the ritual location. We need to get loaded up and get moving."

We gathered the supplies and loaded the boat. I opened the book to find a set of coordinates in what had been the United States, but still couldn't get a response from Ian. I hoped everything was OK. Everyone was on edge about this trip. We knew this could be a death sentence for any or all of us.

Kyro and I took turns using our magic to push the boat faster than the sails could. It was difficult for us to hold back and not deplete our reserves. Q had made an excellent point. We would be performing this ritual and potentially fighting the Order at the same time. We needed to get there fast, but not by sacrificing our safety or health.

"Zoey, you have to stop now. It's time to rest. It's OK, there's a good breeze blowing. The boat will stay on course. Come on." Q was insisting that I rest again.

I shook my head, "I'm fine. I can go for a while longer. We need to get there. I can do this. Please, just a bit longer." I could barely stand and was starting to get dizzy, but I didn't want to give up. I needed to make sure we made it to the coordinates before the Order caught up to us.

Mack snuck up behind me and trapped my arms at my sides. "You have to rest now. No arguments."

There was no use in fighting because it was two against one. And I knew Kyro would be on their side as well. "OK, I'll go rest." The words sounded as defeated as I felt.

As much as I wanted to keep pushing, I was glad for the break. It gave me some time alone with Kyro. We had been so caught up in getting to our destination before the Order that we hadn't spent any time together. It was nice to take the afternoon off and just relax. I knew it wouldn't last long, so I savored every minute of it.

We made it to the United States a couple of days later. I knew how incredible this country had been from all the books I read while I was taking care of the museum. It hurt me to see what this planet had become. There seemed to be some hope, though. Plants had started growing everywhere since most of the people had evacuated. I marveled at the power of nature as we walked off the boat.

Q had managed to secure a ride for us from port to Salem. It was a city in Massachusetts. It would take us half the day to get there from where we were. Luckily, the ride she secured was a jet, which made the trip faster than it would have been in a car or on foot.

FIFTY-FOUR

Jack

IT SEEMED STRANGE TO me that I was back on Calliope, and even more strange that I had settled back into my old routine as if I had never left. The only thing that was different was the one thing I wished I could change. I missed my best friends. I knew Race was dead, so he couldn't come back. I was fairly convinced Zoey would never speak to me again, and I really didn't blame her.

I spent some time with Marlene, trying to figure out who had killed Stephen because that still bothered me. I blamed myself. If I hadn't shared my thoughts with him, he might still be alive. It was too late to do anything about it, so I had to focus on what I could do. Namely catching his killer. I made it a point to meet with Marlene in secret because I didn't want her to suffer the same fate as Stephen had.

My days were pretty much the same as they always had been. I got up in the morning, went to my office, and took care of whatever the engineering department needed. I ordered supplies, wrote reports, hired people, and basically stayed bored out of my mind. After work,

I went to the gym and worked out until I could barely stand up. Then I went back to my room, showered, and tried to figure out how to prove Elena had framed Mama Bear. When that train of thought hit a wall, I switched to my notes on Stephen's death. At some point, I would fall asleep with my notes. The cycle would start over the next morning.

I tried to find out what was going on with Zoey and the others but didn't have much success. There were people who knew, but they weren't sharing with me. The only response I could get was that she was fine. It was pretty frustrating. I thought a couple of times that I should have just ignored Elena when she gave me the evidence on Bea. I blamed myself for that too. I should have seen that it was a frame job from the beginning. If I had, then I'd still be on Kyro's boat, pining over the girl I love but can never have.

Wow, that was a pathetic thought. I would rather be near her than so far away. I knew there was no way for us to come back from this. I had turned her mother in for spying after she asked me not to. Zoey knew it couldn't be true from the start. I couldn't just trust her and think about it, though. I had to act on it without giving myself time to figure it all out.

I found myself going to the museum some days on my way to my workout. I knew it was because I missed Zoey, but I claimed it was to look for an engineering or mathematics book. I had to keep up with the newest trends in my job. *Sure, Jack, keep telling yourself that. Like you're not secretly hoping she'll be there. And that book of fairy tales will definitely help you with your job in engineering.* I think I'd read more books since I'd been back on Calliope than I had the entire year before I left.

There had been some issues with the gravity system while I was away, so that was one of my main concerns since I returned to Calliope. I had been working on it for weeks, between investigating, researching, and wallowing. I thought I had it figured out, but it kept glitching.

I got a call that it was acting up again, so I went to the engineering bay to check it out. It was nice to have a mission to focus on, instead of worrying about Zoey and wondering if she was safe. In a way, I felt like I was being ridiculous, enjoying the fact that there was a malfunction on Calliope to take my mind off my personal issues. Whatever works, right?

I got to the bay and started checking the systems to determine the problem. I realized a moment too late that there was a strange ticking noise coming from the workstation behind me.

Ah, shit. What a way to go! That was my last thought before the world went dark.

FIFTY-FIVE

Bea

ONCE I HAD MADE sure no one suspected the director had come to offer me a way out of here, I started planning how I would trap Elena. I needed to either get her to trust me or piss her off so she would confess everything she had done. I wasn't convinced I could do either. But I was determined to try.

I waited until the guard brought my lunch to tell him I wanted to talk to Elena. "I mean it, Dave, I'm only gonna talk to her, so don't bother with anyone else."

Dave nodded as he left my cell. I hoped I had appeared nervous enough that he would go straight to her and not try to get his supervisor instead. I stuck my hand under my pillow and pulled out the tiny listening device. I swiftly attached it to the back of my ear, making it look like I had an itch in case someone was watching the feed from the camera.

"Come on," Dave ordered as he opened the door. "She wants you in the interview room."

"That was quick," I responded.

Dave moved closer to me and lowered his voice. "To be honest, she's been waiting for you to call for her. She's convinced you're going to confess. I really hope you don't. I'm one of the few who still believe in you."

When he was finished speaking, he pulled back to leave some distance between us. It was good to know there were still some people who believed I was innocent. I let him lead me to the interview room, where I walked inside and took a seat.

I knew she'd probably make me wait a while before she came in. It was a technique I taught her to give the upper hand in interrogation by making the person stew for a bit.

I wasn't sure exactly how long I waited, but I felt like it was pretty close to an hour.

When the door finally opened, I took a closer look at Elena than I had in quite a while. I had to admit, I didn't pay enough attention to her when she was my second. If I had, I would have seen the desperation and need for approval. It was written all over her face.

"I hear you've decided to confess. That's a good move for you. It'll make things go a lot easier." She began.

I nodded but didn't respond to her. I kept my gaze trained on her and my expression neutral. I knew it would drive her crazy to not get the reaction she wanted.

She snarled at me, "Aren't you going to say anything?"

I shrugged and kept my gaze pinned on her. I could see it was making her uncomfortable. I wanted to see how far I could push her to get what I wanted. Her expression told me it probably wouldn't take much more.

She reached into her pocket and pulled out her comm device, tapping buttons on it, then turned her attention back to me. "OK, the cameras and voice recording devices are shut off. You can say whatever it was you called me here for now. No one will know."

I raised an eyebrow at her but still didn't speak. I needed her just a little more agitated before I started. She was beginning to get frantic.

"Well, I don't have all day. Are you planning to say anything?" My plan was working. Maybe too well, as she turned toward the door.

"I was wrong about you, and I wanted to apologize." My voice was barely audible, but it stopped her from leaving.

"What do you mean? You wanted to apologize to me? Why?" There was a slight lilt in her tone, letting me know she was intrigued by my statement.

I shook my head and lowered my eyes to the chair across from me. If my plan was going to work, I needed her on my level. Without raising my voice, I uttered, "Please, sit so we can talk."

Her expression revealed exasperation and curiosity, and she took the seat across from me. "If this is a trick, I won't hesitate to have you punished."

"I know," the animosity in my response was hidden by the lowered tone. "Don't worry, you're really good at getting what you want. Why would this situation be any different?"

She nodded slowly, the smirk on her face growing as she leaned forward onto the table.

I considered my next words carefully, as they would either make or break this interaction. I decided to keep my voice low because I liked her reaction to it. I wanted her to pay attention, and maybe to trust me again. "I'd like to help you, but I don't know how to, and you aren't giving me anything to work with."

Her smirk curled into what can only be described as an evil smile. "Why would you want to help me now?"

I trained my expression to stay neutral. "I need to know why you framed me. Perhaps I can help you without going to prison. You know I consider you a daughter to me."

Elena growled in response to my words. "Really? You've never told me that before. Everything has always been about Zoey."

I dipped my head faking shame. "I know. And I'm sorry about that. I should have given you more attention than I did. The gods know you listen better than she does. You never would have just taken off with that bunch chasing after magical items without talking it over with me first."

Her expression softened a bit. "See? I tried to tell you she was going to cause trouble. You didn't want to hear that about your golden child. What changed your mind?"

I lifted my eyes to meet hers. "This isolation has given me a lot of time to think about everything. I've gone over so many moments in my mind. I realize that I haven't been fair to you. I'd like the chance to make it up, but to do that, you'll have to tell me everything."

"So, you want to know everything, huh? Well, I can't see what it would hurt since I've turned off the cameras and voice recorders. It's not like anyone will believe you anyway."

"Then you'll tell me why you've done all of this?"

She nodded. "All I ever wanted was for you to look at me the way you do her. My grandparents weren't exactly the most loving people, you know. At least they took me in after my parents took off. I wasn't angry with them until I discovered the reason they left."

I nodded and feigned interest to keep her talking.

"After training with the Patrol, I hunted them down. I wanted answers. It turns out, they liked not having the responsibility of raising a child. They were doing undercover missions for the Patrol and living their lives as though I never existed."

She paused again, and I stretched my hand across the table to rest on hers for a moment. "Oh, Elena, I'm so sorry. They didn't deserve you."

"I know, that's why I slit their throats in their sleep, and they never even knew who I was. They thought I was some rookie sent to learn about undercover work. It was surprisingly easy. Once that was done, I met up with some operatives from the Order and was offered a place in the organization. For once, I mattered. They would help me gain the respect I wanted, and the power I deserved."

I swallowed the bile that rose with her statement and steeled myself against the words I needed to say next. "It sounds like you did what you had to do to survive. What did you do for the Order in exchange for respect and power?"

She eyed me for a moment, almost suspiciously, then continued. "All I had to do was forward intel on a book they were looking for. It was surprisingly easy since I got assigned to work in the library with your bitch daughter. I sent a message when she found the book and another when she actually started to look at it. By then, they had another in place to take it from her, so I didn't get the pleasure of handling that."

I nodded thoughtfully. I had suspected there were others involved but didn't have proof until now. I wondered if she would give me names but didn't want to push too hard.

"Framing me was another job they had you do? Why? What did they gain from it?"

She smirked again. "That was all me. They needed to know where your spawn was and what she was doing, and I decided if I was going to give that information out, I would have a backup plan for getting what I want. I knew there were operatives in the Patrol who were looking for a mole, so I offered you up on a silver platter. I duped Jack into being the one to turn you in. I knew it would put a rift between him and Zoey, and it would keep suspicion off me."

"It sounds like you thought of everything. What can I do to get out of here? I'd like to help you, but I'm useless while I'm locked up." It pained my heart to offer her help. I wanted nothing more than to see her locked up for treason. I could only hope the recording device the director had given me was working and he was hearing every word.

"Hmm. That's an interesting offer. I'm not sure you could deliver. I think you'd back out the second you realize they want your precious Zoey. The Chairman wants her for himself, and the Boss wants her powers." Her gaze intensified as she studied my reaction.

Lucky for me, I was a pretty good undercover operative. I kept my expression neutral and responded in exactly the way she needed me to, without showing my feelings on the subject. "If they want her, they can have her. What use do I have for an insubordinate child who refuses to obey?"

She considered my words before she responded. "I see. I'll have to think about all of this. You realize that if I get you out, I'll have to frame someone else, and you won't go back to being in charge? Because I'm not giving this up."

I nodded in response. "That sounds fair. I've heard about your work in my former position. It appears you are better able to handle it anyway."

Elena stood, smoothing her uniform, and turned toward the door. "I'll let you know of my decision in a day or so. Until then, I'm going to have you moved to a more comfortable location, though you'll still be on lockdown. Is that agreeable?"

My face lit up like a child being given a gift. "You would do that for me? That is so generous, especially after the way I've neglected you. Thank you."

I could tell she was languishing in the praise, but I didn't want to lay it on too thick. I needed to gain her trust, not push her away.

FIFTY-SIX

KYRO

DURING OUR TRAVEL TIME, Zoey and I didn't get much time together. One of us was constantly using our magic to push the boat faster. I hated it, but I also knew we'd have the rest of our lives together when this was finished. Luckily for me, Q interfered and made sure Zoey got enough sleep. I wanted nothing more than to hold her in my arms and talk to her, but we had to finish this first.

I cherished the few intimate moments we had, though I wished they could have lasted longer. When I was pushing the boat, she was resting or consulting with Ian to make sure we were heading to the right coordinates. When she was pushing the boat, I was either resting or consulting with Ari. I hoped she'd be able to tell us something useful about what was going on or what was about to happen.

Little did I realize that I would come to regret that decision. Ari didn't usually share any information that could change the outcome of an event. It struck me as odd that she insisted on telling me what would happen.

"Kyro, I have to warn you about something, but first I have to tell you...it's dangerous to mess with fate. There could be consequences just for me telling you." Ari paused to gauge my reaction.

I nodded. "I trust you. You wouldn't tell me if it wasn't important."

She continued, "A moment will come. It will be soon. There will be a choice to make. This choice will either protect or destroy the future. An unborn child hangs in the balance. Death looms like a shadow overhead. The Savior's fate will be decided."

"I'm not sure exactly what that means, but I'm sure it will make sense when the time comes. Thank you for the warning, Ari."

I closed the connection and cleaned up the scrying supplies while I pondered Ari's words. It was a pretty ominous warning.

The closer we got to our destination; the more Ari's words weighed on me. I could have discussed it with Zoey or any of the others, but I chose to keep it to myself. I didn't need anyone worrying about what it meant or if there was something we could do to change things.

According to what Ari had told me for pretty much my whole life, there was no way to change what would ultimately happen. Yes, there was a choice, but even if I made it, things would most likely go the way they were fated to. It didn't matter if it happened at that moment or a few years from then. If I was meant to die, I would. There was nothing left to do but accept it and try to make the most of whatever time I had left.

Of course, I could be totally wrong in my translation of Ari's words. Perhaps someone else was fated to die. And I had no idea what she meant about the unborn child. None of the girls was pregnant.

I had to make myself forget about Ari's words for a while, or I'd make myself crazy trying to figure it out. Luckily for me, Q had decided Zoey needed a break. She forced my girl to come below deck and rest for a while. Since we were making good time, I decided to join her.

I'm not sure how much rest either of us would actually get, but I was pretty sure she'd be fine with that.

FIFTY-seven

Gill

TRAV INSISTED WE FIND the others and help. It didn't surprise me he had snagged a comm device from Q and talked her into keeping him updated. It did surprise me they hadn't called us for help, though. He found out about their plan to close the rift because he called to check on the others. It had been a while since there was a message, and he got worried.

Apparently, Q sent him the coordinates, and he told her we'd be there as soon as possible. I was pissed.

"We can't just abandon everything and run to the rescue. We aren't the heroes." I insisted for the third time.

Trav glared at me. "Yes, we can. Yes, we are. And yes, we will." He turned away from me and started walking back to the hut from where we'd been at the river.

"Look, Gill, you don't have to go. I am going. So, you can either go with me, or we can say goodbye. I can't guarantee that I'll make it back, so if you don't go, you may never see me again. I refuse to abandon our friends when they need us." I'd never seen Trav so angry, and to be honest, it terrified me.

We had been talking a lot since we split from the others. Trav shared everything with me about his family and his magic. He said Zoey had convinced him that he should. It pissed me off that he told her before me, but at least she'd had enough sense to talk him into telling me.

He was worried I wouldn't want to be with him. It didn't matter to me which one of us had more power. All I cared about was us being together and taking care of each other. Which was why his rant was unfair. He knew that by telling me he was going either way that I would insist on going too.

"Fine. We'll go. But we need a game plan. We can't just go barging in there like we know what's going on when we really don't. We have no idea if the Order is following them or if they are already there. We have to be safe about this if we're going. Deal?"

A satisfied grin spread across his face. "Deal. I knew you'd see it my way."

That cocky bastard always did have a way of convincing me to do what he wanted. It was a good thing that I was in love with him, or I would have to kick his ass.

Trav seemed distant as we made lists of spell books and ingredients we might need. We packed up what essentials we had listed for the trip. It would take us a week by boat and a few days by train to get to the coordinates. Hopefully we'd have a chance to talk on the way.

He made the travel arrangements while I double-checked bags and organized supplies. I wasn't sure how quickly we'd be able to leave, and I hoped he wasn't disappointed if he couldn't get things lined up instantly.

Imagine my surprise when he came back into the room a few minutes later, grinning from ear to ear. "Well, we leave in the morning."

"Really? You got us on a boat that quickly?" I was impressed but curious as to how he had done it. Usually, it took a week to get that kind of arrangement made. "How did you manage that?"

His grin turned cocky. "I may or may not have used a little tiny bit of magic."

"What? How? Is that another type of magic that you didn't tell me about?"

The grin faded from his face and was replaced by a frown. "It's not like I was hiding it from you, I just can't think of every single possible bit of magic that I can do on the spot like that. I can sometimes charm people with my voice." There was a bit of malice in his voice, and I couldn't blame him.

"I see." Before I could say anything else, he turned and walked away.

I needed to make sure Trav had told me everything about his magic, so we could figure out exactly what we can do to help. We would need to coordinate our efforts to make any attacks more effective. *So maybe I'm not as OK with Trav's powers as I told him. It's not like I'm gonna botch this just because I'm mad at him for lying to me.* I just had to convince him that showing me all of his powers was the best idea.

I knew I had to reign in the jealousy and hurt, but it was hard to do. I only got one type of magic, and it looked like he got multiple. And to top it off, Zoey had multiple types of magic too. It just wasn't fair. I just needed to study and get better, that's all.

FIFTY-EIGHT

Shannon

Greg led me towards Salem, claiming it was the only safe place for us because of the energy rift there that would mask his magic from the Boss. It still seemed strange to me to think of him as Greg instead of the Chairman, but I guess it made more sense to be on a first name basis with our current situation. Besides, having him in my head gave me some advantages.

I was slowly learning how to manage the extra voice in my head. And he was slowly teaching me how to control the magic. It was almost exactly what I wanted. I guess having part of someone else inside me was a small price to pay for the power I wanted. After all, I had been willing to sacrifice my son for it.

I arrived in Salem and was able to secure a room in a small hotel near the town square. I had heard stories about this being a city, but there were so few of those left that I had never seen one. There were landmarks paying tribute to past witches who had lived here. That made me more comfortable about practicing with my new powers. At least I wouldn't be cast out for them.

I settled into my room, enjoying the way the sun came in the window as it dropped in the sky. I could have requested an east-facing room, but I preferred the sunset to the sunrise any day.

After a few days, I settled into a routine. I slept in until almost lunch then stayed up until almost dawn. I preferred the night hours to practice my magic when there wasn't a crowd to watch. I was gaining control, but Greg wanted to focus on protection instead of attacks. It made sense, but I really didn't want to spend all of my time creating shields. I wanted to make fireworks, to blow shit up, to make people bow down to me. He was right though. I needed to be able to protect myself or we wouldn't survive.

I spent days working on creating and maintaining a shield. Then he had me focus on cloaking myself so I could be invisible in an instant. It wasn't easy, but I knew it would be worth the effort.

I heard the commotion just as I was grabbing my jacket to head out for practice. There must have been some kind of party going on. *Why didn't I hear about a celebration? You'd think they would do some advertising.* I slipped my jacket on and headed out the door in the direction of the noise. I figured I could check it out, then go find a quiet place to practice.

When I made it to the town square, I couldn't believe what I saw. There were half the people who had been after me, fighting with the other half. Luckily for me, none of them seemed to notice I was there. I hid behind the corner of a building where I could watch without being noticed. This was the perfect time to practice shielding and blending in with my surroundings.

Once I had camouflaged myself the best I could, I started paying more attention to what was happening at the square. My eyes stayed with Kyro and Zoey, watching them fight side by side. It was easy to tell they were in love and meant to be together. He would do everything he could to protect her, and she would go down fighting. There was a part of me that wanted to run to them and help. I knew it was too late for that. I had made a choice years ago and would pay for it for the rest of my life. They would never accept my help now. I was confident they would succeed against these henchmen anyway. I watched the exchange of blows from my hiding place.

I watched as the area in front of Zoey seemed to rip open, with swirling purple tendrils of magic reaching out of the black abyss of the tear. She didn't seem concerned with this development. Instead, she seemed to be focusing on the softball-sized item in her left palm. I couldn't hear what she was saying to Kyro, but he refocused his efforts to shield her from the henchmen who were trying to get to her.

I could see two of their friends off to the left, near the edge of the square, fighting with a large group of henchmen. They both appeared to have elven blood and some pretty impressive fighting skills. I recognized the red-haired woman from the Pit, but the white-haired man wasn't familiar.

Two more were on the right, fighting more members of the Order. I wasn't sure where those two had come from; it seemed as though they materialized out of thin air. It took me a minute to realize that this was Gill and his husband. I knew Gill didn't possess that kind of magic, so it must have been his partner who teleported them in.

I stood there under my shield, hiding from the battle that raged around me, knowing I was a coward for not choosing to at least try to help. I knew which side I should be with, but it was just too difficult to swallow my pride and go crawling back. So I stood there and watched. It seemed that Kyro's friends were gaining the upper hand, and Zoey was chanting something at the object in her hand. I felt certain they would complete their mission soon. I wasn't sure what that would mean for me. I would probably have to stay in hiding, but I would deal with that when the time came. For now, I was just going to see how this played out.

Gill and his mate defeated the group they were battling, then went to join Kyro and Zoey at the void tear. At least that gave Kyro some relief from having to run in a circle to protect her. With the three of them covering her, and the other two holding back the large group on the left, I was convinced this would all be over soon. I almost turned to leave. If I had, I would have missed what happened next.

Just as I was about to turn and walk away, I had the urge to stay and move closer. I darted closer on the right, next to a building where Gill and his partner had been fighting. I probably shouldn't have worried about keeping the magic shield up, but I couldn't afford to get caught now. It would be different once I had control over my powers. I wasn't sure what had pulled me forward, but I kept my eyes on Kyro as the battle continued to unfold. The two elven fighters had finally defeated the horde they'd been battling and joined the others around Zoey. Their presence made me even more confident in their imminent victory.

Suddenly Kyro turned for a moment, as if he was making eye contact with me, then he grabbed Zoey, kissing her while his fingers wrapped around her necklace. There was a small flash of blue light in his palm, then he let go of the necklace. The movement was so quick that I almost missed it. After he released her, he turned back to the henchmen who kept attacking. She continued the ritual she had been casting as if it didn't faze her. I took that to mean that they were close to the end, and the rift would be closed soon.

He turned back toward the fight just in time to see the Boss step out from the shadows. My heartbeat quickened. I knew this wasn't going to be good. He trudged forward with purpose, heading straight for my son. Kyro didn't back down, rather walking forward to meet the Boss head-on.

The moment they connected, there was a flash of bright white light, and I glanced back to Zoey. There was a light blue bubble around her that hadn't been there before. I turned my gaze back toward Kyro. I watched as this monster I had worked for plunged an electrified sword into the chest of my son. The sword cut through him, zapping waves of lightning into his lifeless body.

I heard a bloodcurdling scream and saw a flash of fire blast the Boss. Suddenly he was standing right in front of me. I was the one screaming, and I had figured out how to shoot fire at him. Having no control over the magic, I couldn't hold the shield and the blast, but I refused to stop, even when Greg screamed in my head that we had to leave. I had no idea if this beast was truly the Boss, or if it was some kind of doppelganger or mimic. It didn't matter, because I had killed the thing that had killed my son. Once the monster was reduced to dust, I stopped the flames.

I walked over to my son's lifeless body, lying there on the ground. His face looked so peaceful and innocent, just like when he was a baby. I missed those days. That was before I let the jealousy and greed take over. That was the time when I simply loved my son and his father. Somehow, I had grown to hate them both. I realized now that it wasn't either of them that I hated, it was myself. I hated that I never felt like I was enough for either of them or for myself. I turned toward Zoey, who had just finished the ritual to close the rift. Somehow they hadn't turned their attention to me, yet. The fighting and closure of the rift was taking all of their concentration. I disappeared again before they could engage with me This wasn't my time to grieve. For once, I didn't need to be the center of attention. I couldn't bring myself to leave, but I couldn't interrupt. I stood there and watched.

Zoey ran to Kyro, dropped to her knees and laid his head in her lap. She kissed him gently, then threw her head back and screamed. The others gathered around her, watching but giving her space. She screamed to the gods, then screamed for Poseidon. I knew there was nothing he could do to save his son, the same as there was nothing I could do. I watched as Poseidon teleported into the fountain in the square.

His majestic figure stepped out of the fountain and walked with purpose to where Zoey held Kyro. His eyes met hers, and tears began to run down both of their faces. They had a whispered conversation as he knelt down next to her and touched his son's face. My heart was breaking, but I knew I would have to leave or risk being caught. And since I wasn't sure what would happen to me if I was caught, I chose to once again walk away.

FIFTY-NINE

Quinn

ONCE POSEIDON AND ZOEY finished talking, he picked up Kyro's body and disappeared. I figured that meant he'd be taking care of whatever ritual his people used on their dead. Zoey was inconsolable. She didn't talk for three days. She refused to go back to the boat, so we had to rent rooms in the town. She acted like she didn't care if we were around or not, but Trav insisted on staying with her so she wasn't alone. Gill respected her space, most likely because of what he had done to me.

"We have to do something to help her." Mack and I had been going back and forth on this for the entire three days. I didn't see any reason to stop just because we were getting ready for bed.

He stopped halfway through pulling his shirt off and shook his head. "You can't force her to talk. She'll let us know when she's ready." It was the same stance he had stubbornly clung to since Kyro's death. He finished removing his shirt and sat on the bed, kicking off his shoes, then changing his pants.

I huffed out a breath at him as I pulled on my nightgown. "I don't agree. She needs to talk about it. I need to know that she's OK." I couldn't stop the tears from trailing down my cheeks.

Mack walked over to me and wrapped me in his arms. "I know you want to help her, love, but she needs space right now. Just think for a minute, OK? Did she push you when I was gone? Or did she give you space?"

I wiped my eyes as I answered. "She gave me space. And everyone walked on eggshells around me. It was horrible. Then I ran off, and I'm afraid she will too. I don't think she needs to be alone right now." I couldn't hold back the sobs at this point.

He rubbed his hands up and down my back. "It's all right, love, I'm here. I'm not going anywhere. We'll take care of our girl."

I knew he would do whatever he could to help her, and I loved him so much more for it. "Can we at least try to talk to her about it in the morning? I promise I won't force her to talk or to go back to the boat. I just need to make sure she knows that we're here for her if she needs anything."

Mack smiled as he steered me toward the bed. He sat down on the edge and pulled me down on his lap. "We can do that. First, we need to get some sleep. You're no good to her if you're exhausted, love."

He scooted back so we were both on the pillows, then covered me up like I was a child. I thought it was sweet as I drifted off.

At some point in the night, the nightmare came again. This one was different. I was standing in the middle of the Pit, glancing around to see what was happening. There were so many bodies on the ground around me. I didn't understand what I was seeing. I kept turning in a slow circle, looking at everything around me.

The sword was still in my hand, coated in blood. On my right was Mack's lifeless dwarven body, on my right was his lifeless current body. It didn't make sense. In front of me was Kyro, just as he looked before Poseidon took his body away. My eyes kept searching over the crowd of bodies. I had no idea what I was looking for.

I turned away from Mack and Kyro and took a few steps in the opposite direction, still searching. What am I looking for? What does all of this mean? *My eyes kept moving, searching, darting from face to face. Then they settled on a familiar sight.*

James?! How is this possible? *James couldn't be here, much less dead, but there on top of a pile of bodies, he was. I couldn't believe it. This had to be a dream. There was no way we were all back in the Pit again. James hadn't been with us since we left Spain, so it can't be real. Something about it felt so real.*

I tore my eyes from James' face, still searching for something. I prowled around the piles of bodies, hunting for whatever my target was. Just when I was about to give up, I saw her. Pale blue skin, midnight blue hair, eyes closed as if she was sleeping. Zoey.

I ran to her, screaming. "Zoey, wake up! This isn't real. It can't be. I can't have lost all of you again. Please, Zoey, wake up." The sobs overtook my body as I pulled hers from the pile it was mashed up inside.

She was intact, but so, so cold. I couldn't find a heartbeat, and she wasn't breathing. I searched her body for injuries and couldn't find any. "C'mon, Zoey, don't do this. Please. Come back. I need you." I held her close to me and cried into her hair.

Suddenly, her skin started to glow. It was a faint echo of her power. Maybe there was a way to bring her back. I laid her down on the ground in front of me and looked around for anything that could help, even though I had no idea what that may be. I gave up on my search and sank to my knees in front of her. "What can I do?" I asked in vain.

Her eyes flew open, glowing red like flames. "You can die." And flames shot from her eyes, engulfing me.

I woke screaming, with the image of her face burned into my mind. Mack was out of bed in an instant, grabbing his ax and ready to fight whatever had attacked us.

"What is it, love? Where is it?" He was poised and ready to attack.

I shook my head, drawing my knees up to my chest as I shivered. "It was a dream. It was just a dream." I said it more to myself than to him, but it didn't help.

He dropped the ax and hopped back into bed at my words, drawing me into his arms as he settled back against the pillows. "Are you all right? Do you want to talk about it?"

I wiped the tears from my face. "I don't know if I can. It was horrible. So much worse than the usual one." I shuddered at the memory of Zoey's face just before the flames hit me.

Mack didn't push the issue, just held me and tried his best to reassure me that everything was fine. I wasn't sure what the dream meant, if it was just my fears come to life, or if it was a warning for future events. Either way, I didn't want to take a chance of that becoming real.

We waited until a decent hour to go see Zoey. Trav answered the door when I knocked. "How is she?" I asked, knowing the answer before the words even registered.

"About the same. She's just been sitting by the window, staring out at nothing. I can't get her to talk. She'll eat if I make her, but it's not much." Trav's concern for her was apparent from his tone.

I nodded thoughtfully. "Have you been here all night?"

"I have. Gill and I slept in the bed across from hers, but she didn't even seem to notice he was here. We were initially concerned that his presence might upset her, but I don't even think she knows *I'm* here." He hung his head and his shoulders sagged forward.

I ran my hand along his arm from elbow to shoulder. "Why don't you and Gill go rest in our room. We'll stay with her for a while. Everyone needs a break."

He nodded, then walked over to where Zoey was sitting by the window. "Zoey? It's Trav, remember? Gill and I are going out for a bit, but Mack and Quinn are here to stay with you. Please let them know if you need anything, OK? Or if you need me to come back, you just say the word, and one of them will come to get me, OK?" He leaned down and hugged her, though she didn't even flinch at his words or touch. It was as though she couldn't even sense our presence.

I stood next to her as Gill and Trav left. I noticed she looked as though she was clean and groomed. It was sweet of Trav to take care of those details for her. I tried to volunteer for taking care of Zoey, but Trav wouldn't hear of it. He had told me Mack needed my attention and that it was his responsibility to take care of Zoey now. I didn't understand it at the time, but maybe he was right.

"Zoey? You look very nice today. Trav did a good job styling your hair. Are you feeling OK?" I knew she wouldn't answer, but I had to try.

My questions were met with silence. Even though it was expected, it still hurt. It was so hard to see her go through this alone. She wasn't physically alone, but emotionally she was so closed off that she might as well have been alone. I felt like her isolation was killing me inside. I turned to Mack.

"I can't take this. We have to find a way to get through to her. She can't just shut down like this. It's not healthy."

Mack nodded and took my hand. "I agree. She's blocking everything out because of the pain. We need to find something to get her attention."

"I know we've avoided physical contact to avoid upsetting her, but maybe it's come time for that." I grabbed Zoey's arm as I spoke. To my surprise, she turned to look at me, her eyes hollow and rimmed with dark circles from not sleeping.

Her voice was almost inaudible. "Q, how nice of you to come."

I couldn't help being shocked. "Seriously? Three days of ignoring us and *this* is what you have to say? What the fuck, Zoey?!"

Her expression didn't change. It was blank and unemotional. "I'm sorry to have upset you."

At this point, I was livid. "Zoey! Stop apologizing. Please talk to me. You can't block everything out just because he's gone. You have to deal with it." I couldn't stop the venom from seeping into my tone. It was harsh, and I regretted it instantly. "I'm sorry, Zoey." The words came out in a hushed whisper.

She actually looked at me and smiled. "It's OK. You're right. I've been ignoring everyone and everything since Poseidon took Kyro away. I can't go out there, and I can't return to that boat. I just can't.

It's too hard. Please don't ask me to." Her bottom lip quivered, as though she was barely holding back the tears.

I pulled her to her feet, took her in my arms and cradled her head to my shoulder. "Just tell us what you need, and we'll take care of it. We're all here for you."

She nodded against my shoulder. I turned to see where Mack was and found his arms coming around both of us. He held us both for a while before dropping his arms and taking a seat near the window.

Zoey pulled away and sat back in her chair. For a moment, I was worried she'd clam up again. Then she spoke.

"I think I need to leave. I can't stay here." Her voice remained almost a whisper, but Mack and I hung on every word.

I looked from her to Mack and back again. "Where do we need to go?"

She shook her head. "Not we, just me. I need to leave. I need to go back to Calliope. I think that's far enough away that I won't see him everywhere."

Mack spoke before I could collect my thoughts. "Are you sure that's the best idea? To be alone without your friends to help you might make things harder. If that's what you really want, then we'll arrange it."

I turned to him and whispered my concerns. "How can we just send her off into space alone?"

Zoey interjected before Mack could respond. "It's not your decision. I don't even know if I can go back, but that's what I want. Please, could you make the arrangements?" She directed the question to Mack instead of me, and I took that to mean she wanted to talk to me alone for a minute.

Mack nodded and excused himself to make some calls. I was pretty sure he was going to discuss the whole thing with Gill and Trav before he tried to make the arrangements.

"Will you and Mack take care of the boat? I can't handle it myself. Poseidon told me I can have all of Kyro's belongings, but I can't even make myself go back there, much less collect his stuff."

It pained me to agree, but I did because I knew it would ease her mind, and honestly, I didn't want to go home either. "We can do that. I think we can find a nice port town and settle down."

She looked up at me and chuckled. "When I met you, I never thought you'd say those words. I'm glad you and Mack found each other."

"Me too. Do you think you could go back to the boat and get your stuff if Trav and I go with you? Or do you want us to go get it for you?"

"If you don't mind, I'd rather you did it. I let Trav stay with me because it kept Gill close. I still don't trust him. So, they can stay here with me, and you can take Mack with you to collect my stuff if you don't mind." I hugged her close, then she turned back to the window, staring off into the distance.

I walked across the hall and explained most of what had just happened to the guys. Trav took Gill and went back to stay with Zoey while Mack and I headed to the boat.

SIXTY

Mack

I COULD TELL QUINN wanted to talk to me about something from the way she explained her conversation with Zoey. I knew she was leaving something out. I decided if she was holding back, there had to be a reason, so I'd wait and ask her when we got to the boat.

"OK, spill it. What aren't you telling me?" I started as soon as we hit the gangplank.

She laughed. "I knew you'd start on me as soon as we got here."

"Well? Don't make me tickle it out of you." I wasn't going to let her change the subject.

"She wants us to take the boat. And the only reason she's let them stay with her is that she doesn't trust Gill. We have to keep an eye on them if they head out with us."

"She really wants to go back to the space station? She doesn't want to be here with us?"

Quinn shook her head. I could see the tears forming in her eyes. This was a little too close to home for her, given that she'd been through it not too long ago when I'd died. "It's too hard for her right now. She sees him in everything. Trust me, the pain is unbearable. We have to let her do this and hope that at some point she decides to come back."

"OK, but I don't like sending her up there alone. There's too much that can happen to her and no way for us to know if she needs help."

"I don't like it either, but it's not our decision. Funny how we've had this conversation in reverse for the past three days, huh?"

I nodded because the irony of the situation wasn't lost on me. "What are we doing here? Just getting her stuff together?"

"Yeah, but Poseidon gave her all of Kyro's things, so I'm probably going to slip a few into her stuff just so she'll have something of his. She may not want it right now, but she will."

I agreed. We set to work going through Kyro's room, packing most of it up to be shipped to Calliope with Zoey. Then I came across the book. "What about this?"

"Maybe we should keep it here. If she wants it, she'll let us know and we can deliver it. Then we'll have an excuse to check on her."

"I like the way you think, love." I put the book back in the hiding spot Kyro had shown me after we rescued Zoey from the Pit. Packing up my best friend's belongings was the hardest thing I'd done since I threw myself on Quinn's sword. To be honest, the sword may have been easier.

The closer we got to finishing up, the more anxious I became. I knew this was probably the worst timing ever, but I suddenly felt compelled to give Quinn the ring in my pocket.

"Love? Can I talk to you for a minute?" I gestured to the bed, asking her to come and join me.

She looked up at me quizzically from the box she'd been packing. "That sounds ominous but sure." She cocked an eyebrow at me as she walked over and sat down.

I stood in front of her and took her hand. "Quinn, you are the most amazing woman I've ever known. You know that I love you. I need to know if you'll be mine, forever." I knelt down on one knee and pulled the ring from my pocket, offering it to her.

Her eyes grew wide, and for a moment, I thought this had been a really poor decision. Of course, she'll say no, why wouldn't she? Why would she want to tie herself to me?

"Oh, Mack! Did you make this? For me? It's amazing." She took the ring from me and inspected it before putting it on the third finger of her left hand.

"Wait, does this mean..." I couldn't finish the question because she had tackled me and was kissing me like there was no tomorrow.

"Yes, you silly, crazy man. I can't believe you ever doubted it." Then she was kissing me again.

At some point, we stopped celebrating our engagement and finished our task at hand. For me, it was a bit cathartic, allowing me to say a final goodbye to my best friend. We discussed it and decided that we wouldn't move into Kyro's suite. Instead we would be keeping it exactly the way it was for Zoey when she decided to come back.

We finished packing Zoey and Kyro's things, then called Quinn's contact on Calliope to make sure we could get her safely transported back there. She put the comm device to speaker mode so I could hear the whole conversation.

"Frank, it's Q. I need to get someone back on Calliope."

"Hey, Q. What do you mean back on? Who is it?" He sounded as wary as I felt about the whole situation.

"It's Zoey. She needs to be able to come back. She's been through some stuff down here and needs to be as far away from it as she can for a while. I know she didn't exactly leave via the correct process. I don't even have her ID. Can you help me?"

"I can probably arrange it, but it'll mean 'finding' some documents to make the legal aspect of it go away. And it won't be cheap. You know the usual rate? Double it, and we have a deal."

Quinn didn't even hesitate. "Done. I'll transfer the credits to you today. Text me the travel instructions to get her there safely." Then she disconnected the call and pressed some buttons on the comm device.

"Was it a lot?" I was trying not to seem nosey but genuinely wondered if Quinn had the money.

She shook her head. "Not for what I asked him to do. Besides, I would have paid double what I agreed to if necessary. I have more than enough, and if it helps Zoey, it's worth any amount."

"That's so generous of you. I would have helped. Still can if you tell me how much you need."

"I've already sent it and got the confirmation. It's fine, I promise I'm not broke. I have plenty left. And I know you would have helped, but I got this one." She leaned over and kissed me, probably to shut me up.

We got all the boxes and bags together in Kyro's suite and headed back to the inn to wait for Frank's message.

We waited for two hours before Frank messaged Quinn. While we waited, we arranged for Zoey's boxes and bags to be moved as soon as we knew which shuttle she'd be taking. Frank sent directions to a shuttle, an electronic ticket, and a temporary electronic ID card. Quinn transferred everything to a spare comm device for Zoey to take with her. Then we relayed that information to the company responsible for moving Zoey's things. Gill and Trav met them on the boat to oversee the loading.

"You're sure about this?" Quinn asked Zoey as we walked to the shuttle bay.

Zoey nodded, clutching the comm device to her chest as though it might escape. "I'm sure. I've thought about it, and this is the only way. It won't be forever."

I helped Zoey find her seat on the shuttle. "Here it is, and a private compartment at that!" It was nice that Frank had set her up to travel alone.

"Good. Now get settled in, the shuttle will be taking off soon. We'll miss you." Quinn hugged Zoey quickly and bolted from the shuttle. I knew she'd be a mess of tears when I finally caught up to her, but I'd deal with it.

"It'll be OK, Zoey. We'll take good care of the boat, and as soon as you come back, you can come to get it. And we'll stay in touch." I reassured her as much as I did myself. I hoped this wasn't the last time we'd see her. I walked off the shuttle and took my place next to Quinn to watch it take off.

SIXTY-ONE

Zoey

I WOKE SUDDENLY FROM the nightmare and took a few minutes to realize where I was. I sat up and shook my head to clear it. I flipped on the lamp and looked around the room. The familiar room should have been a comfort to me, but instead, it reminded me that he was gone and that the life we had imagined together would never be.

Part of me wanted to stay in bed all day and wallow in my grief. I pushed myself out of bed and walked across the carpet into the bathroom. The cold tile on my feet helped pull me back to reality. I turned the shower on and waited for the water to get as hot as possible before I stepped under the spray. I was hoping it would warm me and chase these chills away.

As much as I wanted to give up, I knew I couldn't. Jack needed me. It didn't matter that he had betrayed me, and I was still angry with him. We were family, and that's what you do for family. I would stand by him until he was awake and healed, then we could argue about what he did. Until then, I would go and sit by his side every day and talk to him. I had no idea if he could even hear me, but the doctor seemed hopeful that it would help him recover.

I finished my shower, threw up a few times, got dressed, brushed my teeth again, and headed to the hospital ward. Maybe I'd talk to the doctor and get something for my nerves. I'd been getting anxious and sick at my stomach all week. There had to be something the doc could do.

I walked slowly down the hall to the hospital ward after realizing that walking faster made me dizzy. I'd definitely have to talk to the doc. Right after I saw Jack. Then I'd be able to go to work and get the library reorganized. It was a mess from the time I was gone. I had thought Elena was a capable library assistant until I came back.

I entered the hospital ward, and my jaw dropped as soon as I saw Jack. They had taken him off the breathing machine. I started to panic. How was he going to breathe without it? I ran to him, freaking out until I realized he was breathing on his own. Tears streamed down my face and I laid my head on his chest, listening to his heartbeat. It was such a relief to see he was getting better.

Once I had calmed down, I pulled my usual chair over and began to tell him about everything. I started by telling him again about his accident, then I would tell him about how I ended up back on Calliope. It was actually comforting that I had started the conversation out with happy tears since I was pretty sure it would be ending with sad ones. I needed to tell him about Kyro and might as well do it today. I'd been avoiding it so far.

"Hey, Jack. It's Zoey. You're in a coma because there was an explosion in the engineering bay. The doc says it happened a month ago. You had been working on the artificial gravity generator when something went wrong, and it exploded."

I paused my story because he started to twitch. I ran to get the nurse, who checked his vitals and decided that he was fine. She told me to keep an eye on him and let her know if it happened again. After she left, I started my story again.

"So, you've been in this coma, while the rest of us were on Earth dealing with the magic rift. I think we got it sealed. I couldn't stand to stay and make sure though. While I was performing the ritual to close it, Kyro and the others were fighting the Order."

I had to stop again because I started crying. I took a few minutes to calm down, just sitting there holding Jack's hand. Then I continued.

"He didn't make it. Kyro. He was killed by one of them. That's why I had to leave. I couldn't stay down there without him."

At this point, I thought I felt Jack squeeze my hand, but it had to be my imagination. He hadn't moved without help from the nurses since the accident. They worked his muscles every day to make sure he didn't get blood clots.

"I didn't even know you were on Calliope until I arrived. Once I was checked in, I got a notification that you were in the hospital ward. I've been coming to see you every day since I got here. I've been such a mess though. It's making me sick that he's gone. I don't know how to deal with it. I'm going to talk to the doctor today and see if he can help. I really hope you wake up soon, Jack. I feel so alone here. It's like home, but it's not."

I don't know how much longer I sat there holding his hand while the tears spilled down my cheeks. A while later, the doc came in and asked how Jack was doing today. The nurse had already told him about the episode earlier. He claimed that meant we were getting closer to time for him to wake up. Then he turned the questions to me.

"And how are you holding up?"

Since he was my doctor, I had already told him about Kyro and that I was having trouble sleeping.

"Well, doc, I don't feel well. You know I'm not sleeping well, but now I can't eat and the past couple of days, I've been throwing up. Do you think it's a bug?"

He nodded thoughtfully. "Come by the office when you're done visiting Jack. We'll run some tests. I'm sure you're fine."

"Well, Jack, I'm starting to worry that you're not listening to me. I need you to wake up before this baby gets here. I told you that Kyro is gone, and I can't do this on my own." I rubbed my growing belly as I spoke aloud to him.

I stood up and began to pace around the room as I rattled on about my day, in hopes that it would get a reaction from Jack. So far, nothing had happened.

Doc Wilson came in to check on us. "Any change today?" He asked, motioning to Jack, then to my bump.

I shook my head. "Neither of them is being very cooperative, but everything is fine. Should I be worried that Jack hasn't woken up yet?"

"We've run every test possible. All the results show he's physically fine. His injuries have healed. By all accounts, he should be awake."

"Is there anything else we can do?" The baby started kicking, and I doubled over in pain for a moment.

"Are you OK? Come sit down. I'll check you out." Doc pulled out a chair for me, and I sat down next to Jack's bed. Doc took my blood pressure and pulse.

"Really, Doc, I'm fine. This kid is gonna be one heck of a soccer player though." Unless he or she comes out with a mermaid tail. That would be a difficult adjustment.

I never considered the ramifications of Kyro and I having children. When I found out I was pregnant, I was overjoyed and terrified. As the months rolled on, I began to consider all the ways this could turn out badly. This was why I needed Jack to wake up. I couldn't take it if something were to happen to my little one.

And I needed his help to clear my mom. He had been the one to turn her in for spying on the Patrol. He needed to be the one to nail down the proof to go with his theories. It was crazy to think that I wouldn't even know about his investigation to clear Mama if Doc hadn't sent me to Jack's room to get more socks.

I wasn't sure if it had been a ploy or if he really had needed socks. It didn't matter, finding his notebooks had softened my heart a bit. At least he had realized his initial decision was wrong. Mama would never betray us like that.

SIXTY-TWO

Jack

I WOKE IN A daze. It felt as though I'd been asleep for so long that I couldn't feel my body. Of course, I guess being in a coma would do that to a person. It was the strangest sensation. I could sense everything going on around me, and I could hear every word that was spoken, but I couldn't respond or even move. I knew Zoey had come back to Calliope and that Kyro had been killed. I remember her telling me that she was carrying his child and that she felt like she couldn't make it through these challenges without me.

Her visits were what kept me holding on. Her words made me fight harder than I'd ever fought against anything before. Zoey needed me, and I wasn't about to fail her again. I would recover and spend the rest of my life fighting to make sure she was safe. I would also resume my search for proof that her mother was innocent. I had to show her how much she meant to me. It didn't matter if she never returned my feelings, I needed to be there for her and take care of her.

I woke up to complete darkness. The clock on the wall said 02:00. It was obviously the middle of the night. I slowly pushed myself up to look around the room. If I hadn't been aware of what had happened to me, I would have been terrified.

I was lucky that the doc and nurses had kept working my muscles while I was out. Otherwise, I would be stuck here until someone came in. As it was, I was barely able to pull myself up and climb out of bed.

After a couple of fumbled attempts at standing up, I was able to use the wall to brace myself and hobble to the bathroom. I faintly heard the high-pitched noise that signified I was no longer in my bed and knew the nurse would be in here soon. Hopefully I could take a piss and put on some pants first. I knew it didn't really matter, as they had all seen me naked at some point or another during my comatose state.

I closed the bathroom door behind me and continued along the wall to the toilet. Luckily, there were rails along this wall to help with just such a trek. As I was taking care of my business, I looked around the bathroom. There was a pair of pajama pants hanging on the back of the door. They'd probably be a little short as they were hospital issue, but it was better than letting everything hang out.

I exited the bathroom and came face to face with the doc. "I didn't expect to see you."

Doc grinned, "I didn't expect you to get out of bed on your own when you woke up."

I walked over slowly and let him help me sit in a chair next to the bed. "So how bad was it, Doc? And seriously, why are you here? It's the middle of the night."

Doc sat on the edge of my bed and looked around before he answered. "I've been taking over the night shifts since I caught one of the nurses drugging you to keep you under. Zoey has been here all day every day and asks all kinds of questions, so I didn't have to worry about you then."

He paused, then continued. "Honestly, Jack, I think someone is trying to kill you. I couldn't get any info out of that nurse, but she's locked up now, and won't get out any time soon. I'm pretty sure you'd still be out if I hadn't walked in at just the right time."

"I think you're right, Doc. That means you're in danger now too. And that's my fault. I don't understand it, though. I thought Zoey's mission was successful. That should have eradicated the Order and fixed everything." I wasn't sure if I should have spoken that out loud, but I felt like Doc could be trusted.

"I have no idea what you're talking about, Jack. I do agree that you aren't safe here. I'll call Zoey and let her know you woke up. We'll get you moved into her suite as soon as possible." Without waiting for a response, Doc left the room. I wondered if he and Zoey had discussed me moving in with her while I was out or if this was just an idea he had. I wouldn't have to wonder for long, because within five minutes, Zoey was in the doorway to my room.

Her face lit up when she saw me. "Jack!" She ran over and threw herself into my arms. "I didn't think you were ever going to come back to us. I was so worried!"

"How long was I out? I know it's been a while, but I also know you've been here every day talking to me about everything that's happened." I gestured at her growing baby bump.

Zoey grinned up at me. "You were in a coma for four months, Jack. Doc says I'm five months along, so don't worry, I won't try to say it's yours." She chuckled at her little joke, not realizing that I would kill for this child to be mine.

I returned her bear hug and smiled down at her. "You can tell people whatever you want. I'll agree with anything you say, as long as you don't hate me anymore."

She pulled back a little bit. "I never hated you. I was hurt. It doesn't matter now. I read your notes, which are safely tucked away in my room now, and I know that you're trying to clear Mama's name. Also, I think I may have a theory about that Stephen guy you were investigating, but we'll talk about that after you've had a few days to recover."

"Doc said I was moving in with you...Is that right?" I felt awkward asking, but it was the only way I'd know if he had forced or guilted her into it.

She nodded, a grin spreading across her face. "The moment I got here, they told me you were in a coma. I talked to Doc at length about it and insisted that you'd move into my suite when you woke, no matter what."

That made me feel better about the whole thing. I didn't want to be a burden, but I also didn't want to go back to my room. It didn't feel safe anymore. I'd sleep on the floor at Zoey's until we got everything sorted out.

SIXTY-THREE

Zoey

WE SPENT THE DAY getting Jack settled into my suite. He kept insisting he wouldn't sleep in the bed. I know I'd convince him otherwise. We needed each other. It was as simple as that. Besides, we'd shared a bed platonically off and on our entire lives. It couldn't be that hard.

Doc told us it would be good for Jack to exercise, but to ease back into it slowly. I used that as an excuse to run him back and forth around the suite until he was worn out. I got him tucked into bed and curled up beside him.

"Are you sure this is OK?" He asked again.

I rolled my eyes at him. "I've told you a dozen times. It's fine. We've done this so many times before. I don't understand why this is any different."

He opened his mouth to speak, then closed it again.

"Just tell me. Whatever it is, we'll figure it out."

"I don't want to disrespect him. I know nothing's going to happen between us. It's not that. It just feels like I'm trying to replace him. And I don't want that."

"Oh, Jack. I love you. You know that. You could never replace Kyro. I know you'd never even try. You're doing him the biggest favor ever by taking care of his widow and child."

Jack sat up against the headboard. "I've always loved you. I saw what you had with him, and that's not something I ever want you to lose. I'm honored that you'd let me be a part of your life, that you'd trust me to be a part of your child's life. I just don't want to mess this up again."

I took his hand and held it gently. "No promises, no regrets. Just family. Now get some sleep." I let go of his hand and rolled onto my side facing away from him. He shut off the light and laid back down.

I hadn't considered how being this close to Jack again would bring up our unresolved feelings. I wasn't sure I was ready to address it, either. I hoped he meant what he said, that he was happy to just be part of our lives. The whole thing coupled with pregnancy hormones was just too much to think about right now. I was lucky enough to have two amazing men who loved me, and now I wouldn't have to choose between them.

Sometime in the night, I began to dream. It was strange yet soothing. Almost as if it was real. Kyro was there holding me. We were back on his boat in our room.

"I thought you'd like to come back here for a bit. Though I understand why you left." Kyro's voice held a sadness I'd never heard from him before.

"Is this really a dream?" I asked, knowing it wasn't.

He shook his head. "No, it's real. It's our last night together, so we need to make the most of it." He kissed me tenderly.

The kiss deepened and our passion took over. Making love to him seemed like the most natural thing in the world to me. It didn't matter that it was in a dream realm. After we had thoroughly expressed our feelings, Kyro held me close.

"You have to give Jack a chance. He's still in love with you. He'll take good care of you and our son."

"What? You want me to be with Jack?" I was already certain the baby was a boy before Kyro's announcement, so I didn't question that part.

He nodded. "If I can't be there to take care of you, I think he should be. He's never done anything but try to keep you safe. Even when you didn't see it that way."

"Are you sure you're OK with it? I'm not sure I'm ready." I stretched up to press my lips to his.

He smiled as he kissed me again. "I would rather it was me taking care of you, but since that's not possible, yes. I think Jack is the best choice. I know you love him. It's OK. Your heart is big enough for us both."

I didn't respond. I couldn't find the words to explain what I was feeling. I held onto Kyro until I felt him fading away. "I love you, Kyro. Forever."

The last words I heard him say echoed in my head as I woke from the dream. "I love you, Zoey. Always remember that."

A few nights later, I dreamed of him again. Or I thought it was him. I saw a young man on the docks and could have sworn it was Kyro. I ran to him. When I got there, I realized that this wasn't a man, but a kid. He couldn't have been more than four years old. The kid had reddish blond hair, olive skin, and the deepest chocolate eyes I'd ever seen. In an instant, I knew he was our son.

"Logan, where have you been? I've been searching everywhere."

The boy smiled up at me with his daddy's grin. "I'm sorry, Mama. I was out here talking to Daddy. I can hear him in the waves."

My heart raced as I hugged the boy tightly and realized that in this dream, I was pregnant again.

When that realization hit me, I woke with a start.

"Zo, are you OK? Is there something wrong with the baby?" Jack pulled me close and held me.

"I'm fine. And he's fine too. Logan just wanted to show his mama a bit of the future."

Jack looked at me with a puzzled expression. "Logan?"

I smiled back at him, "Yup, it's a boy, and his name is Logan."

Jack looked puzzled. "I feel like I've missed something here."

I laughed, "It gets better. Logan won't be my only child, and we aren't staying on Calliope permanently. Or maybe we are, but we'll be visiting Earth. Which would make sense, given that Poseidon will want to meet his grandson."

"Wait, how do you know he won't be your only child? What are you trying to say here?" Jack sounded exasperated.

"It's OK, Jack. You'll take good care of us. We'll be one big, happy family. Don't worry. Kyro told me as much."

"Zoey, are you feeling all right? You know Kyro is dead. You couldn't have talked to him. I'll call the doctor and have him check you out."

I grabbed his arm before he could climb out of the bed. "I'm fine, Jack. And I did talk to Kyro, in the spirit plane. We both had the ability to astral project, which allowed his spirit to come to visit me one last time. We had a fantastic talk about the future, and he wants you to take care of us. He knows I love you, and he wants us to be together. I would feel the same if I had been the one killed. He just wants us to be happy and to know that his child will be cared for."

Jack settled back against the headboard and pulled me close. "I promise you and Kyro that I will do everything in my power to make sure you and Logan stay safe. I will protect you both. I'll give my life if I have to. I love you."

I laid my head on his chest. "We know. It's going to take time, but we'll be fine. Let's rest now. It's been a long night."

SIXTY-FOUR

Bea

Elena was true to her word, and I was moved to my room after our conversation. I was still locked up, just in a more comfortable way. I wasn't allowed to leave or have contact with anyone. At least I could shower, wear my own clothes, and sleep in my own bed.

She waited three days to get back with me about my offer to help her. I wondered if she saw through my acting or if I had fooled her. I needed to obtain as much information as I could that proved she was working for the Order. That was the only way to clear my name.

Elena waltzed into my room as if she owned the place. "Bea, I trust you've been enjoying your freedom?"

It took everything I had to not scoff at her question. If she thought this was freedom, she had no idea what prison was like. "It has been nice to be in my room again, yes."

"Good. Now we can talk without anyone listening in or recording us."

I nodded but didn't speak. I still had the recording device attached just behind my ear and knew the director could hear everything we were saying. It appeared my acting had worked.

She continued without any prodding. "I told you before, this is all your fault. You paid way too much attention to her, and none to me. I had to find a way to get some recognition. So, when I was approached by someone in the Patrol who also had connections in the Order, I jumped on the chance."

"Then is that why you framed me?" I kept the animosity out of my voice, but just barely.

Elena laughed. "I framed you because you pissed me off. I worked for you for years and got no recognition. I was supposed to be in control of the museum, but you gave it to her. Every promotion I was supposed to get was handed to someone else. I got no explanations, no excuses, no apologies. I was sick of it. I created those documents on your devices. It was easy, really. You trusted me way too much and didn't bother to keep track of what was on your devices."

"What is the Order giving you for all of this?" I was genuinely curious about her motives.

"I'm respected there. And they are going to make sure I'm respected here, too. When they take over the Patrol, it will all be mine. I will be the director. I will finally be in charge. People will answer to me for a change."

"I can understand that. What made you change your mind about me?" I wanted to know but was afraid to push her too much, for fear that she'd actually kill me. It no longer mattered to me that the director was listening in, I wanted answers for myself.

She sat down in a chair across from me and stared at me for a moment. "Who says I have? You are in no position to hurt me. No one will believe anything you say. So why shouldn't I enjoy rubbing it in that I've won?"

I couldn't respond to that question. Maybe I hadn't fooled her as well as I thought. I hoped the director was listening to all of this. I might be in more trouble than I expected. Elena was obviously unhinged and dangerous.

She laughed maniacally, "I'm just kidding. I always knew I would end up recruiting you for the Order. It was part of what I used to bargain my way into the organization. I'm impressed it didn't take me as long as I expected. I thought I'd have to have Zoey killed to get you on my side."

"Sounds like you were pretty determined." I didn't let on that her threat against my daughter had upset me. I couldn't risk setting her off. "Surely you're not doing all of this on your own? Don't you have underlings within the Patrol to help you?"

She gave me a knowing look, and for a moment I panicked on the inside. She knew.

"Of course, I have underlings! You just have me all figured out now, don't you?"

I let out a small nervous laugh. "Looks like it. I just figured with as smart as you were, you'd have people to do your dirty work."

"Gold star for you! I have a few connections within our organization and on Calliope. They take care of the stuff I don't want to do myself. Like killing Jack. I couldn't be bothered with that myself, so Jeff took care of that for me. Of course, it looked like an accident. We can't have any loose ends, you know. Down here, Chad and Bret help me, and now I have you. It's so nice to be able to include you in my little family."

Well, she had given me names and admitted to having Jack killed, although the director said he was stationed on Calliope and would be called to testify against Elena. I wondered if he knew of Jack's "accident" and if he really was OK. Jack was like one of my kids, I wouldn't be able to bear it if something had actually happened to him. I guess the moment of fear crossed my face because it garnered a response from Elena.

"Oh, you didn't know about Jack. There's been an accident, an explosion on Calliope, and he's been killed. I'm so sorry for your loss. Is this going to be a problem?"

I shook my head. "No, no problem at all. I'm sure if something was done, it was warranted. Like you said, no loose ends."

It killed me to go along with a murderous crazy woman, but I had no choice at the moment. Any other action would get me killed. I would have to just play along until the director had enough information to arrest her. I had a feeling this wasn't going to be easy.

"Exactly. Why is that concept so hard for people to understand? It's really very simple. Use anyone you can, and when they stop being useful, kill them. Am I right? So easy." Her tone had changed again, and it was like she was talking to an old friend, instead of discussing cold-blooded murder.

"You're right. It's an extremely simple concept. I don't understand why you've had problems with people not understanding it."

"See? I knew you'd get it. You and I are just alike, you know? Peas in a pod, that's us. Now we can get back to business as usual."

"What do you need me to do?" I made sure to keep my voice eager and light.

"Well, I have some documents that need to be reviewed before they get sent over to my contact in the Order. I'll have you do that while Bret keeps an eye on you. I hope you understand that I'm going to have to have you guarded for a while, just to make sure you aren't trying to play me. You'll be able to go wherever you need to and do what you want as long as he's with you."

Keeping my expression neutral, I nodded eagerly. "Of course. I would expect no less. I have nothing to hide."

It took a few days of basically being Elena's bitch before the director contacted me about the evidence I'd gathered. Apparently, it was enough to put her away for a long time. Sadly, the director and I had to have our conversations in my bathroom until he could secure guards to arrest her. He managed to smuggle a secure comm device into my bathroom somehow, and I didn't question it. I just made sure to answer when he called and kept it on silent so Elena didn't find it.

"You know the plan. We're going to arrest her at the morning briefing. She knows I will be there but has no idea why. I told her it's a surprise inspection. She didn't seem suspicious."

"Agreed. She didn't say anything that indicated that she knew what was going on. It's been business as usual. You have guys in place for her and her henchmen?"

"Yes. I have a group of eight of my most trusted guards to accompany me, and they will be taking care of it. I have a feeling I'll need more to take her down than her lackeys, though."

I nodded in agreement. "I think you're right. I can't wait to see her face. This will be priceless."

That night was the best night of sleep I had in weeks. There was no stress or worry that she would just decide to kill me and then go after Zoey.

In the morning, I took extra time getting ready, choosing the perfect outfit, making sure my hair was done just right, putting on makeup. I made sure not to go overboard with it, but I wanted to feel more myself than I had lately.

I walked into the conference room for our daily briefing with Bret at my side. I feigned surprise at seeing the director in the meeting, as that would have been an unusual occurrence. Elena gestured for me to take my seat, and I could tell from her face that she expected me to sit there and keep my mouth shut. I was happy to oblige.

Just before the meeting was scheduled to begin, two of the director's guards grabbed Bret and Chad while two more covered the exits. The remaining four circled Elena, and I could tell from her expression that she figured out what was happening, although she opted to play dumb.

"What's this about? Unhand me, you morons."

"They will do no such thing, you traitor. You're being arrested and will be tried as a traitor to the Patrol. We have all the proof we need, and you won't be able to frame anyone else for your crimes this time." The director spoke with authority, but I could hear the disappointment in his voice as well.

I sat there in my chair and watched the guards take Elena and her goons away, and the director nodded to me as he followed.

"I trust you'll accept your old position back, Bea?" He asked as he walked away. He didn't bother to wait for an answer, which was fine by me, because he knew I would do what I needed to in order to protect my daughter just as I always had.

After getting settled back into my office and taking care of things Elena had managed to screw up while she was in charge, I called the Director and scheduled a vacation. I was going to check on Jack and hopefully find my daughter.

What Next?

IF YOU ENJOYED THIS book, please consider writing a review. Indie authors, even those with indie publishers, can only thrive if word of their books gets out into the world. Reviews matter. They don't have to be overly detailed, just a sentence or two about what you enjoyed.

Thanks for reading!

About the Author

romance that transforms

    M.P. Starkweather is a wife, mother, author, poet, casual on-line gamer, self-proclaimed fan-girl, and full-time nerd. She writes free-form poetry, paranormal romance, sci-fi romance, reverse harem romance, omegaverse romance, and is branching out into contemporary romance. In her free time, she enjoys writing, read-ing, Dungeons & Dragons, table top games with her husband and friends, and playing with her son. M.P. also enjoys tv, movies, and music across various genres.

    To get the most up-to-date information about her latest releases and book signings, check out www.mpstarkweather.com or follow her on your favorite social media site.

Also By M.P. Starkweather

Standalones – Contemporary RH

Standalones - Contemporary RH OV

The Pack Next Door – Contemporary RH OV series

Standalones – Paranormal RH

The Cursed Blade Series — Paranormal w/ different pairings

Digital Blade – RH

Elemental Blade – RH
Vampires at Midnight - Paranormal RH series

Blood Moon

Blood Lost

Blood War

Vampires at Midnight: The Complete Trilogy
VaM/HoF Crossover Novella - Paranormal RH

Blood Wolf— free with newsletter signup
Hunters of the Forest - Paranormal RH series

Wolf Bane

Wolf Caged

Wolf Moon

Hunters of the Forest: The Complete Trilogy
Forged by Magic - Sci-fi/Fantasy M/F series

Hidden

Betrayed

Saved

Forged by Magic: The Complete Trilogy
Daydreams and Sunsets - a collection of poetry

<u>Daydreams and Sunsets</u>

www.ingramcontent.com/pod-product-compliance
Lightning Source LLC
Chambersburg PA
CBHW050408260626
47156CB00003B/921